WILD ONE

BORN WILD BOOK ONE (A WILDS SERIES)

DONNA AUGUSTINE

Copyright © 2018 by Donna Augustine

All rights reserved.

No part of this book may be reproduced in any form or by any electronic or mechanical means, including information storage and retrieval systems, without written permission from the author, except for the use of brief quotations in a book review.

1

Everybody wants to be a superhero. They want to be special, believe that they can save the world and all that blah, blah, blah, bullshit. Well, that would be everybody but me. All I wanted was to save my own ass, and maybe one other person, before I ditched what was left of the human race as soon as I got the chance.

Why? Because when the Bloody Death wiped out most of the world, what it left behind was pretty much crap. I've only known a handful of decent people and I've lived on this earth for eighteen years, give or take a couple of months. That was a large enough sampling size for me.

Of course, because all I'd ever wanted was to be normal, stands to reason I'd end up as anything but that. I've been cursed from the day I was born with this strange gift. You know what was worse than having a power you never wanted? Having one that was absolutely worthless to you when you needed it.

Like right now, being super strong would have been

great, so I could kill the asshole standing in front of me. Or what about flying? So I could escape. But I'm not killing anyone or escaping because, as I mentioned, my power sucks. It was worse than having no power at all.

"You think you can leave here?" Baryn's spit flew between the rotted teeth he had left and a foul odor blasted my nostrils as he screamed. His fist, covered in my blood, waved inches from me, as his pustuled face served as an unwanted backdrop.

Baryn wasn't my curse. He was just the nightmare that kept reoccurring. Every. Damn. Day. And my superpower couldn't do a thing about him.

"You're going to pay for every second my men had to look for you." His face grew as red as that last fall tomato he'd eaten for breakfast.

That was how long I'd been gone too. Since breakfast. Not even a full day. Not that long in the scheme of things, but I guess if you were counting every single second, it added up. "You sure you've got the balls to back up something that big? That's a whole lot of seconds you're throwing around there, *bud*." I hit the B hard, knowing that calling him bud would take him over the edge.

Baryn's bald head gleamed, a bead of sweat dripping a trail to the side of his nose. I might've imagined he was bursting some blood vessels as his heart hammered through his chest. He was entitled to his surprise, considering I was changing things up unexpectedly. Normally, during our times together, he did most of the talking, while I played more of the silent, mysterious type.

But something had snapped in me this morning

when I'd taken a step out of the village, and then a second. It was as if that first breath of free air had seeped into my lungs and then grabbed a hold of my soul with an iron grip that wouldn't let go. All the feelings and emotions I'd kept caged within me, beaten back so I could make myself so very small, halving myself so I'd hopefully go unnoticed whenever possible in my fight to survive—they wouldn't go back in. I couldn't beat them down anymore. It was as if the iron grip had spread out from my heart into everything that was me. That part I'd pummeled for so long, it was refusing to listen to reason. It didn't care if Baryn killed me. Didn't want to hear how it was better to be careful and survive. It couldn't seem to fit inside that little space I'd allowed it.

Craziest part was—I. Liked. It.

I didn't want to beat it back, force myself to shrink within, and the cost didn't matter.

"Don't you ever speak to me like that." His arm pulled all the way back, loading up for another swing.

That wild thing that had broken free inside of me still refused to be cowed. "Fuck. You."

His fist struck my nose. The familiar crunch told me it was broken—again. It was already a mangled lump on my face, so it wouldn't look much worse, and I'd moved past vanity long ago. My head bounced off the wall and then wobbled back. Blood dripping down onto the packed earthen floor, I waited for my head to clear. Waited to see if that thing inside of me, that part that wanted to live large and fuck the consequences, was ready to shrink back into its small box and hide again.

No.

It still didn't give a fuck.

My skull leaning against the wall for support, I angled my head back to get a look at Baryn. "Be careful exerting yourself too much. You're not as spry as you used to be. The ole ticker might get tired out and quit." The nasally tone of my jibe lessened the delivery, but the ragged intake of his breath said it hit its target well enough anyway.

Baryn's biggest fear was death, not that you'd know it the way he wasted his days. The problem with Baryn was the same problem lots of people had. They acted like tomorrow was a guarantee. Yes, logically they knew they could die today, but that wasn't what they truly believed. They walked around as if they had an eternity at their disposal, wasting minutes as if they were nothing. Minutes piling up into hours and days. Years later, they had nothing left but a spent life. Then the reaper knocked on their door and they prayed to the gods of the Wilds for just a few of those minutes back, because *then* they'd treasure them. *Then* they'd do this and that and everything in between.

But everyone has a moment when it all ceases to exist, and the reaper doesn't care if you beg, get on your knees, and cry. The reaper isn't an ex who might give you one last go around. When the reaper shows, it's a date with death.

And the one thing I knew all too well was death. That was my gift, if you wanted to call it that. I couldn't always tell you when the reaper was coming, but I knew how he was going to collect and how ugly it was going to be. I knew who'd beg and who'd go out standing tall. When Baryn's time came, and it was going to be soon, he wouldn't have a chance to beg.

Of all the deaths I'd seen, and hated every glimpse of, Baryn's was the one I'd been waiting for. What a death it would be. Way too grand for the likes of him, but I'd take my opportunity to dance on his corpse any way I got it. Even if it were only for a minute, that minute couldn't come soon enough.

Baryn's face scrunched up as delayed rage finally set in. "Worthless bitch. You deserve everything that's coming for you." His fist connected with my ribs.

The pain was shocking. I didn't care what anyone said, you never really got used to taking a bad beating, but I knew I'd survive. Once in a blue moon, seeing a person's death before it happened had an upside. Long ago, I'd realized that I saw fewer deaths with babies and children. Since I couldn't see my own either, it made me think maybe I only saw the deaths that preceded mine.

Winded from doling out the beating, he stepped back, the bulge in his pants obvious. A beating was his foreplay. The swelling and the blood all added to his arousal. Most people didn't find me attractive, but Baryn did. He got off on the many scars he'd given me through the years. The way my right leg bowed from a crudely healed break he'd caused. The scars that covered my body.

He moved to his bed, sitting with his legs wide open and leaning back, rubbing between his legs. He mumbled and spoke softly, sick words I drowned out in my head.

He wouldn't touch me, no one would—not like that, anyway. That was the only blessing of my gift. There were too many superstitions around my kind. They said I had Death Sight, that I was tainted by the reaper. To sleep with me might bring instant death. But that didn't mean he wouldn't look his fill while he did his business.

His stares and grunting used to make bile claw its way up my throat, gagging me. I didn't feel anything now. Wouldn't let him have that part of me. I stared out the window above me, with eyes that were swelling shut, at the tree tops beyond the wall that enclosed our village. I pushed him from my mind until I was alone with nothing but the stars and the sound of owls hooting in the distance.

What it had been like to run free through those trees. They said that everything out there, in the Wilds, was too dangerous. That bloodthirsty beasts ran the forest at night, killing anything they came upon, and that pirates would kidnap you and sell you at slave markets.

They said the world wasn't what it used to be a couple of hundred years ago, back in the Glory Years, when there were great machines everywhere. Mechanical birds soared through the air and great metal boats cut through the oceans like whales, carrying people all over the world on their backs. And that was only the beginning of the stories I'd heard.

So many people had been alive then that they'd lived in huge cities of towering buildings, and when they walked, they'd bang into each other *accidentally*.

But then the Bloody Death came, wave after wave. And with each wave, the human race became weaker and weaker. Now? We're hanging on to the bottom rung, prey to the beasts and all the other creatures that rose after the fall, and continued to rise.

People said it was safer here, enclosed in five square miles of hell. But those people didn't live my life. Maybe for them it was, but for me, death was preferable.

Since I was a baby, I'd never been outside of those walls—until today. I'd take my chance again as soon as I got it. I wanted to run through the trees with no one watching and no one telling me when to stop or when to start. I wanted to be alone and away from here.

And I had to get away soon. Worse was on its way.

2

I woke sometime near dawn to Baryn's fingers digging into the fleshy part of my upper arm. Eyes barely open, I tried to untangle my legs as he dragged me after him toward the door.

Ivan was waiting for him right outside the door, as always.

"Put her in the circle," Baryn said, and then went back inside.

Ivan did the bulk of the dirty work and was a stellar employee, always doing his duty with a smile. I was handed off, this time by my hair, as I stumbled to keep from being scalped.

Minutes later, I was chained to the post, a half-circle of stones around it. Three inches of iron bit into the skin of my wrist. The circle of shame, they called it. This was where they put you when you did something *bad*, which could be anything from glancing the wrong way or saying the wrong word.

I settled in, leaning against the wood, knowing I'd be here for at least the day, if history told me anything.

I pulled my knees up to my chest, resting my chin upon them and letting white-blond hair curtain my face. People would be rising for their duties soon, and it was much easier to not see them than to pretend I hadn't. It was mutually beneficial, as they didn't want to pretend to not see me either.

I'd gotten as comfortable as I could when Baryn's door opened again. It had a very distinctive double bang when it closed, and his house wasn't that far from the circle. Sometimes I wondered if he liked the view outside his window. I glanced over, and he had that *look* in his eyes as they met mine.

I'd thought he was through with me for now. This wasn't how things went. He'd beaten me. He'd done *that* thing. Normally he'd be content for at least a day and move on to some new amusement. Why was he walking out of his house and toward me?

He paused, looking around the ground near the wooden wall. What was he doing? Maybe he *was* done with me? Except I'd seen that look. I *knew* that look. I'd had nightmares over that look.

Suddenly he was on the move again, but this time in the opposite direction, and I sagged against the pole. It wasn't until I saw the thick branch he picked up, saw him pivot back to me with it in his hand, that I truly panicked. Baryn liked to use his fists. He'd only used a branch one other time, when he didn't think he could get the job done.

I tried to pull my hand from the metal. It scraped over my skin, bunching it like crinkled fabric, but it wasn't enough. I would've broken it if I could've. I would've done anything if it would've gotten me free.

Baryn walked toward me with brisk steps now, determined in his path, the branch swinging at his side.

Ivan, who had been twenty or so feet away, fell into step with him, as they both now charged in my direction.

Baryn turned to Ivan. "Hold her down."

"Whatever you say." Ivan turned to me, smiling widely and probably wishing he was going to wield the branch.

Ivan's steps nearing had me slicing skin from my wrist, but unless I could sever my hand, I was caught. Ivan's foot was planted on my back, shoving me to the ground.

"Flip her over," Baryn said. "I want to watch her face as she gets what's coming to her."

Crows cawed from their perches, mingling with Ivan's laughter. He grabbed a shoulder, swinging me back around. A boot dug into already-hurt ribs and kept me there.

Baryn took the thick branch in both hands, smiling as he swung at the air. "That will be the last time you run. Anywhere."

I should've shut up and lain there, but I couldn't. I just couldn't. That thing inside me, the piece that had broken free, kept saying, *Don't live small. Don't let them rob you of what little you have left. If you're going to die, so be it. At least do it on your terms.* So, instead of shutting up and hoping he wouldn't hurt me too badly, I smiled at him, even as my stomach churned and I choked on its acidic swell.

I took the only swing at him I had left: "Do your worst now, because you won't have much longer."

"Why is that?" he asked, white-knuckling the branch.

"The Bloody Death will be coming for you soon. I can see you in a pile of your own shit and puke after you lie rotting for a week."

He smiled. "Liar. There hasn't been an outbreak of the Bloody Death in years. First I'm dying from a weak heart, now it's the Bloody Death." He laughed like a man whose heart was shriveled and black.

"We'll see," I said.

He was right. He wouldn't die either of those ways. I'd never tell him how he was going to die. Didn't want to give him a chance to stop it.

Baryn used his branch to point at me as he spoke to Ivan. "Don't let her move. This takes very precise aim."

Ivan kept his boot steady, but he was no longer smiling or looking at me. He was afraid of what he'd hear was in store for him. His death was nowhere near as satisfying as Baryn's, so he needn't worry about me sharing.

The branch came crashing down on my shin. First it stole the air from my lungs and then it stole the light from my eyes. If nothing else, I finally got the oblivion I'd longed for.

I HUDDLED ON THE GROUND, MY BACK TO THE wooden wall that circled our village, clinging to any break from the wind I could get. It was cold for fall, and even colder now that night had fallen again.

People gave me a wide berth as they made their way home for the night, no one wanting to look my way and acknowledge me. If they did, they might feel like they had to do something. It was easier to not see me. I kept my eyes downward, so I didn't have to watch the people walking past, pretending to not see me.

The bowl of broth I'd been brought minutes earlier lay turned on its side a few feet away, after Ivan had *accidentally* bumped me.

"Clumsy," he'd said, before walking away.

They wouldn't starve me to death, though. Not on purpose, anyway. They'd already sold me.

Tuesday, the only person left alive I cared a wink about, had overheard Baryn and Turrock, his brother, talking about how much they'd gotten for me. She didn't know to whom I'd been sold, or maybe she didn't want to tell me. Her refusal to look me in the eye was a sure sign she'd been holding back some of the details. No matter how I pressed her, she hadn't said a peep. All she'd kept repeating was I had to leave. That was how I knew whatever was coming was really bad.

Even though I had no supplies, or warm clothing to bear the brutal weather coming, after she told me, I'd decided to run the next moment I got a chance. The plan we'd concocted was flimsy at best, but all we had.

Tuesday had flirted with the guard manning the gate, and I'd slipped out. Even knowing I'd most likely be caught. With my limp, speed wasn't an option, but I'd been determined to escape.

My freedom hadn't lasted long, and with pain shooting up my leg, I wasn't sure I'd ever have another chance. Curled on my side, I let my heart harden a little more, knowing it might be the only way I'd survive.

The last noises finally drifted away, and the only

thing left was the wind whistling as it blew through the gaps in the wall.

Fingers whispered across my scalp, as if fearing to apply any more pressure than a feather.

"Teddy." My name was spoken even softer.

"Tuesday?" I opened my eyes to see chaotic, dark curls framing a pixie face so ethereal that she could have had fairy blood in her veins.

She had big, soft eyes, like Maura's had been before they'd closed for the last time.

Maura—I still felt the loss of her like a knife slashing through my heart, even though she'd been gone for over eight years. I'd known her death was coming, but more often than not, you couldn't escape your time. When the date was stamped deep inside the flesh, not even knowing could help you avoid it.

There was a sickness that had grown in her for a long time. She'd fought it, but death had won, as it usually did. Tuesday, her daughter, the sister of my heart, if not my flesh, was all I had left of her. We'd been raised together, after they'd given me to Maura to nurse.

As I held Maura's hand on that last day, she'd promised me the pain would eventually dull from her passing.

I was still waiting.

"Tuesday, you have to get away from me." I scanned the area.

People were always looking, even if you didn't see them. They were searching for a way to get a few more crumbs for themselves, a ration of meat on the few occasions the hunters brought back more than Baryn or Turrock could eat. If it cost the blood of others, they simply made sure they turned around before they had to see the outcome of their deed.

Last time Tuesday came to me when Baryn had chained me here, she'd caught a few blows herself. The circle was isolation. A spectacle to be seen by all but not approached. To cross the stones around the post was to risk being chained here yourself.

She pulled a bun out from under her jacket. "Here. Take this."

"No, you keep it." Food was tight, even if her lot wasn't as bad as mine.

Kenny, the guy in charge of keeping the walls around this place intact, was sweet on her. He'd lightened her lot while he clung to the hope she'd turn equally sweet on him. He'd managed to get her a job in laundry, which wasn't the worst you could do. After all, it kept her clear of Baryn and Turrock.

Kenny didn't seem like the worst as far as people went, either. I'd never seen him look for trouble, but she hadn't sweetened up yet, and she probably wouldn't.

She shoved the bun back toward me. "You know you won't get much while you're stuck here. Please take it."

I laid a hand on hers and pushed it back.

"I can't eat it anyway." The inside of my mouth was so chewed up from the last punch that hunger pains were preferable. Besides, my mouth was too dry for bread, but that wasn't something I'd share with her. She'd risk her life to come back with water.

"I'm okay, Tuesday. You've got to go away before someone sees you. Please. I can handle anything but seeing him get to you too."

She was barely hearing me. She stared at where the threadbare fabric of my pants was pulled tight across the swelling of my leg, purple flesh showing through the ripped seam.

"Your leg—"

"Will heal." I'd walk on it again, and refused to think anything else.

She forced a smile even as her eyes nearly flooded, tears pooling on her lower lid. She squeezed my hand. "But you almost made it."

Not even close. I tried to smile anyway, but the effort made her grimace, the gash on my lip straining. I dropped the pretense and returned the squeeze instead.

"Next time, I will."

That was the plan. I'd escape one day. I'd settle somewhere far away and send her a pigeon in a month or two. Then she'd follow. She could leave here whenever she wanted. It was me who was trapped, but no matter how many times I'd told her to go, she wouldn't.

Part of it was fear. I didn't begrudge her that. If I had her life, this place might have been just enough to keep me here. Nothing good, but nothing too horrible. Just enough. Maybe you could do worse than getting by in this horrible place if what they said about everything out there was true. Or maybe this place was truly hell.

Would she be brave enough to set out into the Wilds without me beside her? I didn't know. But dreaming about it for hours was one of the things that had kept us both going, so I didn't delve too deeply into reality. I didn't have the strength to strip the colors from the mirage when the mirage was all we had. So we'd talk about the day we'd get out of here and neither of us said a word otherwise.

A last squeeze to my hand and she stood, making her way back into the shadows of the buildings. I watched for flickers of movement from hidden watchers as she did. If a beating came her way tomorrow, I wanted to know who to blame.

Sometimes I wondered if hate drove me more than hope now. It didn't really matter. Maybe hate was better, stronger. I had something to fuel the hate. Yesterday, when I'd run through those trees, I had hope. Somehow, it made the fracturing of my dreams that much worse. Hate was so much easier to hold on to.

I was still huddled against the wall, wondering how much longer they'd leave me here, when the gates creaked open. It was surprising they worked at all with the way they groaned at doing their job. Maybe they were trying to do their part and warn off newcomers.

At this late hour, it was probably Turrock returning. I didn't look up, lying limp, too injured to come awake. He might go inside his house and get settled then. If I looked alert, he'd be drawn to me for sport, just as his brother was. Whatever their sickness, it seemed to run in the blood.

The night grew silent again. The danger had passed. My head on the ground, I tried to sleep, tried to ignore the pulsating pain that refused to stay in my one limb.

I didn't know anyone was near me until I heard the crows caw and then a gasp. I cracked the eye that would still open to see two men, halted about eight feet away. Strangers, probably here to see Baryn or Turrock.

One of them had crazy blond hair that reminded me of a lion's mane, like I'd seen in Tuesday's picture book. He was staring in my direction, oblivious that he'd step over the stone ring as he stood in leather pants too rich for anyone I knew. It might have been the white-blond shade of my hair that was a curiosity, or sometimes it was the scars. I was a walking sideshow.

His stare wasn't the dirty kind that made my skin crawl, but pity. As much as the lion wouldn't look away, his friend seemed to have the opposite problem and wouldn't look at all. That I was used to.

There was a time in my life, when I was younger and naive, that I would've asked for help. I wasn't that girl anymore. I hadn't been her for so long that it seemed as if she'd never existed at all. The only one that was going to save me from this hell was me, and I would. I didn't know how yet, but the time was coming and I didn't need anyone. I'd be my own savior. I'd leave this place one way or another, if only to watch it burn to the ground from a few feet away.

I laid my head back down again, trying to ignore them.

"Koz, come on. We don't get involved in other people's business. She's probably a thief or something. Leave her be."

I didn't need to open my eyes to see the scene, but I did anyway. The one who couldn't look tugged at the arm of the lion who was fixated on me.

"I don't know if I can," Koz said.

There was something in Koz's voice that tugged at an innocence within I'd thought I'd murdered a long time ago. I couldn't afford expendable emotions. Innocence and trust were among the first that had to go.

But maybe, just maybe, this one would be different? It wasn't like there hadn't been a few others that had tried. Nothing ever came of it, though. There'd always been a price to pay, either in their blood or mine. Usually both.

But what if he had the strength others hadn't? He looked strong, much tougher than most of the men here.

"Koz, we need to handle our business and go." The other man tugged at Koz again. "Come on. It's not the same."

Not the same? Same as what?

I wished they'd go about their business. I needed to forget them and not get crazy ideas, like asking for help. If they turned me down and then told Baryn, I might end up so bad off that I wouldn't even be able to crawl from this place.

"Isn't it though, Zink?" Koz asked.

Zink's head angled slightly toward me but didn't complete the turn. Then he gave me his back, shutting the door on my situation. "She's one of them. Their business. Not ours. You know Callon's rule. We keep to our own, take care of our own."

I finally took a long, hard stare at this Koz. He didn't break eye contact and took a step in my direction. He wanted to help, but that didn't matter. People wanted to do a lot of things that they didn't do. But if there was even a chance, how did I not take it?

Zink took a few steps away, waiting for Koz to follow him. "Come *on*."

If Koz kept staring at me for even a few more seconds, I'd do it. I'd ask.

Our eyes held, my turquoise to his brown.

Did I dare? His eyes hardened, as if he were gearing up for action. My heart pounded with life and I opened my mouth, silently forming the word "help" on blood-stained lips.

"Koz," Zink shouted.

His eyes shuttered, Koz turned and walked away.

My heart slowed, then stuttered out into a sluggish beat. I laid my head back down. It had been nothing but wishes on the breeze, as Maura used to say. Not worth the air it took to utter them before they blew far away, as if they'd never been said at all.

3
———

A boot nudged me in the ribs, bringing me awake. I knew it was Baryn before I opened my eyes. I could tell by the rancid smell of him. Turrock liked to bathe, even if it was simply because he enjoyed watching the serving girls lug the hot water buckets as they splashed and burned their skin. "Boiling hot," he'd yell. "The water must always be boiling. Then you add the cold."

He said it was better that way, to steam the room before he was ready to bathe. It was bullshit. Hard to steam a room with windows wide open.

Turrock liked the subtle tortures, though. An artist of abuse, he took a chisel and hammer to his victims, slowly whittling them away, piece by piece. Baryn was more direct.

It was Baryn leaning over me now. Baryn and Turrock were the only ones allowed to go near me. Every scar on my body was due to one of them.

My good eye opened a small slit. The place was sleeping and a full moon had risen, making his shirt look blood red.

I'd never seen this shirt before in person. Only in my mind. It was the one he'd die in. In my vision, it had been vibrant and clean, just as it was now.

His death would come soon. Maybe even tonight? I took the rest of his form in. He was wearing his prized ring on his pinky finger, the one that looked too feminine for him, as if he'd taken it from a woman. I had a hunch that the blood-red ruby hadn't been the only bloody thing when he'd acquired it.

The shirt.

The ring.

The full moon.

It was happening. Would it happen tonight? Could it line up this perfectly and not?

He squatted close to me. "What do you know of Turrock's death?"

He'd never asked me about his brother. Did he think to kill him? Not surprising that he wasn't even loyal to Turrock. I needed to make something up. Baryn was obviously up to something. Was he planning on killing his brother? How would he do it? It wasn't going to work, but Baryn couldn't know that.

I swallowed, trying to act natural. Baryn must not read the worry in me. His wasn't a death that had to happen. His wasn't going to come from within. This one could be avoided. I needed to act normal.

He. Could. Not. Know.

"Answer me when I talk to you, girl, unless you want two bum arms as well."

Think! Baryn would make it a gruesome death, that was for sure. "There's a lot of blood."

"What else?"

He'd be sneaky about it. Poison. He'd definitely use poison. What happened when you poisoned someone?

He raised his hand but then paused as a growling sounded nearby. We both turned, listening for the noise that seemed to come from the other side of the wooden wall. It disappeared as quickly as it had come, but that sound would linger in my head for a while, maybe forever.

We were both still frozen when the wall exploded, sending chunks in every direction. The wood splintered around us.

A blur of fur and claws flew past me as something barreled through the huge hole in the wooden wall. A beast lunged at Baryn. Its massive jaws clamped down on his neck and then severed his head in one bite. It was exactly as my vision had shown, right down to the spurts of blood shooting from his body and pouring onto the dirt as the beast pinned what was left of him to the ground.

It had happened. It finally happened, and there was a gaping escape route right behind me. There was also a beast crouched in front of me.

I remained frozen at the sight of it. I'd never actually seen a beast, and to see one up close was terrifying. Its fangs hung beyond black gums, blood dripping from the tawny fur of its jowls. Claws the size of my fingers were partially sunk into Baryn's still chest. It was a perfect killing machine.

This creature would never be vulnerable. I should've been repelled by the creature, but I wasn't. It wasn't only terrifying. It was amazing.

Its head turned and its body shifted toward me,

claws leaving pools of blood behind. Red eyes burned into me.

I nodded slowly in Baryn's direction as I watched the beast.

"Thank you," I said, even knowing I might be next. Maybe it was my time, and what a death it would be. Much more worthy a death than the life I'd led. I'd lived in a whimper, but I'd die with a roar. It wasn't what I would've chosen, but it was something. If I died now, at least I could go knowing Baryn was dead. Years of torment lay bleeding in front of me.

The creature stared at me, then the chain that led to my wrist, and I could feel the growl in its chest vibrating outward. Blood still dripping from its muzzle, it lunged for me. I squeezed my eyes tightly shut, waiting for teeth to dig into already-battered skin. The bite didn't come, just a graze of wetness. There was a clanking of metal as the weight of the iron fell from my wrist. My eyes snapped open, looking first to my free wrist and then the mauled three inches of metal lying underneath it.

I was still staring at the metal when the beast's claws wrapped around my bicep. It leapt forward, yanking me backward as it did and then dragging me through the hole in the wall. The last view of my village was the horrified faces peeking out from behind buildings as they watched a beast carry away its dinner.

The startled faces were soon forgotten as soon as I was dragged over the first bump. My broken leg was jerked over a log, then a stone and a list of other unidentifiable objects as I was pulled like a rag doll through the forest at a pace no human could hope to match. If not for adrenaline pumping thickly through my veins, I would surely have passed out immediately.

I'd survive this. I'd survive. I had to survive. There were too many deaths I'd seen that hadn't happened yet. I wasn't sure *how*, or in what shape I'd be, but I would.

I reached out with my free hand and managed to graze my fingers across a stick. It was too slick to catch and we were moving too fast. I reached for another, but missed again as the beast continued at its crazy pace. Every new bang and bump crowded my vision with black spots until there was nothing left.

4

I woke to the moon shining through the tree canopy and the forest floor chilling my back. The smell of dead leaves was the sweetest scent ever breathed, and I was hungry to suck it deep inside and hold it there. I was alive. But was I alone?

There was rustling in the distance and the air got stuck in my lungs. Was the beast nearby but taking a breather before it made a meal of me?

"I can't do it, Callon. Look at her and then tell me that." It was a man, not extremely close, but near enough that I could hear every word clearly. The voice sounded like that man from my village earlier—Koz, his friend had called him. I could still picture his lion's mane of hair. How did he end up here? Had he found me after the beast had abandoned me? Had the beast tasted me and decided I wasn't a good meal?

I didn't feel any bites. Nothing felt *that* much worse than it had. Considering I'd seen it bite through a solid chunk of metal like it was a twig, I'd probably be dead if it had bitten me.

"It doesn't matter what she looks like," Callon answered. I'd never heard his voice before. I would've remembered. It was too deep and had a distinct gravelly sound, almost like a rumble.

There was a long pause.

"Won't you just look—"

"It can't happen," Callon said, cutting Koz's plea short.

They weren't from my village, but that didn't mean they weren't a threat. It just meant the coin toss on which way they'd flop hadn't revealed itself yet. I'd listened to stories my entire life of the perils that waited beyond the walls. If they were even partially true, I could be in worse shape than before I'd left. Just because Koz seemed remotely human meant nothing. There were people back at the village that had been a little human, too. Plus, Koz clearly wasn't in charge.

I tried to survey my options without moving, afraid of drawing attention that would probably be coming soon enough. Trying to run wasn't an option. The leg Baryn had hit was worse off than before I'd been dragged through the forest, and I hadn't been up to standing before then.

Flight was ruled out. It left only fight. I glanced around as much as I could without making noise, looking for a large stone or stick, anything that would help dismal odds.

"She's awake," Callon said.

Damn. Time was up.

Footsteps approached, and I sat up, still keeping an eye out for a good stick, not that it would do too much against two men.

Except there were four. Koz and two others

approached me, while one was hanging back. I tried to make out as many details as I could with only the moonlight.

I recognized two, Koz and the one who had been at the village with him, Zink. Zink was a finger shorter, but with a look about him that said he didn't lose fights very often. He was scrappy enough that I'd rather take on the larger Koz.

The other one, with dark auburn hair and a lean, wiry look, seemed to be walking over to see the spectacle but not partake in the games.

Then there was the other one, who lingered farther away. I didn't have to hear him speak to know he owned the deep voice and was the one in charge. His face was all sharp angles and shadows. I wasn't sure if I'd call him pretty or rugged or just *male*. Testosterone poured off him thicker than water down rapids. Everything about him oozed the Y chromosome, so much I wondered if he'd gotten an X at all.

His eyes glazed over me without seeing, the way so many others had in the past. It wasn't only the sharp angles of his face or the breadth of his shoulders—I'd never seen such a shade of blue eyes, other than in pictures of glaciers, so bright even in the darkness. It made his hair seem even blacker, his skin that much tanner.

Good. He could keep his distance. I didn't want any part of him.

I grabbed for the nearest tree, only a couple feet away, dragging myself up even as every movement, every inch, was paid for with a new round of teeth-grinding pain. Not that they'd hear a single moan.

I forced the man with the deep voice and deeper

eyes out of my mind for a minute and turned my attention to Koz. He'd wanted to help me when I first saw him. Maybe he still would. I was free of the village, for now, but that didn't mean much. I'd been free before and it had been short-lived. Turrock might come for me yet.

I didn't know how long I'd passed out for, but it probably hadn't been that long. If Turrock and Baryn had sold me, Turrock wouldn't let a beast stop him. He'd still try to collect, even if it was by handing over a mangled body or my half-chewed bones for some coin. I needed to get as far away as I could, as *soon* as I could. I didn't even know how far away I was.

Maybe this Koz would help now?

"I saw you at my village," I said.

"I was at a village earlier, but I don't recall seeing you." He shook his head a little too quickly.

The guy was clearly lying. He'd stared straight at me, and I wasn't one to be mistaken for another. Even if he'd missed my bloody face lying there, a spectacle for all, or if it had been too dark to see the scars, he couldn't have missed my hair. I'd never met another person with hair as blond as mine.

It didn't matter. His lie was safe with me. I wouldn't force an issue with my only possible ally in this group. I had more important questions.

"Did you slay the beast that had me?" I asked.

"No. We found you here," Koz answered.

Zink was staring with narrowed eyes, and the other unnamed man made a huffing noise, as if something amused him.

"Shut up, Hess," Zink said.

"I'm sorry, but I take my amusement where I can."

Hess shook his head and walked back to Callon, as if their game had become boring.

I didn't care if Hess was bored. All I could wonder was: why hadn't the beast eaten me? Why had it dragged me here to simply leave me? That made no sense. Maybe it had figured out what I was somehow and decided it didn't want to get that close to death?

And where had it left me?

"Where am I?"

"Not far from the nearest village, which I guess is yours? Maybe ten miles or so," Koz said, then looked back toward where Hess was now standing beside Callon. Something was playing out with them, and Koz didn't like it. I had a feeling I wouldn't like it either.

I'd heard stories of what happened to people in the Wilds, especially women on their own. This could be bad. Would they rape me? Enslave me? Tie me to a tree and offer me as a sacrifice to the beasts who'd already turned up their nose at me? What if I'd been dragged to my freedom—by a beast, no less—only to die the same day at the hands of men? I looked about the forest, finding the clearest path. Odds that I could run weren't on my side. But I'd already beaten the odds once tonight, so obviously luck was.

"Koz is bringing you back to your village. He'll have you there before daybreak," Callon, the man with eyes so cold they burned, said from his safe distance away, still not looking at me.

No, no, no. My fingers dug into the branch I was using to stay upright until bark was poking under my nails. It was way worse than anything I'd imagined. There weren't enough nos in the universe for this situation.

"You're not bringing me anywhere, and neither is he," I said to Koz.

Koz looked back at Callon.

I leaned forward, trying to figure out how to take a step toward Callon, knowing he was calling the shots. I stumbled to the ground as soon as I put weight on my leg.

Koz reached forward, and I scrambled back, half crawling, to the tree I'd been holding on to before he could reach me. He stopped moving as soon as I jerked away.

Zink looked at me for a moment but then walked over toward his boss, saying, "This is your mess, Koz," as he did.

Koz was the only one who hadn't moved away from me, and I feared that was only because he was the one ordered to bring me back.

He stood there, his eyes grazing my face and then my leg.

"Callon, I can't do it," Koz said, but not firmly enough to chase away my need to run.

"You can leave me here. I'm not your mess," I said, using Zink's word choice. I'd hang on to the tree for dear life if he tried to bring me back.

Koz didn't answer me but angled his head down and toward Callon "There's bruises on top of scars on top of bruises. I can't bring her back there. They'll kill her."

His face was strained, and I didn't know if he was arguing with Callon or himself at this point.

"Then leave her," Callon called back. He probably would've said kill her or eat her or string her up by her toes as long as Koz got rid of me. He and his other two men had already moved on from my situation, and that was fine. I didn't need them or want their interference.

"It's like the dog all over again. He can't help himself from picking up strays," Zink said to the other guy.

They could call me anything they wanted. I wasn't going back.

A movement caught my eye, drawing my attention back to Zink. He grabbed the hanging bag from his side and brought it to his lips. He guzzled it, letting drops carelessly fall to the ground when he was done. He laughed at something one of them said as he hung the bag back at his side.

My dry tongue darted out, licking cracked lips.

"You need this?"

I jerked back. Koz had moved closer and was holding out a bag of his own.

Callon was still a good twenty feet away, adding sticks to a fire in the center of what looked like a camp. The other two were talking amongst themselves, close to him.

"It's okay. Take it," Koz said, inching the bag closer.

When I didn't immediately take it, he squatted down, placing it near my feet, then backed away with his hands up.

"What's your name?" he asked, giving me plenty of space.

"Teddy." I glanced down at the sack.

I took it and fumbled with the cap before I chugged it down. Cold water washed over a scratchy throat and a tongue that was slightly too large. I was nearly choking but couldn't bring myself to slow down, wanting every drop.

I was vaguely aware of Koz drifting back to his group while I was still emptying his supply, only taking the briefest break to breathe.

Koz had stopped beside Callon. "You know I'm loyal to you. You're my brother. But I can't leave her to die and I can't bring her back there."

My head dropped back down, the bag finished. By the time it was empty, I realized Callon's stare was in my direction, on the bag I'd just finished off. His jaw was even more squared, if possible. His attention was short-lived.

Zink edged closer to Koz, my only hope in this group. I wanted to think I would've liked Koz right from the get-go, but that would've been a total lie. I didn't like anyone from the start. Sometimes I didn't like them for years. Most of them I *never* liked. But if Koz saved my ass, I'd swear up and down until I died that I'd known he was good to the core as soon as I laid eyes on him.

Zink stepped in front of Koz. "Look, it's not a good time, and you know that. Just take her back."

"Leave me be. You don't need to do anything with me. I can take care of myself." Would it be easier if I had someone like Koz helping me? Yeah. I couldn't even walk. But I'd figure it out. I didn't *need* anyone.

Three heads swiveled to my battered form. Callon was more interested in the fire he'd started.

"Maybe if we built a shelter and left her with some food?" Koz was weakening. That question near reeked of capitulation, proving once again that you couldn't depend on anyone to save you. They wouldn't.

Hess, the one who hadn't said much, finally weighed in. "You really want to help her, that's not the way. Something will sniff her out and kill her. She can't even fucking stand. She won't be able to get fresh water. You're better off taking her back. Once we're done, if you still feel like it, go get her then, and you can take her wherever you want."

Koz would never come back for me after he forced me back to my village. I knew it, and so did the rest of them. People didn't come back, ever. And if some miracle of miracle proved that Koz was the one in a million who would come back, I wouldn't be there. There would be no one left to rescue. I'd already have been sold off like livestock to a new nightmare.

"I'll be fine. Just leave me." I laid Koz's water bag on the ground and then turned to find the next tree or branch I could hold on to. I made it one step before I landed with a thud, hands and knees in the dirt. A sound tore from my chest before I could smother it.

I wasn't a crybaby. I got a grip on myself while I was still facing the ground, getting my good leg back underneath me.

"Koz, you need to bring her back," Zink yelled.

"I can't," Koz screamed.

"You have to," Hess said, joining the fight.

"I'm not doing it."

The arguing continued, only Callon's voice silent. Let them argue. I'd leave in the meantime and fix the issue for everyone. I couldn't walk, but I'd crawl away if I had to. Turrock would send people after me, but I'd find a cave to hole up in, one with a tiny enough opening that his men couldn't see me, or get into even if they could.

I wasn't going back. Not ever.

I hopped, reaching for the next tree, pushing faster as I waited for the sound of someone following.

Would they follow? They didn't want to be bothered with me anyway. They'd let me disappear.

It was silent behind me. They'd stopped talking. I didn't know if that was good or bad, and I didn't have time to think about it. I was already breathing heavily after a few minutes. I lunged for my next tree and the mud stole my shoe, sucking at my foot and taking me down again. I sucked in a few deep breaths, shoved my hands into mud, and forced myself up.

"Stop." Callon's voice wasn't that close, but was clear across the distance.

I didn't stop. Why should I? So they could escort me back to hell? He wasn't in charge of me.

"I said, stop."

He'd closed the gap a bit.

No. No. No.

"Go fuck yourself!" I screamed, and managed a few paces more with the help of a nearby branch before falling. I'd run until my leg fell off before I'd let them take me back. I was getting the hell out of here.

Leather-clad legs blocked my way. I shifted to the right, going for the next closest.

Gripping the tree, I dragged myself up. Callon was there again, in front of me. He was larger than Koz even, my head only reaching his shoulders. His breadth looked unmovable. Raising my eyes, I tilted my head back, letting him see exactly what I thought of him for getting in my way.

He might think he had utter control of everyone and everything, but I wasn't going to lie down and take orders from some man I didn't know. That had *been* my life, but not anymore.

I waited as he really looked at me, taking in every

detail. His eyes shifted to my mouth and stayed there for a few seconds. He wasn't looking with desire. I knew how I appeared—that my lips were partially disfigured from one especially brutal beating, and that right now they were worse than normal. The scars that ran across my face made my one eye look permanently half shut, even when it wasn't swelled up. That my nose was dented and crooked. He took it all in, every horrible bit, from the threadbare pants to the way my fingers on my right hand were crooked from the time Baryn had held my hand in the door and slammed it shut.

He read my history in a glance. No pity showed, or anger, because this man was nothing like Baryn or Turrock. He was cool calculation. If there were feelings there, they were buried too deep to see the light of day.

I found myself wanting to look away, hide the pages of my life from his casual perusal. Hated that so much of what I'd been through was there on display for anyone to see.

The more I wanted to curl within, the more something rebelled and pushed back. Strength filled my veins, forcing my chin up, locking eyes with his.

Fuck being small.

"You can't crawl your way out of here." His words were biting. I wasn't entirely sure if that was the way it was meant or if he was too cold to know how brutal he sounded.

"If that's what it takes, then that's exactly what I'm going to do. So get the fuck out of my way." I'd seen enough little guys in the village bluff their way out of a fight to know bravado occasionally worked. Considering the tools left in my box, it was my only shot.

It also felt damn good.

"What happened to you?" he asked, his eyes narrowing.

I pressed my lips together. He didn't deserve answers.

He didn't budge, watching me with no emotion I could read. If he tried to force me to go back, it wouldn't end well. I could sense the other men closer, everyone frozen, wondering which way this would go.

A chill wind blew my hair forward, catching a strand and carrying it forward until it grazed his shirt.

His nostrils flared as he breathed in the crisp air.

Something flickered across his face. The first emotion I'd sensed, but damn if I could put a name to it. It was hard to read him by the slight tilt of his head and enlarging of his irises. Surprise, maybe? But why?

"Why did they beat you?" he asked.

"Does it matter why?" The last thing I was doing was telling this man about Baryn and his sordid desires, or why I'd drawn his attention in the first place. Callon already didn't like me as it was. I wouldn't press my luck by telling him anything that might encourage him to kill me. Unless he'd already decided?

I hadn't sensed death from any of them. Did that mean mine was imminent?

He opened his mouth, as if he wanted to answer that, but then said nothing for a moment. Finally, he said, "We'll take you to the next village on our way. Then you're on your own."

My entire body wanted to sag onto the tree beside me, but didn't. If he saw even a hint of weakness, he might change his mind. He'd become afraid I'd be too much of a burden to him.

5

The next village was way too close, but it was a step, *many* steps, in the right direction. No point in telling them my plan. I'd let them drop me off at the front of the village and then I'd continue on my way out the back. That shouldn't be too much of a problem. From what I'd heard about that place, they could barely keep the people they had fed.

Unless Turrock got word to them first to hold me. They wouldn't go against him. So, maybe they'd drop me off at the front and leave before I went inside. I'd figure something out.

"Okay." I nodded at Callon, who was still staring at me.

He nodded back and then took a step toward me.

I pulled back.

He turned his head to the side, his chest rising and falling, then turned back to me. "I'm going to help you over to the fire."

He over-enunciated every word. I had plenty of

issues, but I wasn't hard of hearing. "I'm good," I said, using the same method of speaking he had.

He raised a brow.

I ignored him. He didn't matter. He wasn't my ally. He was simply another obstacle I'd need to climb over.

Thinking of climbing, where was my shoe? The mud had sucked it off my foot but hadn't eaten it. It had to be here somewhere. A shoe would be a good thing, as there was a lot of walking to be done.

Koz leaned down, pulled a lump out of the mud, and held it out, dangling by his finger.

I leaned forward and plucked it from him as my other hand still gripped the tree. "Thank you."

Koz bowed his head slightly.

I shook off the muddy shoe and then realized I couldn't get it back on my good leg without sitting on the ground—as they all stared at me. I tucked it, mud and all, into my waist. I was pretty much covered anyway. A little more wouldn't make much of a difference.

They continued to stare, as if what I'd do next was some great amusement to them. "I guess I'll go sit by the fire until we get moving again."

Callon nodded, watching to see how I'd accomplish that. I'd gotten this far on my own. He didn't need to look so skeptical.

Koz held out a hand. "Do you need something to lean on?"

"I can do it." I looked over to where the fire was burning. It wasn't *that* far. If I couldn't do this, they'd wonder how I'd make it to the next village. I looked for the closest tree. Five feet away. If I leaned just right, swayed at the right angle, and the wind didn't work against me, I could make it.

I hopped a little ways toward it, still holding on to my current tree as they all watched.

Callon stared, arms crossed, both eyebrows raised.

Zink shook his head and walked back to the fire. Hess was scratching his head.

"You got this." Koz stood beside me with a wide smile and a thumbs-up.

It was hard not to smile back, but my cracked lip stopped me short. I pushed off the tree and managed to get my fingers wrapped around the next one.

Koz moved forward with me. "There you go. You did it."

"Oh, for fuck's sake," Callon said before an arm wrapped around my waist. I stiffened immediately as I was held against a hard chest. I might've screamed or fought, except all I managed was a squeak as his arm pressed against sore ribs. His arm shifted down immediately, removing the pressure, as if he'd known from that small noise, and might've cared.

Not even five seconds later, I was set down by a log in front of the fire. As fast as he'd lifted me, his arm loosened slowly, allowing me to get my balance before he let go. I reached a hand out, using the log as support as I lowered myself to the ground, knowing it would be easier if I took a seat in front of the log, where I could stretch the broken leg out.

Callon was standing in front of me, arms over his chest and eyes running their way up and down my frame. His jaw shifted slightly as his eyes moved from my leg to my midsection then up to my face. "How bad?"

I hadn't looked at my leg, or my ribs, mostly because

I hadn't wanted to. It was dark. He couldn't know that it wasn't a sprain and some bruising with my pants covering most of it.

"Not horrible." I looked away, signaling that the conversation was over.

He squatted in front of me, near eye level, making it impossible to not see him.

"I *said* I'd take you." He continued to stare at me, as if he could force me to believe him.

"Sure." He couldn't. I'd been told a lot of things in my life, and words didn't mean diddly, especially if I met you five minutes ago and it took you much longer than that to look at me.

Koz had made his way over to Callon's side, standing slightly behind him. He gave me a short nod, silently backing Callon. I didn't know Koz either, but he had tried to help me. He was the only reason I wasn't getting dragged back to Turrock. Still, I squinted at him, silently asking if he was really sure about this.

He nodded again but stopped as soon as Callon looked over his shoulder. "What are you doing?"

"Nothing," Koz said, shrugging and walking around Callon like nothing was amiss.

Callon turned his attention back to me, his shoulders blocking the fire. "Your leg?"

"I think it's broken." That Koz guy better be right about trusting Callon or he was going to get a big punch in the nose as soon as he slept.

"How long ago?" Callon asked. His hand was getting a little too close.

I shooed away a hand that got too close. "Don't touch it."

"I'm still looking. How long?" He angled his head this way and that, looking at it from every angle.

"About a day. Why?" What was he going to do to it? I looked over at Koz, who nodded.

Callon's hand moved in my leg's direction again.

"I said, don't touch it." I slid back toward the log, away from him.

His cool eyes met mine, his forearms resting on his legs. "I need to see it."

I didn't let my eyes flicker away from his stare this time. "Why?" I demanded.

He broke the stare first to shoot a look at Koz. I knew that look. I'd given it to Tuesday many times. It was something along the lines of: *You really fucked us good this time.* Apparently, Callon's only emotions came wrapped up in sarcasm.

Koz shrugged and gave him a surprised expression, as if having no clue what he meant.

Callon turned back to me and let out a slow breath, as if girding himself, before meeting my accusatory stare again. "The next village is twenty miles away. I need to set this before we get there, or it might heal like that." He pointed at my leg but didn't touch it.

I didn't need to look to know what he meant. My leg had been butchered. I was lucky the bone hadn't broken the skin. If I wanted a chance of being able to walk on it again, setting was a good idea. I knew that Marc, the healer from our village, always did that. Except when limps were the intended purpose of the break.

What he was saying added up. If I had two bad legs, life would be a lot harder.

I met his eyes and said, "Fine," before I could think about it anymore.

He gripped the hem of my pant leg and tore it up the center, all the way to my knee, before I could stop him.

"Did you have to do that? It's the only pair I have." They'd picked up more tears when I'd been dragged through the forest but had still been in one piece—mostly.

"I'll get you another pair."

He acted like there was a little old woman sewing them under the tree a mile down the nonexistent road. "From where? You aren't going to be able to get me new pants."

"I do what I say. If I say I'll bring you to the next village, I will. If I say I'm going to get you a pair of pants, I will."

We were so busy arguing that it took both of us a minute to look down at my leg. But as soon as he turned his attention there, so did I. I'd never had a weak stomach, but I was ready to retch all over the place. My leg was mottled all different colors and nearly twice its normal size. Then there was the strange bend.

He shifted so more of the firelight hit it as he stared. And kept staring. "How did this happen? It looks like—"

"Does it matter? It's broken." I knew exactly what it looked like. I'd been there when it happened. I couldn't imagine another way a person would get a break that precise in that place, unless it was a freak accident or intentional.

He didn't argue when he glanced up at me, but he knew. And I hated that he did. It made me want to retreat back into that place and be small again, where no one saw me.

I couldn't do it. My chest tightened and I blinked

enough to look like I was sending out secret codes into the night, but not a single tear dropped. I held them all back.

He sat quietly for a second, corded forearms resting on his legs again, his hands fisted. His profile silhouetted by the fire was hard to read. Was he mad at me? Was he going to tell Koz to drag me back again because I was too much work?

I didn't ask him to fix my leg. It was his idea. This was why I shouldn't have told him. I knew it. Now he thought I was going to be too much trouble.

"You don't need to do anything. I'm fine. I didn't ask for your help."

"I know that." His words were as sharp as a knife's edge. "And I can see what happened."

It wasn't my fault. I knew that. So why was I suddenly mortified? Why did I want him to think anything else but that someone had done this to me?

"I fell. I tripped on this…"

He turned back to me, his fists unclenching but his stare nearly burning my flesh. The fire made his eyes look like there was a strange reddish glow to them.

"Bad shit happens. You get better, you move on, and hopefully you kill everyone that hurt you." He looked into the woods for a moment. "That last part about killing isn't really necessary, but it tends to grease the wheels for the 'moving on' part."

It was the last thing I expected. Pity, irritation over how useless I was—that I was ready for. Suggesting I kill all my enemies? Totally unexpected. If I didn't already hate him, I might've actually liked him. Or parts of him.

"This is going to hurt. Hess? Give her your stash and don't tell me you don't have any left." Callon stood and walked around the place, grabbing some sticks. I'd seen splints before, so I knew what he was about.

"Got plenty." Hess walked over and held out a small silver flask. "Take whatever you need."

I took the container but paused halfway to my lips. "Is this going to knock me out?"

Easing the pain wasn't worth getting caught again if Turrock and his men snuck up on me in the middle of the night.

Hess glanced at my leg and then said, "You're not that lucky."

His words were just sardonic enough that I believed him. Koz came and squatted beside me. "I'll wake you up if you pass out."

Callon came back with some strips of fabric and sticks that he laid beside me. "Koz, brace her upper leg,"

Zink looked at the strips for a second. "Is that my shirt?" he asked.

Callon ignored him, looking me square in the eye. "I'm going to have to pull it straight to fix it."

I'd figured as much, but that wasn't really his point. He reached forward and put his finger underneath the flask, urging it closer to my lips. The message was abundantly clear. This was going to hurt. And bad.

I finished lifting it to my lips and took another sip. Then a few more.

Koz leaned forward, wrapping both hands around my leg, right above my knee, and I forced myself not to jerk away. The last time I'd had this many male hands on me, it hadn't been to help.

I put the flask down. Callon didn't give me any

warning as he pulled my ankle and Koz braced my upper leg.

The pain felt like a million hammers all hitting me at once. It might've been worse than when it was broken in the first place. Luckily, or unluckily, I had some experience with pain and managed to hold it together by the thinnest thread.

I kept my eyes closed, waiting for it to ease, and didn't open them until I was back under control.

When I finally opened them, Callon was lining up the sticks and wrapping my leg.

He glanced up, pausing.

He nodded at me, so slightly I wasn't sure if I was supposed to have even noticed. But I had, and it felt like a pat on the back. The worst part of it was that something in me swelled at his approval.

I didn't need his approval. It had to be the booze.

Not knowing what else to do, but knowing I needed to shift my attention, I held the flask up toward Hess. "Thanks."

He waved his hand toward me. "Finish it. You need it more than I do," he said, walking away.

"Try not to move it until we break camp tomorrow morning," Callon said, standing and walking to the other side of the fire as if he was happy to put a little space between us.

Wait, did he just say we were staying here tonight? In the Wilds, in the middle of the night, with no shelter? How were these guys alive if this was what they did? There was a beast around. I'd just hitched a ride with it.

"Here?"

"Yes," Callon said, his back still to me.

"But what about the beasts? We know one is nearby.

He didn't eat me the first time, but that doesn't mean he won't change his mind. Maybe he was just full?"

Callon laughed. "It'll be fine."

I caught Koz making a funny face, like he'd heard a bad joke.

No one else said anything.

I was stuck with crazy people.

6

Koz was poking at the fire, where a big chunk of meat cooked on a makeshift spit. I didn't know where the meat came from, but Koz had mad hunting skills. He'd left for ten minutes and managed to catch a turkey in that time. My mouth wouldn't stop watering, my taste buds screaming in anticipation, because I knew he'd be the one person here who'd share.

I was watching his hand turn the stick when it went still. His head turned, and tilted slightly, raising his ear skyward. Zink and Hess, both sitting on the other side of the fire, got to their feet. By the time I located Callon, all I saw was his back as he walked into the woods.

Turrock was here, or more likely his men. They'd followed me, even into the night. They hadn't waited until dawn. How much were they getting for me that they'd risk the beasts that roamed the Wilds after sundown?

Callon didn't want me here to begin with. He'd surely hand me over for a loose coin or two, no matter what Koz said.

Or maybe the beast had returned? I hoped it was the beast. He hadn't liked the smell of me the first time, so he wouldn't come for me. He'd try and eat one of them. Maybe he'd eat Zink, the one who'd talked about me like I was another dog Koz had picked up. I couldn't say I wanted Zink dead, but I wouldn't complain if he had a nip or two taken out of him by the end of the night.

They were all waiting for Callon to come back. I was waiting to be dragged away—or hear screams. Callon didn't look the type to carry on, though. He'd probably go down silently if the beast got him.

Hess and Zink didn't move, but Koz dropped his stick and came closer to me. His eyes stayed on the trees but his hand patted the air in my direction. I ignored his *all's good* gesture and surveyed the area for a stick of my own in case it was Turrock's men. I couldn't hop reliably with this leg wrapped, but I'd get a couple good swings in before they got me.

There, a few feet away, was a nice-looking one, good thickness and length. I shuffled my butt over. My fingers wrapped around it just as a scream, "Get off me!" cut the silence.

"Tuesday?" I clambered up to my good foot and immediately wobbled.

"Teddy, what are you doing?" Koz grabbed me under the arm.

I tried to hop forward, Koz moving with me, as I followed the sound of rustling in the woods.

"Teddy?" she yelled back.

A second later, she crashed through the woods. Callon was behind her, gripping the back of her shirt. He wasn't looking at her or me. He was staring at Koz, with the *you really fucked up this time* expression back on, as loud as if he screamed it across the camp.

"Great. It's multiplying," Zink said.

"Holy shit, it *is* like the dog," Hess said.

"This is *not* my fault," Koz said.

I didn't care how pissed off Callon was, or how Hess was saying we were like some dog. I didn't care if they all had a meltdown. Tuesday had braved the Wilds after sunset to help me.

I yanked my arm away from Koz, who was distracted by all the grief heading his way. I took a nose-dive halfway there but didn't crash-land. An arm looped around my hips, swinging me back up before I hit the ground. I knew it was Callon's without looking down. Somehow his smell had already imprinted on my mind. It was probably some deeply buried instinct to register danger. At least he was avoiding my sensitive spots.

Instead of letting me go, he hoisted me a foot off the ground as he walked away from Tuesday.

"Let me go!" I grabbed at his arm, trying to dislodge it from me.

"Teddy!" Tuesday screamed from somewhere behind us.

He turned back around, and then I was facing Tuesday again. I didn't know what Callon looked like, but I saw her jaw drop. Her fists froze as she took a good look at her opponent.

"Stop. Hitting. My. Back." He hoisted me up another couple inches and pointed with his free hand. "See that leg?" He waited until she nodded. "I'm not resetting it because she's drunk and falling all over the place. You can have your reunion after I put her over there."

He pointed to the log I'd been sitting by.

"Oh." Tuesday's fists dropped.

"Okay, then." I dislodged my nails from his arm, with only a minimal amount of his skin underneath them and a very small amount of blood.

"Thank you," Callon said, not sounding appreciative at all as he marched over and placed me on the aforementioned log. He didn't linger after he disposed of my body, heading straight for Koz.

Tuesday immediately sat beside me and wrapped her arms around my neck, as if her intention was to strangle me. I could barely breathe and I didn't care. I hugged her back even harder.

"You're taking care of them," Callon said to Koz, not ten feet from us.

"To give him his due, he *did* feed the dogs," Hess said as he stepped over to them.

Tuesday's grip loosened as she leaned back. "Are they calling us dogs?"

"Ignore them. You ran into the Wilds?"

Her face broke into a wide smile I hadn't seen since she raided Baryn's private stash and got away with it.

She leaned in and sniffed. "Are you drunk? You do smell a little bit like booze."

"Barely." I held up two fingers with a sliver of space between them. "How did you get here?"

"I saw the beast drag you out and I followed while the rest of them were too busy trying to find wood to block the hole. They were scrambling around and screaming when I slipped out. The thing moved too quickly to keep up, but your body left a wide trail. Once I lost the trail, I wandered."

Tuesday had been known to scream at a mouse on

occasion. She could say whatever she wanted. My heart warmed ten degrees.

I threw my arms around her again. "You could've been killed."

"Don't give me too much credit. It was running away from me, not *at* me." She shrugged in my hug. "I sure as hell wasn't staying in that hellhole alone."

How many times had I told her to go, find something better, and she'd insisted she wanted to be there? That she didn't think the place was that bad, so she'd hang out and wait.

I pulled back but kept my voice low, very aware that we weren't alone. Callon was still busy giving Koz a hard time, but he wasn't delusional. That man saw everything. I had a hunch that the more you didn't want him to see, the more his evil eyes focused. He didn't need to overhear our business. "So you're sure no one followed?"

"I didn't see anyone." She looked me over. "How did you end up in one piece? I thought beasts ate people?"

"I don't know. It grabbed me and then I passed out. When I woke up, they were there." I tilted my head toward the guys.

Tuesday turned, taking in the men, her eyes lingering on Callon. She scooted closer until her shoulder brushed mine.

"Some of them look a little scary," she said. "But it looks like they set your leg, so I guess they can't be that bad."

I could feel Callon's eyes boring into me. The Zink guy was laughing to himself. Koz was saying something but I couldn't make it out.

I focused back on Tuesday. "We won't be with them

long. They're going to bring me, now *us*, to the next village."

Her eyes crinkled. "That's *close*."

My fingers squeezed her arm. If we could hear them, they might be able to hear us.

"It's not where we would've planned, but it'll be nice," I lied, tilting my head so no one could see my face but her. I mouthed, *We aren't going to stay there.*

She nodded. "Yeah, I'm sure it'll be good. No, *great*. I've heard wonderful things about that place. The people in charge are supposed to be so nice, and you get a lot of days off from your work, plus…"

She kept going, but I turned back to the guys, hoping they weren't paying attention. Instead of a sprinkle of good words, she was hauling buckets. She'd bury it so well there'd be a mound of bull a mile high. Subterfuge was never Tuesday's thing.

Koz walked over with food, distracting her from covering her tracks and saving us both in the process.

Koz handed me a chunk of meat large enough for both of us.

I took the offering. "Thank you."

"I'm Koz," he said, smiling hesitantly at Tuesday.

She smiled like her jaw had just been greased. "Tuesday."

He paused for a second, and they took each other in before he nodded and then walked away.

Tuesday kept staring. "He's handsome," she whispered. "And his teeth are so pretty. We don't have anyone who looks like that at the village. He's so big, too. I bet he's a really good protector."

I wasn't so sure about that. Koz might be a little too nice. If she wanted protection, she was better off setting her sights on Callon. He looked the type to kill without hesitation.

"Maybe." Didn't matter either way. We wouldn't be with them long enough for any of that.

I ripped the meat in half, or sort of, and handed Tuesday the larger chunk. I had to nudge her with my elbow to get her attention off Koz.

"How far is this village we're going to?" she asked, her voice a little softer.

"They say it's about twenty miles from here. Not enough time for anything." I broke off a tiny piece of meat, putting it on the good side of my mouth while I watched her rip into her piece.

She choked down her first bite.

"Is that where they're from?" she asked, still looking at Koz.

She took another huge bite, while I was still working on my first.

"I don't know where *they're* from." They, not us. That was the important thing here. We weren't on the same team, and she better not forget that because of a good head of hair.

Tuesday lost the whimsical look and her forehead bunched. For a split second, I thought my point had sunk in.

"The scary one is watching me eat," she said.

She was staring right at Callon. She had a point. He was watching her eat.

"Maybe he doesn't like to share food? Chew quicker so you don't keep reminding him he's sharing."

Afraid of giving up her food, she shoved a piece in her mouth so big that I was afraid she was going to choke. She was done in a matter of minutes.

After a few more tiny bites, I handed her my piece too. If the guy did have a thing about sharing, we were better off finishing up quick. I didn't need any more fights about how Koz should bring me back.

"Too painful?" she asked, taking mine too.

I nodded. "I'm fine. Not that hungry."

She took the meat but struggled a little more with this piece.

Koz, with a last smile in our direction, settled down in front of the fire on our right. Hess and Zink did the same not too long after.

Tuesday stretched out, getting comfortable as well.

One by one, I saw them drifting off, until only Callon was left awake. He stood in front of the fire for a little while. I wasn't sure what he was thinking about as he stared into the flames, deep eyes watching it as if he saw something that I couldn't.

I turned on my side, removing him from my vision so I'd stop being so curious. A few minutes later, he walked off into the trees. I didn't know who should be more nervous, him or the beasts.

I listened for soft snores before I nudged Tuesday's arm to get her attention, knowing she wasn't completely asleep.

"If it gets ugly, we should split up," I said in hushed tone.

Tuesday was shaking her head before I finished. "No."

"Tuesday, I'm dead weight. You might—"

"Nope. I'm not doing it."

I didn't speak, hearing nothing but crickets for a minute. "We'll talk about it—"

"Never. Not talking about it ever."

I didn't say anything else. When Tuesday was in one of those moods, which she certainly was now, there would be no talking. As the minutes of silence ticked by, we both accepted the truce. I wouldn't bother her now, but she knew I'd harass her later. She'd then repeat what she'd just said and refuse to discuss it. Sometimes I wondered why I bothered. Once she'd made a decision, there was no going back.

She stirred next to me, nearly twenty minutes after I thought she'd fallen asleep. "Have you seen anything? You know, that stuff?"

"No."

Tuesday hated to say I saw death, let alone believe it. She'd told me once that it was too creepy and that I wasn't creepy enough, so it just didn't work for her. When we'd been younger, she used to pretend it was all in my head. I used to do that too in the beginning. By the time I was ten, the body count had piled up too high and I'd gotten past denial. She was still clinging, but she had that luxury.

"Really? None of them?" The whisper was softened further by confusion.

"No." I wasn't always a hundred percent, but I never struck out four times in a row. I should've seen one of their deaths. What did that mean? Was it me or them?

"Can you still see mine?" she asked, probably thinking the same.

"Good point." She knew my theory about only seeing deaths that happened within my life span. If I was right, and I could still see hers, we'd both make it out of this mess. *Or* my untested theory was a joke. I preferred not to believe that.

We'd only talked about her death once, even though

I'd seen it plenty. I grabbed her hand, giving it a bit of a jump start with a skin to skin connection. I didn't normally need help, but familiarity tended to dull the visions, and hers was a comforting one I didn't mind. The familiar sight flashed in my mind.

"Is it the same?" she asked.

"Same."

I didn't have to tell her what I saw. She knew. Old and grey, dying peacefully in bed with family all around her and an expression that said she was ready. She'd live a long and full life. The most comforting was she'd be around for a long time to come.

Those were the kinds of deaths I could deal with. Too bad there were so few of them.

7

I woke to the wind blowing in my face and the smell of trees. I breathed in forest air and sat up, listening to the birds. For the first time in eighteen years, I didn't envy them. I couldn't fly, but I was no longer caged. Baryn was dead, even if Turrock might still be out there.

Tuesday stirred beside me as the smell of meat cooking drifted over. I didn't see Callon, but Hess and Zink were walking out of camp with their water bags while Koz worked his spit.

I moved my hand and it knocked into a pair of sticks, both with forked tops chopped short and stubs sticking out about halfway down. There was a piece of fur wrapped around the top of both to cushion them.

I'd seen things like this in the village, when other people had been hurt. I'd just never had a pair. I'd used a regular stick once, without the luxury of leather. Baryn had broken it in half when he'd seen it. I hadn't bothered again.

Tuesday hadn't stirred from beside me all night. She

was still rubbing the sleep from her eyes, so she hadn't left them there.

There was only one other suspect. I looked over at Koz.

He smiled. "They're not the best, but they'll help you get around."

"Thank you." I ran my fingers over the fur.

Koz waved a hand. "It wasn't a big deal," he said, looking back to the fire, his eyes darting back to me as I checked them out.

Tuesday, still yawning, sat up to see what we were talking about.

"He made you crutches," she whispered, awe in her voice. Her eyes shot to Koz, looking at him as if he were a god walking among mortals. "You made her crutches."

He shrugged and smiled at her. Their eyes met and glued. I didn't care. I was too busy wanting to play with my crutches to worry about their crush.

I stood up on one leg, dragging the crutches up with me and putting one under each arm. It took a little maneuvering, but I got a few steps down. The next few weren't nearly as klutzy. By the next handful, I was cruising.

I listened for the sound of water and hobbled my way toward it.

"Hang on, I'm coming with you," Tuesday said.

I slowed down, but it took some effort on my part. I moved better on these than when I walked normally with my limp. Tuesday fell in beside me and we followed the sound of the stream, only having to stop a few times to untangle weeds from my crutches.

I balanced with one crutch at the bank of the stream. The cold water rushed over my hands, freezing, and all I wanted was to plunge into it, because I could. There was only one stream that ran through the village, but I hadn't dunked myself in it since Maura had died, not even in the boiling heat of summer. Everything had gotten so much worse once Maura had died.

Sometimes I wished she could come back for a single day, or even an hour, so I could thank her for all the things I hadn't known she'd done. She'd been a buffer between me and Baryn for years and never said a word.

And what it had cost her, I hadn't known that until even later. It had taken older eyes and a string of bad experiences to piece it together. Even Tuesday didn't know the extent of what Maura had done for me, and I'd never tell her. I couldn't bring myself to, for her and for me. Tuesday didn't need to carry that knowledge around with her, and I didn't want to see the way she'd look at me if she learned the truth.

Tuesday flicked some water at me, drawing my attention to the present.

"Can you believe we're out of there?" Tuesday asked, as she knelt beside me, enjoying the stream.

"No. I really can't." I dunked my arms in past my elbows, splashing it over every inch of skin I could. The cuts on my face burned and I splashed more, relishing in the abundance.

She sat back on her heels after another few minutes. "I wonder if Koz has a girl back where he comes from?"

Ah shit. I flicked some water back at her and she scrunched her face.

I ignored the look.

"Don't get attached. They're dropping us off at the next village. We can't go with them." If it had been Koz alone, it might've been different. But he had the other three, and one was more hardened than the next until you worked your way up the mountain to the man of granite himself, Callon.

"Maybe they would take us with them? It's not like we've got somewhere to be." She dared me to say she was wrong with almond eyes, large and demanding.

"Callon calls the shots and he's not going to do that. He wants us gone. Even if Koz agreed, it wouldn't matter."

She crinkled her eyes but stopped talking. She leaned back over the water, not saying anything. Silence was never good with Tuesday. Never. Not since we were little kids. Silence meant she had decided to stop talking to you because she didn't like what you had to say. It meant nothing about what she was going to do.

Did I pretend nothing was wrong or try and persuade her?

"Tuesday—"

She sat back up. "I don't see why we couldn't try."

"I think we're better off on our own."

"You really so sure? Have you looked at us lately?" She was staring at me as if I'd gone daft. As if I didn't know that I was lacking two good legs and she hit as hard as butterfly wings.

It was such a comical face that I might've laughed if I hadn't caught a hint of movement across the stream. "Did you see that?"

She followed my gaze. "I don't see anything, but that's exactly why we need them." She hooked her thumb back toward camp.

I kept staring into the shadows across the way. It might've been a deer or something. Or plain old paranoia. Paranoia wasn't such a bad thing right now. It would keep me on my toes, where I needed to be. Maybe she was right that we could use a little help, but it didn't change anything. We didn't have willing help. It was us.

"We can't have them. They're not an option. But if you want to try, go ahead—just don't get all broken up when it doesn't happen." Was that a branch in the shadow of a tree?

Tuesday smiled so wide that I could see her molars. "Good. I will."

I dried my hands on what was left of my pants, now more wet than dry. Tuesday helped prop me back up on my crutches. We made our way back to the camp, my skin still tingling with the buzz of invisible eyeballs watching me. We might not have company for much longer, but I'd feel better with them around at the moment.

I didn't even mind when Callon stopped speaking to Zink as we approached. Obviously they'd been discussing *us*, but at least he didn't try and cover up with some stupid chatter. Koz was the only one who smiled as we made our way over and settled down in front of the log.

Koz grabbed some meat off the spit and brought us two pieces of something so blackened that I couldn't identify it.

"We eat a large breakfast because we don't stop for lunch."

His smile had gotten a little something extra since last night.

"Thank you," Tuesday said. "I'm sure it's wonderful."

Tuesday's smile was the same, but hers couldn't

handle anything extra. It was already packed full. Between the two of them, I was about to get a stomachache.

"Koz," Callon called, breaking up the moment.

I wasn't the only one catching the vibes buzzing back and forth between them, or maybe he really did need to speak to him at that very second.

The meat, some dark red stuff I couldn't name, smelled like heaven in spite of its aggressive cooking. I took as much as I thought I could choke down and handed Tuesday the rest.

"Still?" she asked, taking it.

I swallowed the small piece I'd put in my mouth with as little chewing as possible. "It's been worse. Probably only another few days."

She nodded and then went back to devouring her share. For as slim as Tuesday was, she ate with the ferocity and gusto of a three-hundred-pound man.

I was still focusing on my tiny pieces when I sensed her stiffening beside me.

"He's watching me eat again."

I glanced up. Technically, Callon was watching both of us. He didn't look angry, but he did seem awfully intent. He really must not like sharing.

"Eat faster."

She shoved half the piece in her mouth, using her fingers to push it back in when it threatened to escape.

I was listening for choking sounds when I heard Hess talking to Callon. "Should we make a sled? She's going to take forever with those crutches."

Huh? I thought I was doing pretty good! I took a couple more tiny bits of meat as I split my attention between listening for choking sounds to come out of Tuesday and their conversation.

Callon shook his head. "No. We'll carry her. It'll be easier, and Hera isn't too far."

Carry me? Like, miles? Ugh. That sounded absolutely horrid, and I wasn't even the one doing the lifting. I was small but I wasn't *that* light. I'd probably only have to put up with it for a little while before they realized it was a stupid idea.

Koz stopped kicking dirt onto the fire's ashes to turn toward Callon, as if this deserved his full attention. "We're going to Hera?"

That was a good point. Who was Hera? And why would we go there?

"Who's Hera?" Tuesday whispered, as if I'd have an answer. Sometimes Tuesday thought because I could see death, I had some unlimited source of information.

I gave her the *shush face* so her talking wouldn't ruin my eavesdropping.

"It's not that far out of the way," Callon said, as he moved through camp.

Koz looked like someone had told him a riddle.

Hess and Zink moved in a bit closer, seeming pretty interested in this as well.

"But why?" Koz asked.

Callon's gaze moved to my leg before going back to Koz. "If we don't, they might not take her like that."

Then no one said anything else about it. After a minute of awkward silence, they all went back to business as usual, breaking down the camp and leaving me stumped.

Why would they bring me to someone else for my

leg? What else was there to do? Callon had set it already.

"Who's Hera?" Tuesday asked, loud enough for all to hear.

Tuesday had a strong immunity to the *shush face*, and for once I was glad.

Koz walked over to where Tuesday was sitting beside me and knelt to our level. "A witch. She has her drawbacks, but she might be able to heal it completely. Callon has a point. The next village will be more willing to take you if you can walk without crutches."

I had no intention of going to the next village, but it didn't matter. Healing my leg completely? That might make all the difference in the world.

Turrock was still around to collect on how much he'd sold me for, and he wouldn't be satisfied with the story of a beast dragging me off. He'd want to see the eaten bones of my remains. I couldn't stay around here, and having my leg healed would help us keep moving.

Except the witch would want to be paid, and I had nothing but empty pockets. "I have no coin."

"I'll pay," Callon said, from far enough away that I hadn't realized he'd been listening.

I turned toward his voice. He was staring at my shirt.

Maybe dowsing myself in the river hadn't been a logical decision, but it had still been the best decision. My hair was dripping puddles onto it, making it worse.

Callon walked to his bag and grabbed out a piece of hide. He tossed it so it landed by my hip. "Use that. They won't take you sick, either."

He'd do just about anything to get rid of me, even spend his coin. I turned toward Tuesday and raised my brows. *They are not good people. You must see this, right?*

She was too busy staring at Koz to notice my glares. I wasn't sure why I bothered. She was sunk. She was going to try and sink her claws into Koz so deep that she'd put the beast that killed Baryn to shame.

Callon walked over and stopped in front of me.

Without warning, he leaned forward, and I jerked back, knocking my crutches over from where they were leaning against the log. His hands followed me until one was around my back and the other under my legs.

"What are you doing?"

"Carrying you."

Of course he'd be the one carrying me. I tensed even more, waiting for him to jerk me upward now that he had me in his clutches. He was slow in his movements, as if aware of how he might hurt my leg.

Okay, maybe he wasn't a total ass. He'd set my leg and he wasn't unnecessarily rough. But that was it. He wasn't getting anything else from me. Not even for smelling good.

"Wait, my crutches!" I tried to squirm out of his arms to get down and grab them.

"You aren't going to need them," he said as he continued walking.

I was taking it back. He was a complete ass.

"Tuesday!" I yelled, looking over his shoulder.

She was already grabbing them and then waved one in each hand.

"Don't worry! I got them, Teddy! I got them!" she said, as she fell in behind us.

Hess turned to Zink. "At least the dog wasn't weird and could walk on its own."

Zink nudged Koz with his elbow. "Yeah, Koz. Couldn't you just get another dog?"

Koz didn't respond. He was too busy smiling in Tuesday's direction. If I wasn't up close and personal with Callon, I would've groaned. We were not staying with these men, even if she figured out a miracle. Not going to happen. I refused to end up with Callon for a day more than necessary.

8

It happened. Tuesday was going to get her way. She wouldn't have to conjure up a miracle, and I didn't even see it coming. There'd been no sign of trouble on the horizon when we started out.

The first hour on the road with them wasn't too bad, even though I was pressed against the chest of the one man here who unsettled me the most. I hadn't had this much constant physical contact in maybe my entire life.

Within two minutes of this ordeal, it became clear that it was almost impossible to look anywhere but at him, at his lips, his jaw, his eyes, his hair. Unless, of course, I wanted to turn my head constantly and mess up my neck, one of the only properly functioning body parts I had left. So, I stared past him, focusing on the scenery, and pretended his head wasn't. Right. There.

Unfortunately, my nose was working well too. He had this crazy blend of cedar, orange, and cardamom that made me want to lick him to see if he tasted as good as he smelled. It wasn't natural. He'd been traipsing around the forest. It went against all logic.

Forget about the little zings of energy that shot through me every time he shifted me in his arms, like some weird sort of built-up friction between us.

So I focused on the trees. Trees and trees and more trees. Trees everywhere. I didn't know what I'd expected would lie outside the village, but something more than this. The grass beneath us had flattened out strangely in the last mile or so, like we were walking through a valley of trees. Every so often, I caught sight of a patch of concrete or a strange growth that rose twenty or so feet out of the ground and seemed too square to be natural. Then I'd spy a stone structure peeking out of the vines and realize it was all still here. The world the Bloody Death hadn't been able to completely wipe out of existence, a ghost still haunting us. You only had to look hard.

Once Tuesday and I were on our own, we'd find one of these overgrown buildings, clean off all the vegetation, and make a home, like I'd seen in pictures. We'd have little pots filled with flowers and a fire roaring in the winter. We'd hang fabric over the windows. The past would eventually fade away.

I was eyeing up another hidden building when I caught sight of Koz walking closer.

"You want me to take her for a while?" Koz asked, as he fell in beside us.

My rigid frame relaxed. Koz was safe, easy. He wouldn't churn out energy like a supernova and shoot off sparks.

Callon stopped walking and turned toward Koz, leaning over and about to pass me off. Then he straightened, his arms tightening around me and his chest grumbled.

"It's okay. I'm good." Callon turned and started walking again.

What? Huh?

"You sure?" Koz asked, looking the way I felt —stumped.

"Yes," Callon barked at him.

My mouth gaped. If I hadn't been stuck in his arms, and had two good legs, I would've stomped a foot.

"Don't you need a break?" I asked. I sure as hell did.

"He'll walk too slow," he said, jaw tensed and not looking at me.

What was he mad about? Koz trying to help him? Me? What had I done? I was the one who was supposed to be mad.

He didn't have to keep carrying me. I hadn't wanted to be carried. I could've used my crutches and been fine.

A little slower, but fine.

I clamped my mouth shut, and neither of us talked for the next hour. I focused on a healed leg. I didn't know what he was thinking, and I didn't try to find out. He was obviously annoyed about something, but it was his problem.

On the upside, every step we took away from Turrock took my anxiety down a smidge. It didn't even matter where Tuesday and I ended up. Anywhere would be better than where we'd started, and if I had to be carried away from that place by *him*, then so be it. I'd deal.

A group of crows flew overhead, cawing in agreement. Or that was what I thought they'd said. I wondered where they'd been. If they laughed, I swore I was going to throw rocks at them as soon as I got my legs back underneath me.

"I swear, these are the same birds that were at the camp. I think they're following us," Hess said.

I'd missed them at camp. Maybe they were finally respecting my space a little?

"Hess, do you know how crazy that sounds?" Zink asked.

Tuesday's eyes went round, but she pressed her lips firmly together.

"What did you do back in your village?" Koz asked Tuesday, looking for an excuse to sidle up next to her. "Did you have a job?"

"Laundry. It wasn't bad. Passed the time."

"What about you, Teddy?" Koz asked.

He was asking me for one of two reasons. He felt like he should after he asked her, or he was trying to hide that he was crushing just as hard as Tuesday. If he was doing the former, it would've been nicer if he'd ignored me.

"Laundry," I blurted out. "It wasn't bad, like she said."

Tuesday glanced over at me but seemed to be holding on to her streak of newfound silence.

Koz said something else to Tuesday that I couldn't hear, and I didn't care. He'd moved his attention solely back to her, and the other two had stopped talking about the birds. Things were back on track.

Callon, on the other hand, turned his head toward me. My position made it hard to ignore the sardonic expression plastered on his face.

Okay, so he knew I was full of it. It didn't matter. "What?" I asked, going with an offensive position.

"We're almost there," Callon said, looking ahead

again, as if he'd decided it wasn't worth delving into my lie.

We hadn't gone much farther when the sound of water running could be heard underneath the birds chirping and the sound of fall leaves blowing off the trees. It wasn't the gentle trickle of a stream but a massive tide. Did that mean we were going to the Gathering? It had to be. I'd heard stories of the place. People from our village, mostly the men, would come here and trade for other goods.

We turned, and the gap in the trees widened. I could see it. It was exactly as I'd imagined: an island in the center of a river that ran wide and rough. A wooden bridge spanned the water. I'd heard that it was pulled in every night to keep the beasts out.

The place was cluttered with colorful tents and small wooden buildings. There were carts and the smell of food, but there weren't too many people, luckily.

They had a guard on duty, a crossbow and arrows slung across his back. He nodded in our direction as we crossed the wooden bridge, as if he recognized most of our group.

Callon stopped as we got off the bridge. "Koz, I'm bringing Teddy to Hera. Go find new pants for her while I do."

Koz nearly tripped in his rush to turn around. "Me? How do I know what pants to buy? I've never bought stuff for a girl."

Every part of me groaned, and I didn't need to look over at Tuesday to know she was smiling. With those two sentences, Koz had declared himself single.

"I don't need pants. I need a needle and thread." Tuesday didn't need alone time with Koz and his *I want to help* attitude. In the end, Koz would listen to Callon and then they'd dump us. I was quite happy about that, but the more time Tuesday had to stare at Koz, the worse it would be for her.

"I ripped them. I'll replace them."

He didn't even look at me when he spoke half the time. Just barked what was going to happen.

"I don't need—"

"I. Don't. Care. Throw them in the river, but you're getting them."

Throw them in the river? What kind of crazy person would do that with brand-new pants? Was he so delusional that he didn't realize how valuable new clothes were? Even if I was annoyed, I'd never do that. He was bossy and wasteful.

"If you get them, how can I possibly—"

"Tuesday!" Callon shouted over to where she'd already walked off with Koz.

"Yes?" she asked, running back to his side a little too eagerly for my liking, as if he were in charge of her now too.

We were going to have to talk. I'd thought she'd understood that anyone not "us" needed to be treated with supreme caution, with the exception of Koz. Even Koz should be deemed neutral at best. Callon was in charge, so it didn't matter if Koz was single.

"Pick yourself out some, too."

He hadn't ripped hers. Why was he getting her a pair?

"Why are you doing that?" I asked. It was a move designed to win her over, but why bother? We'd be parting soon, so what would be the point?

"Because I can."

I huffed loud enough to make sure he heard it. I could've told him he didn't have to buy her anything. Let her hang out with Koz and that was all she needed. She'd nearly danced her way over to him, and the pep in her step had nothing to do with clothing. Koz stood and waited, a more-than-willing partner.

Zink was shaking his head as he watched the duo walk off. At least somebody understood. Zink turned, noticing my eyes on him. I shook my head and he nodded. I might not like Zink, but at least him I understood.

I made sure to look at Callon now, narrowing my eyes. "You know she's not one of your men."

"And yet she follows orders so well?" His eyebrows dropped and he squinted, as if it were all a huge mystery to him, too.

I turned my head, hoping we'd get to the witch soon, or my neck was going to get a horrible crick. Even his face was too much to tolerate at the moment.

I'd never seen so many faces at once. There had been one good thing about the village. I didn't meet a lot of new people. I tried not to focus on any of them, hoping I wouldn't pick up their details, the deaths that would come. Callon weaved in and out of tents, and every head turned to look our way, but most kept their distance, which kept the visions to a manageable dribble.

Still, it was nearly impossible as people passed to not pick up something. A stabbing here and a strangulation there—it was a wonder there were any humans left.

I kept my head down, not wanting to see the victims' faces, but it was hard to avoid them. They all stared at me as if they'd never seen someone scarred before. Kind of ironic, considering the bloody deaths piling up.

Who needed to look at the rainbow of tents, anyway? They were just fabric. I turned and studied Callon's jaw instead, the thick stubble that had scratched my hand earlier when I'd brushed it by accident.

Callon shifted, and I found myself a little closer to his shoulder and neck. "This happens everywhere I go. People can't seem to help themselves around me," he said, face as straight as an arrow. He kept looking forward, as if he were the target of all the attention.

Handsome or not, he knew people avoided locking gazes with him. He looked like he'd kill you if the wind blew wrong. It was me they stared at. I choked back a snicker. Maybe he wasn't a total jerk. There might've been a sliver of a decent guy in there, at least when he wasn't telling people to get rid of me or acting like I was the biggest burden ever carried.

By the time I looked around again, we were coming upon a bright yellow tent. If I were to live in a tent, that was the color I would've chosen. It made me think of a big ball of sunshine. It was back, spaced farther away than the rest of the tents and building. It was part of the community, but I wasn't sure if the community was thrilled about that.

Callon carried me inside, the flap making us known.

"Hera," Callon said.

Hera turned from the young lad she'd been talking softly to, who had the same black hair and deep eyes she had. Her gaze took in my leg, then the bruises on my face.

"What can I do for you, Callon?" she asked, as if it weren't obvious.

"Can you fix her?"

Callon stepped closer, which meant I got closer too.

I knew immediately that she had a few decades left, but not the boy. He'd be lying on that same pile of pillows she had in the corner, not very long from now, his skin unmarred by the luxury of a full life but ravaged by sickness. His life would seep out as she kneeled beside him crying the way only a mother could over a child, her entire body racked in the pain of it all.

"If you're paying." She walked over to a table with candles, her red skirt swaying. She lit up a stick of weeds, the smoke billowing as she took it and walked around the tent.

"I always pay. You don't always fix." Callon carried me farther into the tent.

"What are you paying with?" She narrowed her eyes. "Newco money is nearly worthless since the takeover. I'm only accepting gas or gold now."

"Gold, like I always do. But this time, the healing better stick," he said, turning with her as she walked around the tent.

"That wasn't my fault. You knew it was a possibility." She pointed to a group of pillows piled up on the floor. "You putting her down or what?"

Callon didn't move. "How long will it take?"

"Can't say until I see how bad. Maybe immediately, and maybe not until tomorrow." She stepped closer, waving her smelling weeds at us, making me cough.

"Get that shit out of my face," Callon said. "I want this done today."

She moved the stick but hesitated to move away, staring at me so intently that I wanted to bark at her too and ask what her problem was. I would've if the possibility of my leg being healed wasn't dangling.

"Then you best be putting her down and giving me my space," the witch said.

He walked over toward the pillows and kneeled, setting me down. He didn't get back up right away, though. That was when I realized my arm was still around his neck, as if it had its own mind and didn't want to be left to the ministrations of this woman.

I pulled it back quickly, not sure why I'd done that in the first place. I turned toward the witch, pretending it hadn't happened.

His eyes rested on me for anther second before he rose. "Why do I need to leave?"

The witched huffed, as if it were obvious. "She's a lass. I need her to strip, and you don't need to be seeing that."

"I think I can handle seeing her without clothes."

Could "handle" it, like a chore to have to suffer through. I wasn't naïve. No man, or one of normal tastes, at least, would want to see my scarred and disfigured form. I knew what I looked like now.

Either way, it didn't matter, as I wasn't looking for a man's attention. I didn't want anyone, but he could've said he'd turn his back or something.

Hera's hands went to her hips. "But maybe she would like a little privacy?"

"Leave me here." My voice came out stronger than intended. I'd meant to act nonchalant, not like I was ready to throw down in a brawl. I just wanted him gone. If my scars were that distasteful, he didn't need to see them.

Callon slowly turned back toward me, eyes narrowed and standing still. What? Why did he look so surprised? Did he think I'd be happy he was willing to tough out having to see more of me? Did he expect me to be flattered he was going to stay in the room with me and bare my ugliness upon his eyes? I didn't want him either, but being reminded I was disgusting wasn't endearing.

Chin up, steel in my shoulders, I stopped looking at him and put my attention solely on Hera, which was harder than you'd think with the way Callon sucked up all the air in a room. Honestly, he was near overbearing. I wasn't sure why my arm had latched on to him. Probably a muscle spasm or something.

"Shout if you need me." His tone didn't lend itself to thinking there'd be help on the other end if he heard it.

She waited for the silence of his steps, and then some, before she knelt beside me. "I know who you are and I know you've got magic."

That niggling sense of unease blossomed into full distrust. This hadn't been about giving me privacy. I'd known she was off. Dammit. I should've made Callon stay, even if he did bruise my pride a little.

I opened my mouth to yell before he got too far away, but she stopped me. "Just hear me out."

I swallowed as she stared. One of the guys might not be too far away. Would they hear me if I did yell? Would they come? Callon might think it for the best to have this problem taken from his hands. Maybe I was better off letting her speak while she still thought there was someone out there willing to save me.

"What do you want?"

She laid a hand on my good leg. "I don't want to harm you. I know you've been sold and I know the one you've been sold to. What I'm going to do is save you, but I'm going to need something in return."

What were the odds that this woman knew anything? Logic said word hadn't spread that fast, but that didn't stop my heart from pumping so quick and hard that I thought my ribcage would burst open.

"I have no idea what you're talking about." This two-bit witch was not scamming me just because my face and body screamed that I was desperate.

"I saw how you looked at my boy when you came in. You're the one." There wasn't a shred of doubt in her eyes. She was so intent that the boy in question edged closer, wondering what was going on.

"I didn't look at him strangely." I scooted back on the pillows, dislodging her hand. Was I going to have to use my good leg to kick her in the gut while I screamed bloody murder?

She followed, nearly leaning over me. "Tell me what you saw."

"I didn't see anything." All I needed was to get out of here. The break would heal eventually. I didn't need whatever crazy this witch was selling.

"The monster who comes for you will never let you go. If you want to survive this, I can help you." She took my hand. "I'm going to save you. That man who carried you in, I know him and his people. He's your answer. He could keep you safe if he had to."

There was truth there. I'd seen it myself. Callon didn't even fear the beasts. Turrock would be nothing to him. There was just enough bait on that lure to hook me into the conversation, even after I'd decided I wanted no part of it.

"But he doesn't have to."

"I can make it so that he does. I know what's coming for you, and this is your only chance. I've heard things.

The one that's coming, he won't give up. You won't find another that can help you. It must be Callon."

How many times had I heard crazy rumors at the village that had been all lies? Was I really going to let some woman claiming to be a witch with crazy eyes and a dying son lure me in?

"You know what? I think you're full of it."

She grabbed my shoulders. "Listen to me. You're right. Do I sometimes take a coin I didn't earn? Yes. I do what I have to, and so will you. Because I'm telling you, I know what is coming for you, and if you do this thing for me, I will help save you from this evil." She released me and waved toward where her son was hanging back a few feet.

He made his way to his mother, and she put her arm around him. "I'm a witch. I know the power of words, and I swear, all I say is true on the life of my son."

I'd seen her sobbing as he'd lain suffering in my vision. The agony his death caused her. She believed everything she was saying.

And now, so did I.

Chills shot through me. "What's coming for me?"

"A man, if you could call him that. He's more monster than anything now. There's not many that would be able to protect you, but Callon and his men can."

"And you can force him to protect me?"

"Yes." She said it with desperation, as if her life was on the line.

But force? The word tasted like bitter poison on my tongue. How many times had I been forced to do something? Years stolen away, and I was going to turn around and do it to someone else now to save myself? Someone who, other than not wanting me around, hadn't wronged me in any way? Was paying to have my leg healed? I might not like him, but he didn't deserve this.

I shook my head, not trusting myself to say the word no, the temptation was so great. But I couldn't do this to someone else.

"This has to be done, and we don't have time. That smoke will block whatever things might be watching, but not for long. This must be done now." Her hands were back to gripping me, fingers digging into my wrists.

"I can't—"

"If you don't, it will kill everyone and everything around you to get you. You *must*." Her voice was frantic, her eyes scary.

Tuesday. My heart stopped beating. My skin grew clammy. Tuesday would never leave my side. I might not be willing to sacrifice Callon for me, but I'd sacrifice him and his men to save her. I owed her that. I owed Maura even more.

"What would I have to do?" I said, knowing as soon as the words left my mouth that I'd taken the first step toward hell.

Tuesday was going to get her wish, and she wasn't even going to have to conjure up a miracle to get it. I'd made a deal with the devil instead.

9

I walked out of the tent on two good legs, and yet I was rockier on my feet than before she'd touched me. Callon would probably assume Hera had done a lousy job healing me, and I'd let him. It would save me telling him the true reason I felt like I'd been deboned. As for the shaking hands, I'd blame it on exhaustion and not the shock coursing through my body.

Had that really happened? A tremor shot up my spine, aftereffects leaking into my arms. I shook it off. I'd done what she'd told me. That was all. *Don't think of it. Do what you have to and think of what happened later, much later. Maybe never.*

I walked across the packed earth, where Tuesday and Koz were waiting by themselves.

Tuesday saw me first. She squinted, as if the light were ruining her eyesight, and then her jaw dropped. Koz followed Tuesday's stare.

I turned to Tuesday. Tears were streaming down her face. "You're beautiful. She took it all away, every bad thing."

"Teddy?" Koz asked. "I didn't know Hera could do that kind of magic. She didn't even heal the last bone right."

My fingers went to my face, feeling the smooth skin. I'd known she'd done something to my face because I'd felt the tingles as the magic had burned there, and everywhere else. She hadn't asked if I wanted my scars gone. She'd just done it, saying it was safer. She'd said it was one of the things people would be looking for as they hunted me.

Once upon a time, I'd dreamt of having a pretty face again. Being admired and beautiful. Now, as their eyes burned my skin, I wasn't sure this was better. They weren't seeing me anymore. Every mark was still there, carved into my soul so deeply that they'd never go away. The only thing that had changed was that no one else could see them. I felt like an imposter in a stranger's skin.

"What's going on?" Callon asked, coming up from behind me.

Keeping my back to him, I launched into what I'd been told to say before I lost my nerve. "Hera said the leg was on her because she owed you for the last thing that went wrong."

She owed him even more for what we'd done. I wasn't ready to break that to him yet. Wasn't sure when I was going to be able to break that. That girl who'd wanted to live large and rage against the world was even telling me we weren't quite ready for this fight yet. Plan. Think it through.

Telling him was going to be bad, worse than breaking a leg. Might be worse than breaking every bone in my body. I wasn't sure what the fallout would be yet, but it would be intense. Had to be, because Callon was. I still couldn't quite believe I'd gone along with this.

I heard more footsteps and then a gasp.

"Holy shit, what did she do to you?" Zink asked.

Callon stepped in front of me to see what the deal was. For someone who didn't show much emotion, his eyes flaring was the same as Koz running around and screaming.

My skin grew warm. Why I was embarrassed over not having scars? Still, my face grew hotter and hotter until I must've been beet red. When I couldn't stand it anymore, I knelt down, tying a lace that was already tied.

"It's not a big deal. She's healed, is all," Callon said, walking until his legs were in front of me.

"Hess can't help himself. He doesn't get close to too many girls," Zink said, picking up on Callon's vibe and moving the conversation along.

"Excuse me, but I think we all know how untrue that is—for me, anyway," Hess said.

"You think you get more ass than me?" Zink shot back.

When I stood, Callon was facing me and his broad shoulders blocked me from the others. "Tuesday has some new stuff for you. Go duck behind a building and change before we take off."

If he'd suggested that an hour ago, I would've rebuffed his gift. Now, I couldn't wait to get away from them for a few minutes.

Tuesday's hand was on mine. She tugged me behind the building that was closest. It backed up to the river and had a few trees around it.

She shoved a pair of pants, a new shirt, and a

sweater at me. "Are you all right? You seem weird for someone who has, well, had some good shit happen for once. Why aren't you smiling?"

"Yeah…" I gnawed on my lower lip, not saying anything about the amount of clothes I had. Bigger problems and all that.

I started undressing while I decided how I was going to break the news to her before we went back.

Tuesday leaned forward, staring. "Wow, they're really all gone. That's amazing."

I yanked the new shirt on so quick that my arm got jammed up from not aligning with the sleeve right. And I could still feel her staring. My head poked out and I grabbed the sweater next. Layers would be good, considering this newfound scrutiny.

By the time my head popped back out, she said, "What else, though? You look like you did that time right before Turrock got sick."

Figured Tuesday would put that together. She knew me better than maybe even Maura had. It had been my first try at retaliation. I'd taken a piece of decaying meat and put it in his water bucket when he wasn't paying attention. He vomited that night like his insides were trying to escape his body, but he survived. I'd never actually uttered aloud what I'd done, but Tuesday always suspected I'd done something.

She held up the new pants for me. "You can tell me. You know I'd never betray you."

"I know you wouldn't." She had plenty of chances and had always stayed true. She wasn't the problem. It was what I'd done.

"But you aren't ready?" she asked, watching as I put on the new pants. They were leather, like the guys had. I looked at her legs, and noticed she had leather ones too, just as we always said we'd get.

She noticed me looking and struck a pose, pointing out a hip one way and a leg the other way.

I tried to smile for her, but it didn't last. I ran my hands through my hair and then crossed them in front of me. "I did something bad."

Her mouth popped into an O. "How bad?"

"Bad enough that we won't be going to the next village. They're going to have to take us with them. But you can't say a thing yet."

Tuesday's face transformed, and suddenly she was looking at me like she looked at Koz—the *you're a god* part but minus the lust.

"Oh, Teddy, I love you." Her arms were around my neck, squeezing tight while she jumped up and down. "How?"

"By doing some shit I can't talk about yet."

"I don't care what you did. This is wonderful!" She stepped back so she could jump a few more times without me anchoring her down.

"I'm not sure this was a good thing." I gnawed on the inside of my mouth. "You can't say anything."

"I won't." Her hands were gripped in front of her heart. "I'm meant to be with Koz. I *know* it."

I grabbed her arm, trying to weigh her back down to earth. "Don't. Say. A. Word."

"Okay, okay." She shook out her hands and then wiped the smile off her face.

"You're good," I said, hoping she could hold it.

We headed back, and I had to nudge her another five times to keep her from bouncing.

We walked out of the Gathering, and for the first time since I was twelve, I didn't limp.

10

"When will we be getting to the next village?" I called out to Callon, who was about ten feet ahead of me and Tuesday. The rest of the guys followed behind us.

We'd been walking an hour before I spoke. I'd been afraid to ask earlier, as if he'd be able to smell my guilt, know I was counting down the seconds to doomsday. Because when we got to the next village, I'd have to tell him he couldn't leave me there, or really anywhere, and I was expecting one hell of a blow-up.

"Not until the day after tomorrow." He sounded casual enough as he continued walking.

He'd made it sound like the village he was bringing us to was closer. Hadn't he?

Tuesday looked over at me at the same time I was turning toward her. Both of us had the same *huh?* expression. She shrugged. I nodded.

It worked to our benefit, so why bring up the fact that we'd thought it was only twenty miles away? Maybe the witch had been farther out than we'd thought. I wasn't going to complain when it didn't make a difference. He was stuck with us, and if I had a little more time to figure out the best approach to telling him that, it wasn't so bad.

By the time we did stop, the sun was setting. Zink had the flames burning bright, and I edged as close as I could without setting my clothes on fire. Tuesday sat beside me, shoulder to shoulder and hip to hip, while fall felt like it was morphing into winter quicker than it should've. I kept my hands bunched in my lap, resisting the urge to touch my face again. The smooth skin was the only tangible thing I had that proved today had happened.

Koz was off hunting, again. I chewed on some dried meat he'd given us from his pack before he'd left.

"My stomach feels like a monster that can't get enough," Tuesday said, finishing up her last bite.

"Here. You can have the rest of mine." I handed her what I had left. I could finally chew, but now my nerves were taking the edge off my hunger.

"You sure?" she asked, already reaching for mine.

"Yeah." I couldn't eat after what had happened back at the witch's tent. Images kept sneaking in, and I told myself to not think about it.

"He's staring at me again," Tuesday said. "He stares at me every time I eat."

"I told you. Chew faster." I rested my hand on my chin, not looking at Callon. Pretending I didn't feel his stare on both of us. I had bigger issues. If he had a food hang-up, that was the least of the problems. How was I going to tell him that he was stuck with me? Did I just spit it out now and hope for the best?

"Why does he always do that?" Tuesday continued.

I didn't answer. I couldn't focus on Callon watching her eat. Didn't care unless he walked over and grabbed the food from her mouth. He might've had to beat her with it, too, before I could muster up anything for that situation.

I was staring at my shoes when a pair of boots entered my vision. I looked upward until I was staring at Callon's face. Obviously, he wanted something, and since I currently wasn't eating his food, I couldn't imagine what.

There was no way he knew. No way. Right?

"Why do you keep giving your food away?" he asked.

"She was hungry. I wasn't." I put my chin back on my hand and waited for his legs to depart from view. If the guy got this crazy about food, what was going to happen when he heard about the real issue?

He stayed put. There was a flutter of movement as he crossed his arms in front of his chest, and I looked back up.

"I'm not going to carry you because you pass out from hunger."

I leaned back so I could look him in the face. "When that happens, you can say something or just leave me there."

We were really going to fight over food. When he found out what I did…

"I'm saying something now."

For the first time, I realized Tuesday was frozen next to me, the piece of dried meat still in her hands.

Now look what he'd done.

"Eat that," I said.

She didn't move her hand.

"Don't give away one more bite," Callon said to me, ignoring my poor little frozen friend.

What was up with him and food? He was starting with me at the wrong moment. I was a ball of pent-up energy looking for an outlet, and he was opening the door.

"I'll give away every bite if that's what I want to do." I stood up on two sound legs, holding my spot even as he leaned in and crowded me.

That wild thing inside me had napped all damn day and was suddenly bursting with energy, thrilled to find a fight we were in the right about. "I don't take orders, not from anyone."

We squared off, neither of us moving. His chest was rising as rapidly as mine. I knew why I was mad, but I couldn't figure out why he was so angry—not yet, anyway. It wasn't even his dried meat we were eating. It was Koz's.

Tuesday got up and tugged on my arm, putting the meat in my hand. "I'm really not hungry anymore. You should definitely eat this."

"What's going on?" Koz asked, as he walked into camp, a dead turkey hanging from his hand.

"Ah, shit. There's more food. Does that mean the show's over?" Hess asked.

I hadn't realized Hess and Zink had been watching our little drama unfold.

Tuesday took the opening to grab my hand and drag me away a good twenty paces, right beyond the camp clearing. "Don't fight with him like that. We need him. If he wants you to eat your food, eat it. He wants you to stand on your head while singing, do it."

I looked at Tuesday and saw the same worried

expression that Maura used to have. I wished I could do what Tuesday wanted from me. It would be so much easier to be that girl again, but I couldn't.

I grabbed her hand, squeezing her fingers. "I can't do it. Not after everything. I can't."

"Just for a little while?" she pleaded.

"I. Can't. Not for anyone. Not for you and not for me. I don't have it in me anymore." The panic in her eyes made me want to say, *Yes, I'll play the game. I'll swallow anything they shove at me*, but it wasn't an option. I couldn't be small again. I didn't want to be, and damn the consequences.

"I know you're strong, but—"

"This isn't me being strong. I'm too weak. I don't care if it means my death. I'd rather die standing than continue living on my knees. At some point, it's too much."

I grabbed her shoulders, willing her to understand something that I wasn't sure she could. No one could, not unless she'd lived my life.

"Baryn didn't only break my leg that night." I dropped my head, trying to keep it together. I took a ragged breath. "I'm done living on other people's terms, even if that means it's going to end badly for me."

It wasn't until I'd snapped that I realized how close to the brink I'd been for so long. In my desire to survive, I'd nearly lost myself completely to that sad and pathetic creature I'd become.

Surviving had cost too much. I'd rather die than be that person again. Even a hint of taking a step back toward that life made the thing inside me roar in anger.

Tuesday nodded. I watched as she came to terms

with what I'd said. When tears welled in her eyes, I turned my attention back to the camp.

"I should've done more," she said, a suspicious sniffle following.

"You did everything you could." I squeezed her hand. "Don't you dare cry."

"I'm not."

She definitely was, and I couldn't look.

I trained my eyes on the camp, realizing how quiet the guys were. They were still a good distance away, but no one was speaking. Not even a whisper of conversation. There was no way they could hear us from over there, but I would've sworn they were somehow listening. I caught Koz's profile, as if he wanted to turn toward us but didn't.

"Come on," I said, urging her back to the camp, where I knew she'd drop the subject. Koz would come and talk to her and pull her mind away from the horrors of the village. I'd never forget them, but maybe she could.

She dragged her hand over her face and we walked back. Callon didn't say anything else about the food or eating, and I didn't pursue it either. The silence was heavy, though.

Koz's newest roast was finished and sectioned off to all. It was a good thing Callon had dropped the food fight, since there was no way I was going to be able to eat the amount of food Koz handed us. When I tried to hand Tuesday a piece of my meat, simply because I couldn't get another bite down, she held up her hand. It had nothing to do with being afraid of what Callon would do. Her face was tinged a little green from too much food.

I was sitting there stuffed, as Zink ribbed Hess over some girl at some village that he'd gotten involved with. Apparently, the girl was going to be in a very bad mood when Hess saw her again, since he said he'd be returning in a week and it had been several months. Tuesday was smiling beside me, our conversation fading from thought.

Then Callon walked over to Koz and said, "We're better off crossing the river on the north pass."

River. Large rivers meant bridges. Bridges meant pirates. Everyone knew that the pirates controlled every water way in the Wilds. It just was. You were born knowing how to breathe and about the pirates.

The pirates were bad news in general, but even worse news for me. They were well known for taking extra coin to report the comings and goings of people to whomever was paying at the moment. Turrock had connections with the pirates, and there was no way he wouldn't have gotten a pigeon to them by now. I might not be scarred, but I was still recognizable with this damn hair.

"Is that a large river we're crossing?" As soon as I asked, Callon's eyes shot to mine and narrowed.

"Yes. Is that a problem?" he asked, watching, waiting to sniff out something from my response.

He knew something was off with me. Or suspected. I wasn't going to tell him either, not until I was strung up by my ankles and tortured.

"The pirates will charge, won't they? It'll be expensive. Why don't we swim across?" It wasn't a completely crazy suggestion. People who didn't have coin did do that. You wanted to cross a slice of water more than a mile wide, you'd better be ready to pay.

"The water is freezing right now. Why would we?" Tuesday shook her head so fast she might've given herself whiplash.

She couldn't swim, but neither could I. We'd have to figure it out. That sink-or-swim saying didn't come from nowhere. At least some of the people must've swum, or the saying would've been closer to *hey, fuckers, you're going to sink*. Still, a breakdown of the people who managed to swim in any given scenario would've been helpful.

"I'll pay them," Callon said.

I didn't say anything else, afraid to give myself up.

When Callon walked to the other side of the camp, Tucsday whispered, "It'll be okay."

I could see Callon turn his head slightly toward us. Instead of telling her Turrock would follow me until he had my bones in his hands, I only nodded.

Something ripped me from sleep, if drifting with one eye open could be called that.

Tuesday gripped my arm. "What was that?"

"I don't know." I immediately looked around to see if the guys were up.

They weren't just awake but standing and alert, all staring at a spot in the trees.

Callon glanced at me and put a finger to his lips before he walked into the trees.

A low growl rumbled from somewhere in the dark, and I grabbed the stick I slept with.

"Was that a beast?" Tuesday whispered.

My heart thudded as Tuesday's fingers made holes in my arm.

"Shhhh," I said. If it was a beast, I didn't want to lure it right to us. It hadn't liked the way I tasted or smelled last time, but that didn't mean its standards wouldn't drop if it was hungry.

"It's clear," Callon said, walking back into the camp. "There was someone there, but it looks like he ran off. He might've been trailing us."

Callon looked at me, and then three other stares followed suit, in lesser intensity. Why were they looking at me? It might've been my fault, but they didn't know that.

Callon stopped in front of me. "Is there any reason someone would be following you?"

"Not that I know of."

Tuesday said nothing, and I held my breath, afraid Callon would question her next. There had never been a worse liar born than Tuesday. Even something close to the truth would trip her up. Growing up together, before Baryn and Turrock had taken more involvement in my life, Maura had always questioned Tuesday first, and for a reason.

Callon walked away, but I knew he wasn't letting it go. I was just getting a short reprieve.

"I heard growling. Do you think there's a beast out there?" Tuesday asked.

"If there is, he already got his meal. We're probably fine." The beast wasn't my biggest concern anymore.

11

I dipped my hands into the water and brought them up to my face.

Tuesday kneeled beside me, doing the same.

"It's going to be okay." Her emphasis was on the word "okay," and the way she wouldn't look up, screamed she thought it was going to be an epic disaster.

I, on the other hand, was staring at her. There was absolutely nothing okay about the coming situation. "There's no way he hasn't sent word to the pirates. No way. It's been days."

"Turrock might not have had time." She sat back on her heels, pausing. "Maybe." She shrugged, and then shrugged again. If she moved her shoulders one more time, she was going to be in seizure territory.

I splashed some more water on my face, trying to use it to clear my head of the panic that wanted to suck every rational thought out.

I shook the water off my hands. "He would've sent a pigeon to the closest posts. You've seen how fast those little suckers can fly."

"They won't recognize you without the scars." She shrugged again.

She was going to need a branch to bite down on soon.

I grabbed a hank of white-blond hair and held it up. "Have you ever seen a shade like this before? Because I haven't, and I'm pretty sure it's going to be on the list of things he mentions." My finger went to my eyes. "Or these? I almost look like an alien. They're going to notice me. Everyone notices me—always."

Tuesday didn't argue and—thankfully—didn't shrug again. She bit her lower lip as she sat there. Now that she'd stopped trying to convince me it was okay, I felt even worse. I'd been secretly hoping she was right and would find a way to win the argument.

I moved from kneeling to sitting on my ass. Desperation drained all the energy from my limbs so my brain had more fuel to panic with.

She sucked in a loud breath. "I've got an idea."

My attention snapped back to her. "What? Is it good?"

Tuesday didn't usually lack for ideas. It was the caliber that was typically the problem.

"It's something." When her face puckered at her own idea, I knew it wouldn't be some genius anomaly.

I racked my brain and still had nothing. "Give it over. Desperate times and all that."

We made our way back from the stream, as if everything were normal. Koz looked first, followed by Hess, then Zink. Callon, with his back to us, noticed all the attention, groaned, and shook his head before turning around.

I gave Tuesday's arm a squeeze before we continued on. If she didn't speak, we might be able to pull it off. If she talked, we'd be sunk for sure.

"What?" I barked, as if nothing were amiss. All the while, my fingers wanted to reach up and scratch my head. Who knew mud would be so itchy when it was caked on your head?

It didn't do anything for my eyes, but at least my hair didn't shine like a beacon in the dark. Tuesday had done it too. We'd decided it would look more natural if both of our heads were covered.

Callon shook his head again but otherwise ignored us. Zink glanced at the rest of his buddies, judging whether anyone was prepared to comment.

When no one said anything, he spat out, "Why are your heads covered in mud?"

I shrugged. "It's good for body. We do this once a month—sometimes more. You're a guy, so of course you haven't heard about mud."

"That's garbage." Zink's upper lip rose, like he smelled bullshit.

Tuesday's eyes flared. That was her *I'm going crack under pressure* look.

Mine shot to Koz and then back to her. *You want that man, hold it together!*

She nodded, with a bit of a flinch mixed in. Still, she appeared to have shored up her walls. For now. When Tuesday was going to blow, though, she usually blew.

"Zink, let it go," Koz said, then glanced at Tuesday with a small smile.

Zink caught the look passing between Koz and

Tuesday and found something more disgusting to him than heads full of mud. He made a noise like he was going to be sick.

"I'll be back," he said, heading for the stream.

We gathered our things and were on the road soon after, with no more talk of mud.

WE'D ONLY BEEN WALKING A FEW HOURS, ACCORDING to the sun, when the bridge came into view. Two men stood by its entrance, on the horizon. They were still tiny dots, but they were definitely pirates.

I turned to Tuesday and moved my eyes upward, in the direction of my hair. Hopefully it was holding up better than hers, which had left a trail of flaked dirt as she walked, some still on her shoulders.

Her mouth twisted to the side and she held out her hand, giving me a so-so wave. A clump of dried dirt fell in front of my face, making the question obsolete.

Tuesday leaned in. "Next to Callon, Koz is the biggest. Callon will probably do most of the talking, though, so stand behind Koz."

I completely agreed.

Callon stopped and looked back to where Tuesday and I had slowed our pace to talk, as if he had some sort of sixth sense we'd fallen behind. The way he was staring, it was as if he knew something was coming.

He looked calm but he didn't *seem* calm. If I could've risked saying it aloud, I would've hashed it out with Tuesday. She probably would've told me I was crazy because Callon wasn't doing anything in particular that read *high alert*. It was more of a feeling I was picking up on, as if he had super-powerful pheromones that were drifting in the air. It sounded way too crazy even to me.

Tuesday and I picked up our pace at the same time. Guilty consciences probably thought the same way. Callon stood there waiting for us to catch up. The other guys seemed to decide it was a good idea to wait for us too.

"You two, stay with the group but toward the back." Callon turned toward Koz and looked at him for a second too long.

Koz gave the slightest nod, barely a movement at all, but it seemed to be plenty for Callon. Callon turned and walked forward.

Only two pirates stood in the front of the bridge, but there were probably backups nearby. There was talk enough of it in the village, how people had tried to pass without paying, not realizing how many pirates were lying in wait. It made sense. People never knew how many men were hiding, so the pirates didn't need as many. Everyone always suspected there were more. You never knew until you tried to screw them out of their fare.

I'd seen enough pirates coming in and out of the village doing business that I knew these guys had been around for a while. Pirates got a new inch of tattoos for every year they were part of the gang. These two had full sleeves.

As we moved forward, I kept my head down. My hair might be camouflaged, but if anyone looked at my eyes, I was surely done for.

Callon stopped in front of the larger one, digging into his pocket, presumably for gold coin to pay them. I couldn't see how much he retrieved, because that was above my line of vision, staring down at the dirt as I was.

"Six heads, six coins," Callon said.

I shifted, trying to stay in Koz's shadow as he fidgeted, shifted, and generally wouldn't stay the fuck still. Tuesday kept shifting with Koz, trying to fill in the gaps he left. It was a workout for sure, and not worth the effort. She was barely any larger than me.

I should've gotten behind Zink. That fucker wouldn't budge in a hurricane. His stillness was freakish, but worth emulating.

"You five can pass, but I need to see that one," the pirate said.

Tuesday edged back, nearly stepping on my toes in her effort to block me from view.

The jig was up. I was already on the radar. I knew which one of us he was talking about. I was surrounded by four scary guys that looked like a hell of a bigger threat than I was. Who did he look at? Me, less than half their size and with biceps the size of walnuts, not oranges. The messenger pigeon might as well have landed on top of my head and been pecking at my scalp.

Now what? Would Callon throw me to the wolves? He still didn't know the deal with the witch. I still didn't know if what she'd done to Callon would hold up.

At least I could make a run for it with two solid legs. I might be small, but before I was injured, I'd been fast. It was one of the reasons Baryn had broken my leg the first time and refused to let it be set. That had slowed me down a lot.

"I paid your fee. Be smart. Take your coin and be

happy for it. That's all you're getting." Callon's voice sounded lower than normal, almost growly.

I should've known he wouldn't back down. It had nothing to do with me. He was an alpha to his core. Even if he didn't want me with him, he'd still insist on keeping me before he'd let this goon dictate what he should do.

Koz shifted slightly in front of me and then stopped moving, *finally*. He reached out and pushed Tuesday behind him, beside me. Good thing he was a big guy, because it was getting a little crowded back here.

"Look, I gotta check her out. If I let her stroll across this bridge without doing that, I'm dead. Let me get a look and then we'll let you pass," the pirate said.

Tuesday, shoulder to shoulder with me, whispered, "Should we run?"

"Only if it gets bad and there's no other choice. There'll be men in the woods." I'd thought Tuesday would know that, but then again, she hadn't been around Baryn as much. I'd heard a lot when I'd been "knocked out."

Hess edged in on our left and Zink moved in to our right, closing ranks around us. Okay, they were gearing up for a fight. This was a good sign.

Just when I'd thought they were going to protect us —or try—Callon told the pirate, "Give me a minute."

He was changing his mind. I should've known. My blood felt like it was draining from my body, my heart stuttering and dying.

This was it. The pirates would drag me back. Would the spell the witch concocted work? I didn't even know if running would help. Maybe Callon would deliver me back himself, and then they'd find a way to fix what Hera had done.

Tuesday grabbed my hand and squeezed it until my fingers lost blood supply. She thought we were screwed, too.

"Stay near Koz," I said, knowing things were about to turn ugly. "He might save you." If she came with me, it definitely wouldn't end well. At least one of us would get a better life.

"No," she said, squeezing my fingers even harder.

I was going to argue, but we were out of time. Hess moved out of the way to let Callon into the protective ring they'd formed around us. Holding on to Tuesday's hand, I only had one option. Run.

I lunged toward the trees, pulling Tuesday with me. I wasn't getting handed over, and damn if I'd let them get her. Callon's hand wrapped around my other forearm before I could get more than a couple of feet.

"Let me go," I said, trying to yank my arm from his grip.

Tuesday pulled on my other arm, as if she had a shot of winning this tug of war.

"Koz, get Tuesday," Callon said, pulling me in toward him as Tuesday got towed behind me, like a stick floating on the water.

Koz walked around and, with an arm about her waist, detached Tuesday from my arm.

"I can't leave her!" she wailed.

Koz leaned closer and said something that calmed her down immediately. Then they were moving away from us. She was nodding toward me as if to say it was all okay.

I was still trying to pry Callon's hand off me as he said, "Zink, Hess, keep the pirates company."

Zink nodded. "Yeah, can't say I'm sad about that. Need to get a little energy out."

"There's five in the woods," Callon added.

"We got it," Hess said.

What did "keep them company" mean? It didn't sound nice. Something wasn't quite right here. I was fairly certain I had Zink's number. If this was something that the pirates liked, he wouldn't be happy about it. He didn't like making anyone happy.

Callon looped an arm around my waist and then steered me forward at a pace I wouldn't have been able to keep up if I'd had my old limp. We hadn't walked far when shouts erupted behind us. I couldn't twist my body around enough to see what was happening with Callon's hard body behind me, steering.

We didn't stop until we were at a large boulder that was a good twenty feet away from where the pirates had been. When we stopped, instead of letting me go, his hands moved to both my shoulders, steered my back against the stone, and held me there.

"You want to share what's actually going on yet?"

The yelling in the distance escalated, and then there was gunfire. I hadn't known the pirates had guns.

Two palms on his chest, I pushed against him. He didn't budge. I turned my head but couldn't clear the stone. "What's happening?"

He didn't loosen his grip. "Why does Turrock want you back so bad to have the pirates looking for you?" he asked, as if he had all the time in the world and a battle wasn't being waged.

What the hell was wrong with him?

And wait, how did he know Turrock was coming for me and not Baryn?

"Answer. Me."

"Don't you care if your friends are in a fight? *I* care." If they lost, and me and Tuesday got caught because Callon had me pinned to a rock, so help me, I'd kill him myself. I'd have to wait until he was sleeping or find some poison, but I'd get it done.

What if they got Tuesday while I was stuck here? She wasn't as tough as me. She wouldn't be able to handle it. I shoved at him again, and every time I did, he just pressed closer, until his body was an inch from mine. If I breathed too deeply, I would've brushed against him.

Callon moved one hand off my shoulder. "Why do they want you?"

There was a mewling sound in the distance and then there was nothing but the birds chirping, and a couple of crows cawing. The fight was over. Callon didn't bother glancing over to find out who'd won.

He leveled his eyes on mine, as his free hand cupped my jaw and his thumb tilted my chin up. He leaned in close, taking a deep breath as the bristles of his jaw grazed my skin.

I stopped breathing completely. Or maybe he was stealing the air from my chest.

He leaned his head back until his eyes met mine again, searching my face, analyzing it. There was something there, brewing deep in those eyes. It was like his soul was whispering to me, charging me from inside. It called to the core of me, and I didn't know if I wanted to drag his mouth to mine or throw up the thickest wall I could.

"Tell me what you're hiding. You're safe. You can tell me anything." His voice was deep but soft, tingling over my skin, luring me in to some place where nothing could harm me and I didn't need to run. Where if I told him all my darkest secrets, it wouldn't matter. No, it would be better.

"What makes you so valuable that they're going to such lengths to get you back?" he asked in that same tone. It hummed through me and felt like it was caressing every wound I'd ever had. Soothing all my hurts.

I could feel my lids dropping and heavy, my lips wanting to form the words, tell him every secret I had, all the things I'd feared to utter in the dark. With him, it was safe and warm.

And that was what jarred me out of it.

I didn't believe in safe and warm. It didn't exist in my world. It was a fairy tale for the naïve.

I blinked, shaking my head, and pushing off whatever strange trance he'd put me in. This was what I'd sensed in him. I wasn't the only one here with magic, and right now I was nearly choking on his.

"What was that?" I asked. "What did you just do?"

His eyes near burned into mine, and he smiled just a hair as he said, "I'll make you a deal. Tell me how you resisted it, and I'll tell you what it was. Because if you don't tell me why they want you back, I'll go ask Turrock myself."

He backed up, but I stayed still against the stone. Why hadn't he said Baryn, again? He knew my village enough to know who was in charge. He *knew* Baryn was dead, but how? It had just happened, and his people had left the village before it had. I'd been with them this entire time and there was no one that would've known.

"You mean Baryn, don't you?"

"Baryn, Turrock, does it matter? I'm sure either one of them will willingly give me the answers if you refuse."

"It matters and you know it does. How do you know Baryn is dead?" And hell if he didn't. I'd thought I was the one holding out, but as I stood in front of him, I was positive this was no ordinary man. How had I not seen it? Felt it like I did now? He positively sizzled with some sort of deep and earthy energy.

"Maybe I'll bring Tuesday with me when I go?" His eyes narrowed.

Would he really do that? If Turrock knew she'd been with me, he'd torture her. My hands trembled and I crossed them over my chest to hide it, to stop myself from trying to claw his eyes out.

"And if I tell you?"

He tilted his head slightly. "There won't be any reason to go back there."

In that moment, I hated him. I would've killed him right then if I could've. But I couldn't, and it made me want to rage and scream. It made me want to use the only weapon I had and terrify him.

He wanted to know so bad? I'd give him more than he bargained for.

"My mother was a plaguer, someone who survived the unsurvivable. She caught the Bloody Death and lived. Well, it doesn't just change them, it changes their children too. Sometimes the magic passes down in unusual ways—"

He leaned forward. "I don't need a history lesson. I want to know about *you*."

If finding out that my mother had been a plaguer,

something that would send most people screaming, scared him, he didn't show it. Nope, he stood there in front of me with a look of boredom and annoyance.

Well. Fuck. Him. "I'm a Daughter of the Reaper, Reaper Kissed, or whatever else you might want to call it. There's all sorts of names for me, but the bottom line is I know when people are going to die."

The fucker nodded. That was it? A nod? Oh no, that wasn't satisfying at all.

"Give me your hand and I'll tell you how you're going to die."

He smiled. "You mean you don't already know?"

I sneered and grabbed his hand. He didn't fight me, letting me do my thing. I didn't particularly like forcing the visions, but fuck him. He was getting rattled today if it was the last thing I was doing. When I did it like this, even if I couldn't see his death, if I focused hard enough, I'd see if he'd come close in his past. When you stepped near enough to the abyss, it always left a mark somewhere inside. All I wanted right now was to wipe that smirk off his face.

I got a vision, but he wasn't in it, or at least the him I'd expected. A beast, a different one than the creature who'd saved me, limped across a snowy field, leaving a trail of blood in his wake until it lost so much it collapsed. That was all I saw.

I dropped his hand, suppressing the chill that ran up my spine.

I looked at him, speechless.

He smiled. "That's all right. No need to share."

When I'd tied myself to him, I'd made a deal with the devil. I was fairly certain I'd gotten shortchanged.

12

Callon took a few steps away from the boulder and paused. He looked back at me, where I was leaning on it, and raised an eyebrow.

I pushed off the stone.

"I'm coming. You're not that scary." Actually, he was, or should be, but I was too mad that the tables had turned to admit it. He was supposed to be afraid of me after what he'd found out. Hello? Reaper Kissed? Death visions? Most people thought I was haunted. Him? No big deal.

Callon threw back his head, laughing and looking like the demon that lay beneath his skin as he walked.

I'd barely gotten past my annoyance when I was waylaid by the strewn bloody body parts. Not even full bodies. How many pirates had there been? There were arms and legs everywhere, so it was hard to tell unless I walked the area and tried to piece them together.

Hess and Zink were standing there, remarkably clean, considering they'd just slaughtered countless men.

Were they all beasts? They had to be. I'd heard the rumors of beast men, but I'd dismissed it as fiction. There was no other way two of them could've slaughtered this many and that quickly unless they were the same as Callon.

The witch had said Callon could protect me. She'd clearly known what he was. A word of warning would've been nice before she talked me into tying myself to him.

Tuesday was walking toward us with Koz, and I could tell from her wide eyes that she hadn't seen the killing go down either.

She stopped beside us, speechless and looking all around at the blood and gore. She glanced up at Hess and Zink, with wrinkles on her forehead, as if she couldn't quite do the math. She went back to looking at bodies, silently counting.

Callon tilted his head toward me. "She's Reaper Kissed," he said, without any warmup or background like I'd supplied.

"Fuck me," Hess said, shaking his head.

"Of course she is," Zink said, with a huff.

Zink and Hess looked at me with varying shades of wariness. This was a little bit more of the reaction I'd expected from Callon. Maybe if I'd spat it out the way he had, I would've rattled him. No more history next time. It had watered down the punch line.

Koz nodded.

That was it? Only a nod?

Tuesday was oblivious to everything going down and had started using her fingers to keep track of the body count.

"Koz, go up ahead with Teddy and Tuesday," Callon said.

I didn't know if he wanted us gone so he could snack on the body parts or hide them. Either way, I was quite happy to get moving. Certain things I didn't need to know.

Koz walked toward the bridge. Tuesday wasn't paying attention to anything but counting, so I grabbed her arm and pulled her along.

After we crossed the bridge, Koz and I picked up our pace, leaving the dazed Tuesday behind but in sight. She was still shaking her head and mumbling numbers. It sounded like she'd made it to the division portion.

"You know, don't you? I could see the way you looked at the bodies and then us. Are you scared?" he asked in a soft voice that wouldn't carry to Tuesday.

"No." I didn't think I could be scared of Koz, not after what I'd realized today. It was him—the color of his hair was the same as the beast's fur the night I'd been dragged from my village. That night, he'd said he couldn't bring me "back." I'd ignored it then. I shouldn't have.

"You're not afraid I will freak out and…" He made an exaggerated wrenching movement, as if twisting a neck or limb.

"No. I don't think you're going to…" I made a dramatic wrenching movement of my own. "Considering I've slept next to you in camp and the only thing I woke to was handmade crutches, it's a little hard to be fearful now."

We walked a few more feet and I waited for him to come clean. He didn't, and I was pretty sure he wasn't going to, so I said it.

"Plus, you saved me. I don't think you would've

dragged me out of there so you could turn around and eat me. I owe you, big."

Koz looked down at his feet and shrugged.

"I couldn't leave you there, not like that." He finally glanced at me with hooded lids, his face tinged a warmer color.

"Why couldn't you?" I asked. He'd said that as if it were human nature. I'd been left like that countless times. Asked for help more than I'd ever admit before I'd stopped relying on others to save me.

"Could you have walked away?"

Could I? It was an alien idea. "I've never been in a position to help anyone. I guess I don't know."

"I've been in both spots. It's awful tough to walk once you have."

He'd been chained and abused, too. It was crazy to think anyone would've been strong enough to abuse a beast, but I'd heard stories here and there of beasts being captured and tortured to death. I didn't ask for details, and he didn't offer any.

But there was still something weird I couldn't let go of about that conversation Koz had with Zink the first time I'd seen them.

"That night in the village, why did Zink say it was different?" I asked.

Koz laughed. "Because you're human."

"He isn't?"

"Don't tell him that."

I nodded. With Zink, I could believe that.

Koz tilted his head toward where Tuesday was lagging behind, and we both stopped, waiting for her to catch up. She took a while as she walked in sort of a stunned trance.

She finally reached us and said, "I'm missing something big here, aren't I? How did Zink and Hess kill all those men by themselves? There were way too many. And I heard gunshots. You guys don't have guns."

I cleared my throat, hoping Koz would explain it.

Instead of answering, he turned to me. "Is she going to scream? I hate when people scream. It hurts my ears. They're very sensitive."

I couldn't help but look at that statement in a whole new light, considering what I now knew.

"Maybe?" I had wanted to scream.

Tuesday was staring at Koz. "Somebody better tell me what's going on."

Koz kept his eyes on me. "I'm going to lag a few paces behind, just in case." Koz tapped his ears and smiled, all teeth and no happy. He took a few steps away. No matter how hard Tuesday stared at him, he wouldn't look at her.

"It's going to be fine," I said, giving him a thumbs-up, like he would do for me.

The second Tuesday turned back to me, Koz's eyes shot to her. That was when I knew if she freaked out over Koz being a beast, I was going to have to beat some sense into her until she saw what I did.

I grabbed Tuesday's hand, tugging her along with me for the second time that day. "You know how that beast dragged me out of the village and then didn't eat me? I don't think it was because I didn't smell tasty."

"Then why?"

"Remember that rumor about how some of the beasts that roam the Wilds could turn into men? Remember there was a place northeast of here, where they said there were a bunch of them?"

"Yeah, I remember that," she said, and I could nearly hear the gears turning in her head.

"Turns out it might have been accurate."

I made a point of not staring at her while she let it roll around in her head for a few moments. I glanced back at Koz, who was staring at everything but us. I saw the tense line of his shoulders and the way his eyes didn't seem to be seeing anything.

"Are you saying they're…" Her mouth dropped open, and then she squinted. She looked back toward Koz and then to me.

Tuesday stumbled to a stop. I stopped as well. A peek at Koz showed he'd done the same, maintaining his distance.

"Callon?" she asked as it all really sank in.

"Yes."

"And…" Her eyes darted to Koz.

"All of them. Koz was actually the one that saved me from the village."

I knew Tuesday; I knew she was good to her core. I also knew she was scared of mice. *Please don't be scared. Please.* It would slice Koz to his core, and I didn't want to see that. I would've shaken her and said as much, but I knew Koz was listening to every single word.

Tuesday's shoulders straightened and her look turned authoritative as she said, "Well then, beasts can't be as bad as they say. Koz wouldn't turn into something evil. Ever." She tilted her head back to Koz, dark, gorgeous hair falling over her shoulder. "Koz, why are you walking all the way back there?"

He lifted his head, all smile and this one jammed full of happy.

We'd been walking for an hour when I noticed Zink getting closer to me. He didn't normally speak to me, let alone walk next to me. People only sidled up to me for one reason. Now I had to decide whether to screw with him or give him his answer.

It didn't hurt that it was a good interruption from the other thing looming over my head like a guillotine. I'd trapped a beast and he didn't know it yet. So if I vented some of that angst on Mr. Grumpy, he deserved it a little. After all, he had compared me to a dog.

Zink cleared his throat for the fifth time before he asked, "How does that thing you do work?"

"Not sure. Just does." I continued walking and whistled. I'd never whistled much, so it didn't sound very good. I didn't let that deter me.

Ten minutes later, Callon said, "Stop fucking with him, Teddy."

Callon wasn't only a beast that killed animals and probably people, he killed joy. Or tried. I wasn't done yet.

I turned toward Zink. "I'm sorry. Did you want to ask me about something?"

For someone who usually didn't twitch, he was as jumpy as a cricket. "Is there something I should be asking you about?"

"You can ask me whatever you want."

"She didn't see you dead, Zink," Callon said, shutting down my little game.

"How do you know what I've seen?"

Callon was walking in front of me so he couldn't see the lasers I was shooting into his back. It wasn't all Callon's fault that I was mad at him. For the last hour,

I'd been preparing for the fight we'd have once he knew he was stuck. In my mind, Callon and I were already battling it. It was hard to be pleasant when you were in mid-fight with someone, even if they didn't know it.

"If you had, even though he's an irritating fuck, you wouldn't screw with him." His words reeked of confidence, as if he knew me.

He didn't. He was right, but that didn't mean anything. It was a lucky guess. I thought of all the things he'd said to me during our imaginary fight, and man, he was irritating sometimes.

"I'm not dying?" Zink asked.

I let out a puff of breath. "Everyone is dying." His face went white and I knew my fun was over. "But I don't know when. Your fur and fangs throw off my vision. Now go back to ignoring me, if you don't mind." I picked up my pace, but the whistle in my heart was dead.

"Thanks, Teddy."

"Shut up."

Zink smiled.

It made me want to punch him.

I increased my steps until I was walking beside Killjoy.

"Shouldn't we be at the village soon?" I asked, trying to reset my doomsday countdown.

"I'm bringing you to a different one, a little farther away. They're more likely to take you in," Callon said, not even glancing at me.

I stopped. "Why didn't you tell me?"

"Does it matter?" He kept walking.

Of course he didn't need to tell me. That was what

he was saying with his arrogant tone and raised eyebrow. I couldn't even see his face, but I knew that sucker had climbed up his forehead.

He was really giving me a lot of fuel for the next imaginary fight.

13

A two-and-a-half-story house stood in front of us. It was weathered but tended to, repairs made by pieces salvaged from other places, showing in the different-colored shingles and mismatched windows, every difference adding to its charm.

A wooden plank over the wide porch read, "Jim's Eat and Sleep." I'd heard stories of places you could pay to get food and stay over, but I'd never seen one. I hadn't seen much of anything, so that said more about my travels than the scarcity of these establishments.

But why were we coming here now? Places meant people. People talked. Trees didn't.

"I've always wanted to go to an eat and sleep!" Tuesday skipped beside me, as if she'd been zapped by a bolt of energy that was shooting out of her legs.

I would've been more excited myself if I wasn't planning on the talk with Callon. I'd had too much time to think. I'd gone from why I should be mad at Callon—which was pretty flimsy and easy to poke holes in—to thinking about how angry he was going to be with me. His case was a lot solider. If things went well, it would probably morph into a screaming match. If things didn't go well, it wouldn't be my first beating.

Callon walked up onto the front porch of the house, with Hess beside him. Zink hung back, waiting for us. At least one of them always did, as if they thought the boogeyman might jump out of the trees and steal us. In my case, it might happen.

"Why are we stopping here?" I asked Koz, who was at Tuesday's side more often than not.

"Better to stay here than out in the open until we get some more distance."

Ah. They'd get more warning if someone came. After what they'd done to the pirates, and the fact that they knew people were looking for me, it made sense. I'd still prefer the trees, but no one was asking my opinion.

"Come on," Koz said, waving us forward as he went to join Callon and Hess.

Tuesday hung back for a second. "Wait until after we eat. I've never gotten to eat in a place like this. I want to see what we get." She grabbed my arm, dropping her forehead toward me. "If he's really angry. We. Might. Get. Nothing." It was quite dramatic for a whisper.

"Sure, not until after dinner."

It wasn't a surprise she knew what I was thinking. She'd been staring at me for the last hour of the walk, watching me brew. I'd caught myself mouthing the imaginary argument a couple of times. Luckily, the guys hadn't noticed and I hadn't said the words aloud.

"Good." She let go of my arm and skipped after Koz.

I glanced back at Zink, who flung his hand toward the door in a *hurry it up* gesture. But he wasn't rolling his eyes. That was extreme patience for him. The two of us might be making progress.

I walked through the door and Callon was right inside, as if he were waiting for me or something. The din of conversation leaked into the hallway, so I was somewhat prepared for the packed room. It was mostly men, dingy from the road, with a smattering of women here and there, some lacking an entire outfit. A large man with an apron around his waist was placing dishes down and collecting coin as he did. A young woman, who might've been his daughter from the matching freckles and ginger hair, was right behind him, filling tankards.

All looked toward us.

No. I couldn't tell Callon in here even if I wanted to. He wouldn't care if the place was packed and he made a scene. He wouldn't care what people thought of him. He did what he wanted, and fuck opinions. They may not have even registered.

If this was going to get ugly, I was better off doing it outside and in private. Maybe a good fifty feet away, in some thick brush that would muffle the noise. I should probably lead by telling him he couldn't kill me, although that would be a bluff. The witch hadn't said anything about that.

It would be ugly, and deservedly so. I'd chained him to me. Not indefinitely, but she'd said for a year. A year could feel like a lifetime when you were barely into the sentence.

It was uncomfortable sitting on this side of the

scales. I was used to being the wronged one—not the wrongdoer. I almost wished I could talk to Baryn and ask how he dealt with the guilt, except I wasn't sure he'd ever been afflicted with that pesky side effect. The bottom line was that I needed to survive and I'd taken the opportunity that had presented itself.

Callon pointed at a table in the corner, the only one available. Koz made his way over, with Tuesday happy as could be on his heels. I followed as well, trying to avoid the looks I was getting. The scars were gone but they still stared, like they knew I was different or something. Probably the hair. I should've left the mud on it, but it was itchy, so we'd both washed it off at the next stream after the bridge, while Zink and Hess had washed off their own grime of a redder nature.

I went to take a chair, but Callon's hand on my back pushed me forward until I was in the corner. It was the spot I'd been avoiding, in case someone in here spotted me and there was a need for a quick getaway. There wouldn't be now with Callon blocking me in. Wasn't so bad. It wasn't like anyone could ID me with the way he was sitting.

The man in the apron came over and Callon ordered whatever he was serving, some venison something or other, and a table full of ale. Tuesday was nearly bouncing in her seat as I sat there in dread of what would follow the meal.

Hess turned to me with a forced smile. "You're going to like the village we're bringing you to. Decent folk. We've traded with them on and off."

I nodded. This wasn't helping my nerves. Tuesday looked like she was on a date with Koz. Other than ordering food, Callon didn't speak. Zink didn't talk much to begin with, and tonight was no different.

Hess continued to wax on about how great this new village was and how nice all the people were, forcing conversation upon me. It wasn't like him at all, and I finally realized what it was about.

"I didn't see yours either. Like I said before, I can't see past the whole…" I tapped a finger to my pointy tooth. Hopefully, that would end all the chitchat directed toward me.

"Oh, yeah, that's good to know, but I really do like the village." He took a swig of ale that the girl had just placed in front of him.

"Yeah, they're *great* people over there," Zink said, rolling his eyes and buying the bull even less than I was.

"They are," Hess said, losing the happy-go-lucky persona that fit him about as well as a sock on a fish.

"I think you mean she's a great gal. That's the only one you've ever talked to for more than five minutes in the whole place. Actually, have you spoken to her for more than five? Or is it the banging that lasts only five?" Zink asked it as if it were a genuine question.

Zink and Hess soon ignored me, arguing as we waited for food that came out too quick and too lukewarm. I choked it down, not tasting anything, as they all talked amongst themselves.

All except Callon and me. He was watching me, and I didn't think it was because I was eating. I pretended he wasn't.

I struggled through the meal and then said I needed to step outside for some privacy, Tuesday tagging along. Koz got up, shadowing us to the door, and I found myself missing Callon as we crossed the room. He seemed to be better at redirecting stares than Koz. Maybe it was because he looked more likely to kill you. That might be a bad thing, considering the fight to come.

I'd barely cleared the trees when I asked Tuesday, "How do you think this will go when I tell him?"

"I thought you had to pee?" she asked.

"I had to get out of there. He knows something's up. It's like he's got a line directly to my brain or something."

"It'll be okay. He won't hurt you," she said. For a good friend, she sounded quite blasé about the whole thing.

I leaned against a tree as she checked for poison ivy before finding a good spot to squat.

"If it goes badly, don't get involved." I banged my head back against the bark.

"It won't. He steps in front of you all the time."

"Huh?" She was done peeing before I finally came to my senses. "No, he doesn't."

"Yes, he does. He did it tonight when we walked in the place. I've noticed the trend." She walked back over to me. "You know what the nicest part is?"

"What?" I asked, even as I told myself this was ridiculous.

She paused for a second, like she did when she was about to get whimsical. Then her voice got all soft as she said, "He did it even before you were healed. I was thinking about this while we were eating. When we were at the Gathering, and he was bringing you to the witch, I saw the way he was carrying you, like he was shielding you from everyone."

I let her fanciful idea dance around in my head for a

few seconds, relishing in how great it would be if that were true. To live in Tuesday's world must be nice, where there was true love and unicorns prancing in the forest. Rainbows with big pots of gold and happily-ever-afters.

But that wasn't the real world, the one most of us knew. There was nothing soft about my voice as I replied, "You're so crazy right now that I can't believe *I'm* the one who sees death."

She let out a long sigh, one that reeked of *poor, clueless Teddy*. "You might know all about the bad stuff, but you aren't so good at seeing anything else."

"Let's go back. I've got to get this over with. I can't take another minute."

When we turned back toward the eat and sleep, Callon was already outside. Tuesday's shoulder bumped mine "accidentally" as she walked past me, her version of punching me in the arm for good luck. She continued to the porch, giving me an *it'll be okay* smile before she disappeared inside.

I stopped in front of him. "Could I talk to you for a minute?"

His eyes narrowed as he nodded. Those eyes read too much. I didn't know this guy, but he acted like he knew me. It was all guesses, but he was the best guesser I'd ever met.

I shook off my nerves, imagining myself to be a grand oak tree. I might lose some branches but I'd weather this storm, as I had so many others.

I tilted my head away from the house. "Do you mind?"

If this went bad, I preferred my fights in private, or

at least the ones I was sure to lose. Back at the village, I'd never had the choice. Baryn or Turrock would regularly drag me out into the center of everyone, a spectacle for all. They thought it made them look tough that they weren't scared of the girl who saw death.

He followed me to a small clearing just beyond the trees. A crow swooped down, landing on a branch and cawing. Then another joined it. If Callon wasn't there, I would've shooed them away. I'd come out here so I didn't have an audience. The twosome cawed in unison, looking down at me, as if they were saying I was stuck with them.

He stopped a few feet from me and then waited.

He probably thought I was going to plead or beg for him to take me with him. Even if I'd never met Hera, and there had been no spell, there would never be any pleading and begging from me.

I knew men, all sorts of them. Some were weak of body but strong of mind, and some had it the other way around. Some were just weak in everything. Once in a blue moon, there was someone like Callon. He wouldn't crack; there were no weak spots. The fact that he'd relented as much as he had for Koz said more about how close he was with his men than about a soft spot. It spoke of loyalty. I hadn't known many men his type, but I knew in my gut how he was going to feel about what I'd done.

I toyed with a branch.

"Teddy?" His eyes stayed fixed on my face, trying to get a read on what he sensed was off.

"You're going to have to take me with you." I broke the branch with my fingers, not meaning to.

"And why is that?" he asked, taking a step forward.

I had such a bad case of cold feet that I might as well be standing in ice water. "You can't leave without me. The witch, Hera, she did something." I blurted it out so fast that I wasn't sure he understood what I'd said.

He stood so frozen that he had either the utmost control or he was on the verge of losing it. Probably a combination of the two. I would've thought that the temperature had suddenly dropped to negative thirty. Or maybe it was the ice pumping through my veins, chilled by my frozen feet as I steeled myself for the eventual reaction from the wild beast who'd discovered he'd been trapped.

Trapped. It was a horrible word, and a worse reality. I knew what it felt like firsthand, and yet I'd done it to him. He was going to hate me, maybe kill me, and I didn't blame him. There was no going back. The witch was long gone. I'd made my choice and now I was going to live with it. Or die because of it.

"What are you talking about?" he asked, so slowly, his words so distinct, it was impossible to feign misunderstanding.

My heart pounded out the seconds. "You can't leave me behind. You can't go more than a few miles away from me."

He was staring at me, speechless.

"It's only for a year or so. Not forever."

"Hera told you this? And you believed her?"

"Yes."

He threw back his head and laughed. Somehow, that laughter sounded like a fuck you.

"I don't know what you gave her or how you convinced her—"

"I wasn't trying to—"

He took a step forward, and I quickly turned my head to the side. If he attacked anything like Baryn, he'd go for my face first.

I waited a few seconds, but the blow didn't come. I turned back to him, squinting. He shook his head, as if disgusted even further by me.

He wasn't going to hit me?

His jaw was tensed, the tendons in his neck corded as he disregarded my shock.

"It doesn't matter if you weren't trying to screw me. That witch doesn't have the magical chops to pull it off, and she would've needed something of mine to do it."

He was wrong on all counts. I'd seen what had happened inside that tent. That woman had more magic than he could even imagine. And he was wrong about her not having something of his. He'd been carrying me for hours. I'd had one of his hairs on me.

I started chewing on the side of my cheek. Did I agree with him that there was no way Hera had pulled it off, or let him figure it out on his own that she had? I hadn't planned on having to convince him I'd screwed him over. It didn't look like he was going to believe me anyway.

If I were that oak tree, his eyes would've set me on fire and then nailed me to the ground where I stood. He shook his head one time. The slightest movement, but there was something so powerful in it that it nearly brought me to my knees. That small shake had been packed full of condemnation, judgment—disgust. That was all it took to feel like I was the lowest of the low. I'd had so many things I'd planned on saying and yet I couldn't utter a word. He'd slayed me with that one look. A punch would've hurt less. I wasn't even pond scum, but whatever fed off it.

He turned and walked away.

"Callon." He didn't pause or acknowledge he'd heard me call him. I didn't know what else to say as I watched his back. An apology would fall miles short.

I'd been prepared for rage, maybe a beating. Not this. He went back to the eat and sleep. He walked through the door while I was still rooted to the same spot.

My entire past was filled with not being able to do what I wanted. But I'd always known *what* I wanted to do. This was the first time I had a choice and was stumped. After a couple of deep breaths, I forced myself forward, not sure what would happen when I caught up to him.

I was only a few feet from the front steps when Callon walked back out. He went past me as if I were a ghost. The guys followed, looking from him to me, trying to figure out what had happened. Tuesday was last out the door, following them.

Koz looked from Callon to where I stood, silent and suddenly no longer a part of the group. It was the strangest feeling, since I didn't know I'd been part of a group to begin with. Maybe you never do until you're on the outside looking in.

I'd *never* been the guilty party. I wasn't sure what you were supposed to say in these situations. Did I plead my case to the jury?

Koz spoke before I had the chance. "I don't understand. I thought—"

"Change of plans." Callon turned, his eyes accusing.

I found myself staring at the trees behind him, unable to hold his gaze.

Koz stepped closer. "But—"

"Tuesday can come with us, but not the other one."

I wasn't even Teddy anymore. I was "the other one." I crossed my arms in front of my chest and held my chin up. Maura had always told me to keep my chin up. I wasn't sure exactly what it accomplished, but I was floundering right now, so chin up it was.

It might not be my proudest moment, but I'd done what I had to. He acted as if I'd slaughtered all his men in their sleep. Was it really that bad? I'd go wherever he went and he could ignore me. It was a year of my life I was sacrificing, not his. I'd been ready to tell him all of this, too, but he'd been so busy condemning me for decisions he couldn't possibly understand. I knew I'd wronged him, but had I really committed something bad enough for him to react like this?

Tuesday took a step closer to me, broadcasting her position before she said anything. "I go with Teddy."

Koz's eyes shot to hers. Hers to his.

Was this *the* guy for her? It sure looked like it.

I couldn't take this from her. "You should—"

Her arm looped through mine. "I'm staying," she said, even as her eyes remained locked with Koz's, something poignant in them that I could only guess at. It might be an apology, or maybe it was more of a *wish it could've worked out*. Only the two of them knew.

If the witch had done what she'd said, and I was pretty certain she had, they weren't getting far anyway. If the witch hadn't been able to do it, did I want her to be stuck with me when she had a chance at something normal? I was a two-ton albatross on my lightest day.

Anyone attached to me had a good chance of sinking straight to the bottom alongside me.

"Tuesday, you should go with them." I tried to tug my arm out of her grip.

She held on tighter. "No."

I didn't continue arguing. I knew Tuesday. When she dug in, you couldn't pry the shovel from her hands.

"We can't leave them here," Koz said to Callon.

Callon turned and walked away, Hess and Zink behind him. "We can and we are."

Only Koz remained. He dug into his pocket and pulled out some gold coins. He thrust them at Tuesday. "Here. Take these and get a room inside. I'm going to go try and talk to him. I'll figure something out." He covered the hand she was holding the coins with. "Don't. Leave. I will be back."

"I won't," Tuesday said.

If it was anyone else, I would've said they were full of it. They were never coming back. But not Koz. When he wanted to come back, he did. I knew firsthand, and it didn't take a spell to force him.

Koz left and joined up with them as it hit me. If Koz had planned on leaving us at the next village, was it really that big of a deal to part ways now?

He'd had no intention of leaving her.

"Tuesday, did you have some arrangement with Koz?" I asked.

"No, why?"

"Nothing." If Koz didn't make it back, this wasn't the best conversation to have.

We watched their backs fade into the night, and then Tuesday tugged at my arm. "Are you sure about that witch?"

"If you'd been in that tent, you'd believe." I shuddered thinking of the memory. I didn't care what anyone said. Something very strange and powerful had gone down that day. As someone well versed in strange, that was really saying something.

14

We sat on the stoop, watching as the men disappeared into the shadowy darkness of the trees. Koz turned around right before they were out of sight, holding up a finger to tell us it would only be a minute or two. It wouldn't be that quick, but if my guy was right, they'd all be back.

Tuesday perched her elbows on her knees. Her chin hit her palm and her stare was fixated on where they'd faded from view. "What if you're wrong?"

"Then I'm wrong. We give Koz some time to come back. If he doesn't, we leave in the morning. It's not like we planned on staying with them anyway. This changes nothing."

It was even better. It was. I mean, yeah, part of me might've started to like having the guys around a little. But this was better. Definitely. We didn't need them.

A small sigh escaped Tuesday's lips.

"You could still catch up to him." I didn't look at her. I didn't want to see the sad eyes.

Her wild hair brushed my arm as she shook her

head. "No. If he doesn't come back, he's not the one for me."

"I'll understand if you go with him." If she left, I'd be on my own. If she stayed, I'd have company but I'd always worry for her. Koz was someone who would be able to take care of her. The scales in this situation were abundantly clear. She was much better off making a trade.

"I'm not leaving you to go run after some man who might not come back for me." Her words were firm, and they sounded good.

Until sad sigh number two hit.

"Either stop sighing or go. The sighing means you want to go, and I don't want to hold you back."

Her hair hit my arm again. "The sighing is premature mourning of a man who wasn't who I hoped he'd be. It has nothing to do with you. If he leaves me here, I don't want him."

"Then don't mourn yet. He might be back."

"That's not the way I do things." Her voice was a little shrill on that last answer.

To each his own. If she wanted to mourn, I should let her do it. Right?

The pair of crows that had been eavesdropping in the woods found a new perch on the roof and cawed a few times.

Tuesday leaned back, taking in the duo. "Are your crows laughing at me?"

"They're waiting with us. I think they like to stay apprised of all the happenings." Those caws sounded a bit like cackling, but I wasn't going to tell her that. It was bad enough to be possibly abandoned. Mocking crows would definitely bring on another round of sighs.

"They're really annoying me." She stared upward, and from her expression, the crows were lucky she didn't have a ladder.

"Ignore them."

I ignored them all the time. The crows were just a nuisance. We had bigger issues to deal with. The witch thought I needed Callon, but I didn't. Yes, having a beast to protect you might come in handy, but it didn't matter.

If the spell didn't work, who cared? We'd head toward the west coast, as far as the land went. Even Turrock wouldn't span a continent to get me. He'd give up. I could handle this fine without Callon.

I was ten minutes into planning—and Tuesday's chin perch had sunk another few inches lower—when I felt it. I'd begun to think Callon had been right, and all that hocus-pocus with the witch had been a charade, until I felt the tug. It was as if I had a rope was tied around my waist and had been pulled taut.

"Something is happening."

"Really?" Tuesday's head shot up from her palm.

There were another bunch of tugs in rapid succession.

"Definitely." I tried to shimmy back toward the step behind me but couldn't budge, like I was anchored to something. I had a feeling that I'd be able to go forward, in the direction Callon had gone, though. I didn't want to lose my seat while I waited, so I didn't test it.

"What? Why are you making that face? This is good, right?" Tuesday asked.

I felt some more tugs.

"Not only do I think it's working, I think he might be

really mad about it. He was already really mad to begin with."

There were another twenty tugs in less than a few seconds. How was he moving that fast? He must've shifted, trying to push past the invisible wall I was feeling. "Oh yeah, he's mad. Stay near Koz when they get back."

"He won't hurt you," she said, her faith continuing.

"Either way, I'll ride it out. It won't be any worse than what I've already dealt with." What could he do to me that hadn't already been done? Scar me again? I didn't care anymore. There was no use for a pretty face when all I wanted was to go off and live out the rest of my life alone.

Five minutes later, I heard them coming. They were much louder arriving than they'd been departing. Koz was in front, as he broke into our vision with a smile. Hess looked like he was taking a stroll. Zink looked pissed, so same old there.

Callon was last, striding right for me like a bull at a cape. He had no right to be angrier now, just because the witch had pulled it off. I'd told him she had.

Tuesday's eyes were trained on Callon, and she began chewing on her nails like she hadn't eaten in a month. "It's a shock to the system, is all. He's probably not as mad as he looks."

"At least I have two healthy legs to run with."

"Run where?" she asked.

"Out of range? At least your boy is back."

Both of us fell quiet as the raging bull neared.

I got to my feet. If this was going to be a battle, I'd be as ready as I could be. Although, sitting or standing, I'd never be a match for the beast if he shifted.

Who was I kidding? I wasn't a match for the man. A giggle formed as nerves swelled up. The acid burning a hole through my stomach dissolved it before it escaped my chest, though.

Callon was still charging in my direction. If he thought I was going to back up or run, he was wrong. I might flinch, but I didn't retreat.

He stopped an inch shy of stepping on me. Anger rolled off him in waves. "We're going to go see that witch and we're getting this undone."

Ah, shit. He still thought there was a way out. He might be more stubborn than I was. There would be no undoing it, not with Hera. Did I let him work this one out until the end, or did I try and tell him? Telling him hadn't done much for the situation yet. But if we went back there and found out after days of traveling, I didn't care what Tuesday thought—he'd kill me for sure.

Here we go again. "She won't be there."

His eyes narrowed and his nostrils flared. "What did you do?" His voice was soft, the way a lion was quiet before he killed his prey.

My palms were sweating and I had to unstick my tongue from the roof of my mouth. "She's dead."

"She's dead?" Tuesday asked.

Did she have to sound so shocked? I knew I hadn't told her about that part. I'd barely wanted to think about it myself. Still, she wasn't helping the mood here.

"She *could* be lying," Zink said, but he sounded like he believed me.

Callon stared down, his jaw shifting. "She's not. That's how Hera pulled it off. She used the last of her magic to perform a death spell."

As our eyes held, I saw my possible death in his.

That was how much rage showed. The only option at the moment was damage control. "I'll go wherever you want to go. You won't even know I'm there. Nothing will change with your life. It will all be on me."

I studied his face, looking for some sign of softening. There was more softness in the boulder he'd pressed me against than what I saw. My spiel had done nothing.

He grabbed my shoulders, slowly lifting me to my toes and then up further until we were nose to nose. His grey eyes flared red. "Don't you see what you've done? You sacrificed my life to save your own."

Tuesday edged closer to my side, but I waved her back with my hand.

I met his burning rage with steel in my spine. I didn't know where I got the nerve to face off with this man and not crumble. I didn't cry. I'd given up on crying when I was ten, after I realized how much Baryn enjoyed it. Maybe it was all that practice under Baryn's hands that had honed the strength in me. I'd been through worse, and I'd hopefully make it through this.

"You mean promising to follow you around for a year? Is that what you mean? Because it'll be much worse for me than you, that's for sure."

He let go suddenly, and I wobbled as my heels hit the ground. He turned, taking a couple of steps away from me.

His back still to me, he said, "I have two choices. I'm either stuck with you at my side for the next year, protecting you so I don't get caught and trapped in the process, or kill you myself so I can be free of this."

That was where I'd really screwed him. He wouldn't have a choice but to protect me. If Turrock got his hands on me, it wouldn't be to kill me. Whoever he sold me to probably wasn't planning on it either.

Tuesday believed Callon wouldn't hurt me. I wasn't so sure. Tuesday and I had grown up together in the same village, but I'd seen the underbelly of man that she'd often been spared. I knew the lows they would go to. The depths their egos would sometimes demand of them to prop themselves up.

Even if he only intended to beat me, he was a beast. He'd be stronger than most men. What if he broke something in my face, and not just my nose? What if he caved in my cheekbone? Could you live with a caved-in face?

"I did what I had to."

I wouldn't beg for my life. I'd never beg. If this was my time, then so be it. I'd fight like hell and die the way I'd always wanted to live. Fighting.

My life hanging by the merest thread, I waited to see if his claws would come out and snap it.

He stopped moving altogether.

"You crossed a line. Even if I don't kill you, I'm not a priest. I don't offer forgiveness." His voice was gravelly, as if he were warring with himself, but his arms relaxed at his sides. His fingers uncurled.

Did that mean he *wasn't* going to kill me? It didn't seem like he was going to, even though that was probably his best option. He was a beast; he'd surely killed before.

"Then I won't ask for it." Seriously? That was the worst of it? No killing? No beating?

I waited for the relief to flood me, but it didn't come. I should be happier, but I wasn't. He hated me. I didn't think that would taste so sour in my mouth or sit in my gut like a lump of lead.

He turned to Koz. "Watch her while I'm gone."

He disappeared, but I knew for sure he'd be back this time.

"See? I was right. That didn't go that badly." Tuesday smiled, patting my shoulder before her eyes went round as she suddenly realized something. "Does that mean we get to stay here tonight? I've never gotten to stay in an eat and sleep." She turned to Koz. "So we're staying?"

A year. One year and I'd be free. That was it. I could deal with anything for a year. I'd dealt with a lot worse than someone not liking me.

15

I jerked awake the second the door to the room opened. Callon was standing in the doorway. His eyes searched the bed, where Koz and Tuesday formed two lumps. Koz had offered me the bed, but I'd insisted on taking a spot on the floor by the window.

Since the room was so small, Koz either had to sleep in the hallway or in the bed with Tuesday. She had insisted Koz sleep beside her for fear she'd wake and have a nightmare without him. I'd barely managed to keep my eyeballs from rolling right out of my head.

Callon took a step into the room, and Koz lifted a half-dead arm in my direction. "She's over there."

Callon's eyes had already landed on me, and I would've sworn they weren't silver at all now, but a deep red. Had he just changed back? Had he been out all this time as a beast?

The red faded as he headed toward me, but only slightly. I sat up, expecting a continuation of the fight from earlier. I shrank back as he bent forward, but that didn't slow him down as I was thrown over his shoulder.

The last glimpse of the room was Tuesday still sound asleep. She could sleep through a tornado. Her shack back at the village had been right by the gate that had groaned all day and all night. Koz nodded, half out of it and unfazed that I was being carried off.

Callon had finally cracked and was taking me outside to beat the hell out of me. He probably didn't want to deal with Tuesday crying or Koz trying to stop him. I didn't either. I'd take my lumps and deal with Callon on my own.

Callon shut the door behind us as he walked into the hall. I wouldn't scream. I had too much pride to have the whole place peeking out to see what was going on. I'd wait for him to put me down. Then I was going to kick him right in the stones. I wasn't going to just take it the way I used to. The days of sitting there waiting for the blows were over.

He didn't walk very far. Only to the other end of the hallway. He dropped me to the floor. My knees wobbled, but as soon as I got my feet back underneath me, I angled my knee up. Before I could get a full swing, he was pinning me to the wall, a leg in between mine.

His chest pressed against me, hands caging me in.

I looked into his eyes that were definitely still reddish.

"Don't," he said, his canines peeking out longer than normal.

He was right on the edge, and part of me wanted to push him off it, see what would happen if I did. He looked the way I felt every moment of the day. He was walking an impossible line, one I knew that chafed me constantly.

If I pushed him over the edge, would I follow? She'd

every last bit of fear inside me and finally break free of the chains that were woven into me from the day I was born? Chains that felt like they dragged my soul into the ground every morning when I woke?

"Don't," he repeated, and that was when I realized he could see where my thoughts were leading. "I'm not going to hurt you."

He really wouldn't. He was barely hanging on to his humanity and he still wasn't going to hurt me. I exhaled, not realizing I'd been holding my breath.

Did I push him anyway?

No. I'd pushed him enough. I let me body go slack, letting the wall take some of my weight.

He moved one of his hands and opened a door beside us. Then slowly backed away from me until there was just enough room to edge off the wall. He lifted his other hand up, herding me into what looked like something closer to a closet with a window than a bedroom. A pallet lined the floor of the small space that appeared narrower than his shoulders.

"It's the innkeeper's."

I stepped inside, wondering what this was about as he followed me in.

He took off his shirt and tossed it onto the pallet. I edged back, watching him. There were different types of hurting. Just because he didn't hit me didn't mean he wouldn't exact his revenge.

His eyes shot to mine, taking in the way I pressed myself into the corner. "That's not what this is. If I'm chained to you, no one else is going to get their hands on you. Koz sleeps like the dead." He dropped onto the pallet, made a pillow of his shirt, and closed his eyes.

I stood there and watched him for a good five

minutes. If this bothered him in any way, it wasn't obvious. In fact, it was becoming clear I could stand there all night if I wanted. And I really didn't want to. I was exhausted.

I slid down the wall, trying to determine the best way to lie down and touch him the least. In my efforts, I only stepped on him a handful of times.

He sat up. "For fuck's sake, I'm trying to sleep."

He looped an arm around my waist and then tugged me down beside him before closing his eyes again.

I settled into the spot, my blanket still wrapped around me, and he shifted, having to lie on his side to fit in the space. His body brushed mine from shoulder to toe. I could feel the warmth of his skin seeping into me and the feel of his chest, thick with muscles. His breath fanned my neck. The smell of pine clung to him like he'd been born to run through the forest, rule it.

Logic dictated that I should be irritated. He'd stormed into the room and carried me off without a word. But logic didn't seem to have much of a say at the moment, because I wasn't mad.

There'd been a reason I'd lain awake long after everyone else had fallen asleep. I'd felt as vulnerable as I had at the village. Word would spread of the pirates dying, and too many people at the Gathering had noticed me. They'd be coming for me.

With Callon's body flush against mine, my muscles finally calmed. I didn't have to listen for every creak of a board in the hall, every breaking twig outside the window. I could finally sleep. The witch had been right. If I wanted to be free, I needed to be tied to him, at least for a while.

16

I woke alone. It was better than waking up shoulder to shoulder after the best night's sleep I'd ever had. That would've been plain awkward. For the first time in more than a decade, I hadn't stirred. I'd slept like Callon *had* killed me.

I ran an arm across my mouth, realizing I'd drooled. Who cared if I drooled? Callon was a necessity, and one that hated me. Maybe he'd left before I drooled. I stood, brushing myself off and deciding I probably didn't drool until he'd left.

I made my way into the hall, and the noises drifted up from the main floor. I knew they hadn't left me here because they couldn't. Even without the spell, Tuesday wouldn't have let them.

I peeked downstairs, searching the main floor, where people were breaking their fast. Callon looked up from where everyone was sitting at the table. If he was still raging, I couldn't tell. If he was happy, that didn't show either. My legs were stiff as I made them bend to descend the stairs.

Tuesday followed Callon's stare and made her way over to me before I hit the last stair.

"What happened last night? I went to sleep and then you were gone in the morning. Koz said you were safe, but I was still a little nervous, and then Callon wouldn't tell me what room you were in because he said to let you be."

She continued to ramble off each and every little thing that had transpired this morning, but I couldn't take my eyes off the guys where they were talking. Callon might be stone-faced, but the others weren't.

"What's going on?" I knew when things were wrong. I had a lifetime of experience with it.

She glanced over her shoulder before she said, "Someone came around looking last night."

Looking for me? My first reaction was to barge out the door and run, but logic overruled that quick enough. I couldn't run unless I had Callon running with me. And with Callon, I didn't need to run. It was going to take a while to really firm that up in my mind.

Once I nailed down my flight instinct, I asked, "What happened? Did anyone tell the person anything? Do they know where I am?" She whispered something so low I couldn't decipher it. "What?"

She jerked her thumb toward her chest, but she was trying to point at the guys without them seeing.

"Just tell me what happened."

She leaned in close. "I think. Zink. Killed. Him."

"How? What else did you hear?" I kept my eyes trained on Tuesday's face, forcing them to stay there, so I didn't stare at the guys instead.

Her eyes shot sideways, making sure we still had a buffer around us. "He was there when the guy arrived.

He heard this person asking some guy who was lingering outside about a blond. Luckily, the guy hadn't seen you. I'm not sure what exactly happened after that, but they know Turrock sold you. The guys said something about the blond's new owner was looking for her."

"What about the guy that was asking?"

"He's gone. Koz said he. Wouldn't. Be. An. Issue." Her big almond eyes went round, and she nodded slowly, as if to add, *Can you believe that shit?*

No one spoke as we walked. I avoided looking at Callon, and he did me the favor of pretending I didn't exist. We'd gone about an hour before all the guys stopped, as if the spot had been predetermined.

Koz handed over some dried meat. He was always good about having some snacks on hand. I chewed in silence, tricking myself into thinking I wouldn't have to speak at all. Callon and I would ignore each other for the next year and then one day I'd leave, end of story.

Of course, that wasn't going to happen. He confirmed it by walking over and standing in front of me.

"Is there anything else? Who else might be following you? Tell me now or I really might beat you."

He tilted his head toward me as he waited. Even from here, I could feel the heat he threw off, like he had last night.

I swallowed the last chunk of meat quickly. After this, he might take the meat back.

"Speak," he said, as I was still forcing the too-large bite down.

"They were selling me. If they think I'm still alive, they'll probably want to make sure they get me back. You know, so they can get their money."

Callon didn't budge, waiting for me to add anything more I might know. I was slightly relieved not to know anything else.

"That doesn't sound so bad," Koz said.

I'd known everyone was paying attention but couldn't focus on them. I had to concentrate my efforts on holding Callon's stare. *See? Give it your best. Nothing left to hide here.*

"Don't worry. I'm sure it'll get worse," Callon said to Koz, but he didn't bother breaking eye contact with me. "Do you know *who* they sold you to?"

"No. That's all I have." Even his questions were aggressive. If you really thought about it, he was overreacting. This arrangement was much more detrimental to my life.

"They must've said *something* else." He rolled his head, a perfect punctuation to the doubt in his words.

"No. That was it." That was all I'd heard, anyway, and Tuesday was not getting dragged into this conversation. I knew she'd held back on me, and I needed to know the full story before she spilled. After the way he'd flipped out on me, I was done offering up information. He was cut off.

Tuesday stepped forward. She ignored the rapid shakes of my head that pretty much blew the story open anyway.

She didn't stop until she was nearly in between us. "*I* heard them."

"What else did they say?" Callon asked, and it didn't go unnoticed that his tone softened.

Okay, fine, she didn't screw him over the way I had, but still. I crossed my arms, looking off at the trees, letting my foot tap all it wanted.

"I didn't hear a name. I only heard talk that buyers were coming and Turrock and Baryn were getting a nice chunk of gold." Tuesday shrugged.

It was all in the shrug, or the stiffness of it. She always shrugged when she was holding out. I didn't need to see her face to know her mouth was twitching with untold information.

"You're a lousy liar. What else did you hear? I want all of it," Callon said, his voice having a hint of the sharp edge it held when he spoke to me.

Callon was right. Tuesday was the worst liar ever. It was like her whole body stiffened in rebellion. When she'd told me initially, I knew she was holding back and I should've pressed her. I shook my head a few more times as my tapping picked up its tempo.

"There was nothing else important," she said, taking a few steps back, trying to extricate herself now.

Had she not been traveling with us these last days? Had she been so busy staring at Koz that she had no idea who this man was? There would be no retreat. You either stood your ground or triggered his predatory nature by running.

Callon followed Tuesday. "Tell me anyway."

She shook her head, lips sealed shut.

If she started sweating, I was going to have to get involved. I was studying her forehead when Koz stepped closer.

Resting a hand on her shoulder, he said, "Tuesday, if it's going to help us—"

"It won't." Her face was flaming red. Her eyes darted toward me.

Ah, shit. It was bad, but not in a way that was going to divulge my secrets. It was going to open me up for humiliation.

"It might help," Koz said.

"I need to know every detail," Callon said, refusing to stand down.

Koz glanced at Callon, then back to Tuesday, torn by his budding feelings. It didn't help that Tuesday was looking at Koz expectantly. I knew how Tuesday's brain worked. She was looking for a white knight. If he picked Callon's side, I didn't want to think of how bad it would be. It wouldn't matter that Koz had only known her for a short time. He'd called Callon a brother. Reasoning didn't always factor in when Tuesday got on a roll.

Callon looked at Tuesday.

Tuesday grabbed Koz's arm.

This chain of events was about to go bad.

I stepped forward. "Tuesday, just tell him. It's not that important, whatever it was."

Koz's shoulders slumped as Callon's eyes narrowed on me. Seriously? I was telling her to say it all and he was still suspicious?

"Can we talk in private?" Tuesday asked.

I lost my chance to dissect it any more, because Callon tipped his head toward the trees. She walked a few paces away with him and I dropped back a few, to the other side of the clearing. It was cowardly for sure, but I didn't want to hear what was said. If I didn't hear it, I wouldn't be embarrassed by whatever it was.

Still, it was hard not to watch them.

The more she talked, the more animated she

became. And soon it looked as if she *wanted* to talk, as if telling everything to Callon was unleashing a dam.

Her voice grew louder as she was half talking, and now half sobbing.

Her voice grew so loud that it carried to me. "Then they laughed because Turrock said the only one who could possibly get off on a face like that was Baryn. And what was he going to do now that she was gone? He'd have to start from scratch." Her hands were fluttering around. "And he's the one that did that to her, and it wasn't right. But that wasn't even the worst. They were laughing about what this person was going to do to her, and, and…"

I dropped back a couple more steps, afraid to hear what might come out next. As far as revelations, I guess it could've been worse. But damn if I could think of one right now. All I could do was try not to choke on the humiliation of it all. I'd thought no one knew about what Baryn used to do after he beat me. I'd never told a soul, but I guessed he had liked to talk.

"So, Teddy, ever been out by these parts?" Koz asked, loud enough to drown out Tuesday's voice.

It took a second before I answered. "No. Never had the chance."

I appreciated the effort. I really did. But I was having a hard time speaking at that moment.

Callon glanced over at me. I couldn't guess at what else was being said or what he was thinking of it. I turned away too quickly to guess. Tuesday's voice dropped lower a second later.

Callon walked back over and went straight to Hess. "Go to the nearest pigeon place and see if you can get this settled. From what I know of Turrock, he's a greedy fuck. Tell him you'll pay twice what the current buyer paid and wait for a response."

Tuesday was following behind him, dragging her sleeve across her face as she made her way to me.

"Tuesday, it's fine."

She latched on to my neck anyway. She was talking, but I couldn't make out what she was saying. She was mumbling and blinding me with her hair.

I was trying to make out her last words when I watched Koz walk up to Callon.

"Do you need to..." Koz nodded in the direction of the trees.

"I'll be back soon."

Callon turned, his face clear even through Tuesday's locks. His eyes looked downright feral, near glowing as he looked in my direction.

Then he was gone.

17

The temperature must've dropped thirty degrees from that afternoon, and it felt more like forty every time the wind blew. My jaw smacked together so violently that I was expecting to spit teeth out soon. The palm I smashed up against it did little to stop the chattering because my hand was shaking even worse.

I glanced over my shoulder at where Tuesday had curled up beside Koz. If he was anything like Callon, he threw heat off like a bonfire.

Koz stared back. "You don't look so good," he said quietly, to keep from waking a sleeping Tuesday.

"I'm fine." I tried to speak without chattering. I turned back around and used my arm to sweep some more leaves over me.

"Someone needs to sleep with Teddy. She sounds like she's about to get hypothermia," Koz said a second later.

"She's fine," Callon said, the words sounding like they ran over a grate as he spoke.

Footsteps neared and then Zink said, "Humans

aren't that useful, but I'm not sure I can watch her freeze to death."

I squinted an eye open and looked at where Zink stood staring at me, completely comfortable, as if it were a balmy spring day.

"I said I'm fine." I closed my eyes, intent on ignoring him.

I heard a few more steps and then another person walking over. "What are you doing?" Callon asked.

"Keeping her from freezing to death?" Zink offered. "Unless you want to?"

"No," Callon barked, as if having to sleep next to me last night had been so terrible.

I'd slept like a babe, but I guess I snored or something. What if I'd drooled *on* him? I almost hoped I'd freeze to death in the night and wouldn't have to think of that again.

"Didn't you sleep near her last night?" Zink asked, wondering the same as I.

Well, he wasn't wondering if I'd drooled. Who knew you could die of embarrassment at the same time you froze to death?

"I don't need any of you. You can all fuck off," I said. Or that was what I tried to say, but my words came out a mess of stuttering and huffs. I was fairly certain the only clear words were "need" and "fuck," because that was the kind of night I was having.

Zink tilted his chin up and raised an eyebrow my way.

"She told us to fuck off. Not what you're thinking," Callon said.

"Shame. I was just about to revise my opinion that maybe humans *were* good for something." Zink shrugged and then took a step forward, but Callon cut him off.

"What are you doing?" Callon asked.

"I told you. She's freezing, and you, well…"

"You. Can't," Callon said, his voice at a near growl. "That's not a smart option."

Figured he'd let me freeze because he had ice in his veins. Not that I'd die. Didn't need him. I didn't need anyone. I'd make it through tonight with the hate burning in my chest, fueled by every mean thing he did.

"Oh shit. Really?" Koz said, awe in his voice. "What are you going to do?"

"Nothing. It'll pass," Callon said.

I lost track of what they were talking about, and I didn't care anymore. I tried to scoop up more nearby leaves and pile them on top of myself, closing my eyes and trying to burrow under my pile of compost.

There was shuffling near me, but I ignored that too. I knew it was Callon. It was disturbing how I recognized his scent so easily. Made me want to take a hot poker to the insides of my nose.

I squeaked when an arm wrapped around my waist and dragged me onto a fur beside him. We weren't in a good place. I should be rolling right off this fur and telling him to shove it. But damn, I was cold.

"Wouldn't it be better if the fur was on top of us?"

He didn't answer, probably because my question was mauled by teeth chattering.

He reached over me, grabbed the edge of the pelt on my side, and then pulled it until I was rolled into the fur. He turned, taking the edge of the fur with him as he gave me his back, the fur pulling me closer to him.

"Don't complain. I don't particularly care to sleep

like this either. Unfortunately, if you get sick, I'm afraid of what you'll do if I bring you near another witch."

Helping me sounded like it was near killing him, and sent a renewed urge to tell him to go screw. The idea of complaining lasted all of one second before the warmth eased into the arms I had crossed in front of me. His body nearly boiled.

"You need to get closer," he informed me a minute later.

"This is good." Good was an understatement. It was the difference between the North Pole and the heat of summer.

"You can't make anything easy, can you?"

I thought I was making it super easy, so I ignored him.

He growled for a second and then turned to face me, the fur slacking. I edged back, not sure what he was going to do. He shifted, turning toward me and then turning me, pulling my back snug against his chest. It seemed like every inch of my back had part of his front attached to it.

Every. Single. Part.

Every muscle fiber froze, but I couldn't bring myself to pull away as heat seeped into me, thawing me from the outside in. Still, I was as stiff as the icicle I felt like. I closed my eyes, pretending that Callon wasn't lying behind me. I was cozied up to a hearth.

"Relax. We're sharing body heat. That's it. You're as stiff as a vir—"

"Shut up." I jabbed my elbow indiscriminately. It wasn't a hard jab. Partially frozen limbs moved slowly, but it stopped his words.

He lay there silently for a moment, exactly long enough to give me false hope he'd stay quiet.

"Really?" he asked, his breath tingling on my neck.

"Shut. Up." After what Tuesday had told him, the confusion would be obvious. If I'd heard the story, I would've assumed the torment wouldn't have stopped short of the whole shebang too. It wasn't something I was willing to offer a play-by-play on. Living it had been enough. There would be no reliving for his enlightenment.

He gave me another pause full of false hope.

"So, nothing—"

I tried to push away from him, but his arm moved around my waist and was too strong to budge. My body might be freezing, but my face was burning up.

"Calm down. I'm too tired to discuss it anyway."

"You're an—"

"You don't get to call me names while I'm saving your ass."

I would've argued, but every time he spoke, his chest vibrated through mine and his breath whispered over my skin. I'd let him think he was winning this one.

I WAS POKING THE FIRE THE NEXT MORNING, AVOIDING looking at Callon. Waking up next to him had felt much more personal than going to sleep next to him. One good thing had come out of it. When I'd woken with my arm wrapped around his stomach and my head planted to his chest, I'd heard his heart beating. Up until now, I hadn't been sure he had one. I'd untangled myself, and neither of us had said a word to each other since.

Koz's head jerked up and looked East, those beast ears picking up on sounds un-hearable by a human.

Before worry could set in, Callon stood and said, "He's back too soon."

Even Tuesday was paying attention.

I straightened, looking at the woods. I couldn't hear or see a thing, but I followed Callon's stare, fully confident that Hess would walk into the clearing at any moment.

When Hess walked back into camp, he looked like he was towing five tons of stone behind him. He tossed down his sack and exhaled a long, weary breath.

Callon looked at him, assessing.

Zink was squatted by the fire, in between Callon and myself. "How bad?"

I chewed away a piece of cuticle as I waited. Tuesday moved until her arm was brushing mine.

"We can't settle up with Turrock," Hess finally spat out. "There was a message waiting at the pigeon stand when I got there. My guess is, the same message is at every pigeon stand a hundred miles from here."

That was the big issue? That wasn't *good*, but it wasn't *that* bad. Now that I saw what Callon's crew could do to the pirates, was anyone overly concerned about Turrock? Turrock was no threat against what these guys were packing. Actually, if Turrock put up a fight, this might work out to my benefit. A world without Turrock wasn't a bad thing. I'd planned on going back and killing him myself one of these days, and I wouldn't be picky about how his death came. I wasn't a forgive-and-forget person, not when the things I was supposed to forgive were too horrible to ever forget.

"What did it say?" Callon asked, clearly put out over having his easy fix ripped away.

Hess scratched his head, buying himself a second. "The message wasn't from Turrock."

Callon crossed his arms, feet braced apart. "Who was it from?"

Hess let out a breath so strong it blew out his cheeks before he dropped the bomb. "The Magician. And he wants his property returned."

There was a chorus of groans interrupted by the silence of Callon. There were a lot of grave looks passing in between everyone, but no one was explaining why this was so bad.

I glanced at Tuesday, looking to see if she knew something about him.

She mouthed, *I never heard the name.* She shrugged.

"Who's the Magician?" Tuesday blurted out, as impatient as I was to get more details. It made my gut clench to know the person I was now running from unsettled these men.

"You don't know?" Zink asked, and something happened that I'd never thought could. He blanched. Zink had tan skin to begin with, so to see him lose his color was shocking.

"No." Tuesday's shoulder banged into mine. "Who is this person?"

For once, I was glad she was doing the talking.

"I'd use the term 'person' loosely," Zink said. "He might've been human once upon a time, but now the Magician is more monster than anything. He's been on our radar for quite some time, but we've avoided conflict so far."

"Had," Hess added, running both hands through his hair.

Zink nodded toward Hess before continuing. "After the country of Newco collapsed, he filled the power vacuum. The people in charge before weren't good, but it was more of an evil under the radar. The Magician doesn't believe in being so subtle. He's been trying to expand for some time, and by any means."

"Do you think you could…" Tuesday was chewing on the side of her lip as she fumbled her way around phrasing the next question.

"Can you take him?" I asked, helping her out.

"Does this Magician guy know you?" Tuesday added.

Even though Zink had done most of the explaining, I shifted my attention to Callon. This was one answer I wanted from him.

Callon looked at me for the first time that day. "I believe we're on his radar as well."

I nodded, absorbing what he said, and what he didn't. Neither Callon nor the Magician knew who would win, but it would be a hell of a fight.

"We need this settled. I'll head out alone and…" Callon looked back at me, as everyone else was. "That's right, I can't go alone. Fuck. This just keeps getting better and better."

"Now what?" Zink asked, verbalizing what everyone else was wondering.

Callon stood silent for a moment. "I can't bring her with me to negotiate and I can't leave her behind. There's only one person that might be able to undo a death spell. We head to Hecate."

Hess groaned, and Zink and Koz didn't look so hot either.

"Who's Hecate?"

"A witch. If anyone can fix this, it's her."

Great. Another witch.

18

The sun was high in the sky when the guys realigned themselves. Callon, who'd been walking ahead, dropped back until he was behind me and Tuesday. Koz fell in beside him. Zink took the lead and Hess covered the side.

Koz was whistling, and Callon's shoulders looked relaxed, but something was off. I veered off to the left and Koz herded me back into the center. A step to the right and Callon edged me back in.

They could whistle all they wanted. Shit was about to go down. I grabbed Tuesday's arm and tugged her closer to me. She turned, a question in her expression.

I gave a short shake of my head. My hair was still waving with the motion when I was rushed from the back and taken down to the ground. I didn't know what happened, but I instantly recognized Callon's scent when he shoved me into the crevice of a fallen tree, his body on top of mine. Callon was tall and solid, but it was like his flesh was packed with heavy metals instead of muscle, he weighed so much.

His hand went to the back of my head, forcing it closer to the log until I was in jeopardy of chewing on rotting leaves and bark. Shots whizzed overhead, and I decided maybe soggy old leaves wouldn't taste so bad.

Callon was signaling over me, his body moving with the action. Zink crawled over to where we were hunkered down beside a log.

"I got her," Zink said.

Callon rolled off and disappeared into the woods as Zink took his place. I put up a hand before he thought about climbing on top of me too. "I'll stay put. We're good."

"Fine by me," he said, situating himself beside me.

Bullets whizzed overhead, but I knew they weren't meant for me. Odds were we were getting shot at because they *wanted* me. I was the safest person here. I could probably stand up, wave my arms about, and still not get shot.

I scanned the forest and caught sight of Tuesday hunkered down nearby with Koz. I couldn't see Hess. He was probably taking out the threat with Callon, and I had no idea if they'd make it out alive. Yeah, they were tough, but these people had guns.

Very few people had guns anymore—the pirates sometimes had them, but other than that, word was the former collapsed country of Newco had the only large stash left. If they were right and the Magician had filled the power vacuum there, it stood to reason these people were sent by him.

The gunfire stopped after a few more minutes.

There was scuffling and Zink got to his feet. I followed him toward the noise.

Callon wasn't far away and had a boot to a man's

neck, pinning him to the ground, while holding his arm outstretched.

"Who do you work for?" Callon's boot lifted to shift to the man's chest.

The man on the ground shook his head but stopped as soon as he caught sight of me.

"You looking for her?" Callon asked, and then twisted the guy's arm so hard that I was waiting for a snapping sound.

The guy visibly gulped but said nothing. Hess walked out of the woods, a few guns slung over his back and a smattering of blood covering his forearms.

"Tell me," Callon said, and this time I did hear the snap.

The guy's face contorted, turning bright red. "Can't," he said, on a gasping breath.

"He's not going to speak." I stared down at the man who'd stopped looking at me.

"How do you know?" Callon asked.

"Trust me. I do. He's not going to say anything, and then you'll slit his throat." There was no reason to get into the nitty-gritty about how the blood would spurt out. Callon had killed before. He'd know that part. He hadn't walked out of those woods as clean as he did if this was his first time.

Zink raised his eyebrows and shifted a step away from me. I didn't blame him. Times like this, I even creeped myself out.

"Where you going?" Koz asked, as I backed away toward where Tuesday was standing. She'd had the common sense to know this was something you might want to keep your distance from.

"I've already seen this." It had been gory enough the

first time it played out in my mind. A second showing in the flesh wasn't needed.

Tuesday stared over my shoulder, and I knew it was as bad as I'd seen. From the sounds, they were working the man over, but it wouldn't matter. I grabbed Tuesday's hand, tugging her along with me back to the fallen log I'd taken shelter beside. She didn't say much as we sat there, waiting for the noises to stop. After today, I knew there was one less rainbow in her world.

"It's really good we've got these guys to help us," she said after a couple minutes.

"Yeah," I said, giving Tuesday the side eye. Actually, there might be a couple *more* rainbows in her world.

The guy's moaning finally stopped. Koz made his way back to us first. He stopped right in front of me and asked, "How much can you see, exactly?"

I shrugged. "Varies. If I'm lucky, a few seconds. Bad day? It can get pretty long."

"Koz," Callon called out from across the way.

"I know. I got 'em," Koz yelled back.

I stood, knowing the drill by now. Time to walk while they cleaned up the bodies.

19

Zink stared at me from across the fire. "Do you have any family that can do what you do?"

That question got Zink and Koz's attention until the three of them were staring. I hated being the center of attention. Nothing good ever came from it. I never should have said anything earlier about how the guy wouldn't talk. Now they wanted to know things about me.

"I don't know." I took another bite of meat, hoping they'd take the hint. I'd rather spend my time chewing this meat than chewing the fat with them. This shit was the best thing I'd tasted in years, maybe ever. I didn't know how, but Koz could burn some serious flavor into a chunk of meat.

"Are they all dead of something?" Hess asked.

Seriously? My jaw dropped, and I didn't care if there was some unswallowed gristle available for view. Maybe it would give them a hint.

"I don't know." Damn. Last bite. I looked around,

seeing if anyone was getting tired of eating. It was like all the hunger from those missed meals had multiplied.

"Haven't seen them in a while?" Zink asked.

"No." What the fuck? Didn't these people take a hint? The only one that wasn't speaking was Callon, and it was probably because he was too pissed off that he was being hunted by the Magician because he was stuck with me. Or maybe he didn't like me enough to care? Whatever. I'd take the silence.

I looked around. "Is everyone going to finish their meat?"

Three sticks were held out to me. I took them all.

"When did you see them last?" Hess asked.

Really? Were they going to ruin my meal with constant questions? "Holy fuck. The last time was the day I was born. I was sold as a baby for a couple of coins because, from what I've heard, my mother was an attractive plaguer. They thought I'd either be a good whore or have magic, or maybe both. Seeing as how everyone was afraid of me causing them to die prematurely, the whoring didn't work out so well. Anything else?"

I saw *that* look pass from man to man, like the Bloody Death itself. I hated *that* look. The one where they thought they had it so much better.

"I'm sorry, but do you really think what you have going on is *soooo* great? You sprout hair and fangs. The world thinks you pick your teeth with the bones of babies, after you steal them from their cribs. But hey, if you're all cool with it, so am I." I took a big bite out of one of the legs I'd taken.

All three of them shut up. Koz might've turned a

little rosy. Zink's scowl was a little fiercer, and Hess nodded as if he agreed with my statement.

There was silence until Callon broke out into the heartiest laugh I'd ever heard. Figured he'd see the humor in that. He was the one that seemed most comfortable having fangs and fur at his disposal.

His laughter didn't taper off in a normal way. It halted suddenly.

"A representative from the Magician is here."

How could he know that? Were they talking to him and I couldn't hear it?

"Where?" I got to my feet immediately, and Callon tugged me back down. I yanked my arm loose, but his palm landed on my shoulder next. How had I ended up sitting beside him? Big mistake. I needed to watch what I was doing from now on.

His grip was firm as he said, "You say nothing. You don't smile. You don't grimace. Nothing."

"Got it." Actually, I didn't get it at all, but I wanted his hand off my shoulder.

"Teddy," Callon said in a way that instantly insinuated doubt.

"I *got* it. Nothing," I said, ignoring the way his eyes were so sharp they could've sliced bone.

I didn't have time to ask how he'd known who was approaching because the bushes were rustling.

A single man stepped into the clearing, and even if he hadn't been sent from the Magician, I still wouldn't have been able to take my eyes off him. I'd never seen such shiny clothes with flares and ties and shiny buttons. His shoes sparkled, as if he walked above the dirt the rest of us trod upon. Hair slicked back into a long grey ponytail with not a single strand busting loose. That alone screamed some crazy magic.

Everyone was standing but me, who still had a hand planted on my shoulder holding me down. Even Tuesday was standing. To say it chafed was the same as saying sticking my arm in the fire would tickle.

"I'm Harlow. I'm here on behalf of the Magician." Harlow looked at me, his eyes moving to pause on my shoulder and then back to Callon. "The Magician wanted me to tell you that he is aware of your situation and circumstances. He can alleviate the problem caused by the witch. He can reverse the spell if you hand her over."

How did he know about what the witch did? There was only one way, only one person left to speak—her son. Had Harlow killed him? Hopefully not.

I would've jumped up except for Callon's hand still planted on my shoulder. Fucking beast strength. It was ridiculous. What I would've done for a gun or a knife at that moment.

Harlow took the smallest step toward Callon and me. It was enough to make it clear he only wanted to deal with him.

"The Magician knows you weren't looking for this situation. He bears you no ill will. He only wants his property returned." Harlow dipped his head toward "the property."

Fingers squeezing my shoulder kept my lips sealed, but barely. This was the shit I'd said I wouldn't take anymore. Here I was, taking shovels of it. This was why I needed to be alone. I never should've listened to that witch. At least there was another chance if we ever got to this Hecate person and they could do something.

As soon as Callon told this Harlow to go screw, we'd have to double-time it there before this Magician person showed.

"You've already attacked us," Callon said.

"That was an accident. They were only supposed to observe. They were misdirected," Harlow said.

"What guarantee will I have if I hand her over?" Callon asked.

My head fell back to look at him. Had he really said that? Fucking bastard.

His fingers pressed into my shoulder, but he needn't fear. There wouldn't be any jumping up in indignation. There wouldn't be much movement of any kind. It was too hard to breathe through the pain from the knife that had gutted me. Of course Callon would go along with the Magician. Why wouldn't he? He owed me nothing. Less than nothing, after manacling myself to him. Why was I surprised?

"Whatever guarantee you need." Harlow was smiling, as if the deal was done.

"I want time to think it over," Callon said.

With every word, the hope I'd misunderstood died. My shoulders shrank so low that Callon would have to kneel to keep his hand there. Then I was bending forward, resting my arms on my legs and letting my head drop as well.

He'd never agreed to help me. It wasn't a true betrayal. So why did it feel like one?

I glanced over at Tuesday, who was being held back by Koz's arms around her waist. Her eyes were trained on Callon, and they were saying much more than if she'd been screaming.

"The Magician is prepared to give you several days," Harlow said.

Callon took a step forward. "Tell the Magician I'm taking a week."

"I'll pass on your message." The man bowed and then turned and bowed to me as well, that smile still there.

The second Harlow was gone, Koz dropped his hold on Tuesday.

She launched herself at Callon. "You're a monster!"

Koz was on her again, swinging her away from Callon before her nails could meet his face.

Callon remained standing where he was, as calm as he'd been before she lunged. His eyes met Zink's and he tilted his head toward where Harlow had left.

My butt didn't budge off the ground. It was easier to remain sitting than stand on wobbling legs. Plus the movement might make my already-churning stomach decide it needed to empty as my options, or lack of, settled in my mind.

There wouldn't even be a chance of running. As sure as Callon was chained to me, I was to him. The rage turned inward. I'd willingly entrapped myself and handed him the key to my downfall.

The camp was quiet, other than Tuesday crying, her rage turning to sorrow. At some point, Koz's lockdown had turned to consoling as he rubbed her back. It was good someone had it in them to do it. Right now, I was too empty. The only thing filling that emptiness was the urge to take the knife I'd eaten dinner with and plunge it into Callon's heart, in the hopes he might feel a fraction of the pain coursing through me.

Why had I thought part of him had wanted to

protect me? He'd been stuck. That was the beginning and end of it. As the person who'd stuck him, I should've known. From the second I'd met him, everything had revolved around dumping me.

I'd been so stupid. There was no end to the error I'd made. How had I thought I could pull this off?

Zink stepped back into the clearing and nodded in Callon's direction. Callon tipped his chin and Koz let out a sigh of relief.

Callon immediately walked back to where I was, and I finally found the strength to get to my feet so I wouldn't have to look at him. He followed me, blocking my view. I would've kept moving—my feet wanted to run from him—but my pride kept my chin up, shoulders back, and, by some miracle, my eyes dry. Tears had never been my thing, but this situation would make rain in the desert. Plus, that wildness that was growing inside me was poking her head up, getting ready to fight.

If he thought this was going to be the live-and-let-live moment, where he told me he was only doing what he had to, he'd better plan on living an eternity. That was how long it would take for me to get there. I didn't care if it made sense. My feelings right now had nothing to do with logic.

"I'm not going to hand you over. I'm buying time." His voice was short, as if *I'd* irritated *him*.

"You *aren't* handing me over?" Sure he wasn't. I snorted. It didn't make any sense. He wasn't going to risk everyone here to save me. I was nobody to him and he was going to save his own ass, just like everyone always did.

"Although it would be much easier, no, that's not what I'm doing." The ire in his voice was growing.

"Why not? Give me one reason you wouldn't." I nailed him with my full glare, and what a look it was. If he was going to bullshit me, he was going to need to do better than that.

He crossed his arms, muscles tensing and the vein in his neck looking about to burst. "Because I said I wouldn't."

Oh, well, that explained it all.

He couldn't even come up with a reason. I rolled my eyes in response.

Tuesday plowed into me from behind, hugging me. "Thank you!"

Who was she thanking and for what?

She was staring up at Callon. "I'm sorry. It was a knee-jerk reaction when I heard you say that to him."

Seriously? She was believing this bull? Tuesday was back to hugging me, and I didn't have it left in me to tell her how wrong she was. Or argue when she told me I was the one who was wrong.

"Now what?" Koz asked.

Callon spared me one last glare with those steel eyes before he walked over to the guys.

"He won't act on us until after the week," Callon said. "If we take the west pass around…"

I listened to them plan a way forward, and I wondered if he'd tell them it was all a lie once I fell asleep.

20

Trust but verify. There was a guy back in the village who used to say that. No one ever questioned him. He read a lot, so everyone thought that must mean he was smart. I'd silently disagreed. I always thought it should be verify then trust. That made a whole lot more sense. Otherwise, you were running around and trusting everyone. Talk about a setup for disaster.

I'd lost count how many times I'd been lied to. Callon *seemed* like a straight shooter, but that meant nothing. Lots of people seemed okay but weren't. How many times had Baryn told me that he'd let me go? How many times had I believed him when I'd been too young and stupid to know better? Or the people he'd sent in to trick me? I'd lost count of the parade of liars I'd met. But I was supposed to trust Callon, with all those gaping holes in his story? I'd spent the last three hours of our walk peering through them.

"Where are you going to meet up with the Magician in a week to give him his answer? I didn't catch that detail." Because I'd heard the entire conversation, and nothing had been said about that.

Callon glanced at me, as if he knew every thought in my head, before looking forward again. "Stop it."

"Yeah, stop it. You're acting weird," Tuesday whispered beside me.

I ignored her. I had to or I'd start yelling at her, asking how she could believe what he said. Didn't she see it made no sense? He wasn't going to risk himself and his guys for me. It was never going to happen, and that was the biggest gaping hole in this charade.

"What? I didn't hear that detail," I said, hurrying after Callon as he picked up his pace.

"Stop trying to figure out how I'm lying." His voice wasn't raised, but there was a rasp to it that sure sounded like his nerves were being rubbed raw.

"I don't know why you're getting defensive. It's a logical question." Especially if you had nothing to hide. He could be marching me toward the Magician right now, and I was supposed to be a lamb to the slaughter without a peep?

"Getting him a message won't be a problem. He has men tracking us at this very moment." His pace picked up even more, as if he was trying to put space between him and my questions, or maybe just wanted to get the hell away from me.

I still couldn't stop. The fact that I wasn't flat-out calling him a liar was about as much as I could hold back.

"He's following us right now?" I glanced over my shoulder. "Then why aren't we running? Why are we right now walking in the middle of a field as clear as day?" After all, he did say he wasn't going to hand me over. If that were true, we were as vulnerable as could be.

"Because *that's* not the plan." He spoke like he was having trouble getting his jaw to relax.

Oh, so now there was a plan? No one had told me there was a plan. I didn't hear them talking to Tuesday about a plan.

"I'd love to hear—"

He swung around so quickly that I nearly ran into him.

He grabbed my arm, halting my progress. "Don't," he said, his voice low, his eyes a tinge of red swirling in the heart of steel.

Everyone else kept walking, flowing around us like water around a boulder. Water with big, nosey ears and eyes.

I tossed my hair back. "Don't what?"

"Do. Something. Stupid." Frustration exuded from his every move.

It was a cool act, but I'd been swindled too many times before to buy it. I wouldn't stand around waiting to get stabbed in the back anymore.

"I promise, I won't do anything *stupid*."

His eyes burned ice cold, but he dropped his hand. He shook his head, as he had in the past, disappointment thick in his stare and movements. This time I wouldn't let it gut me. I knew what he was now. No better than the rest of them.

Callon and I didn't speak again, didn't make eye contact. I didn't know what his problem with me was, but I didn't want to see his lying face.

We managed to maintain our distance for the entire day. Every hour, his guilt became more obvious to me.

With each foot of distance he maintained between us, I knew I needed to take steps of my own.

Damn if I'd lie down for anyone again. I'd been trampled on for years and it would never happen again, not willingly. The rabid animal inside of me was chomping at the bit, and I wouldn't hold it back.

By the time we stopped to make camp, I knew what I had to do. There'd be a few hurdles, but nothing I couldn't manage.

Callon's attention finally landed back on me. His stare could've burned me alive where I stood. I wouldn't give him the satisfaction of looking back at him.

"I'll hunt tonight," Callon said to Koz, who usually caught dinner. "Keep an eye on things."

After one final stare, Callon disappeared into the woods.

Keep an eye on "things." Callon might as well have said "Teddy." The only thing Koz wanted to keep an eye on lately was Tuesday.

Still, first obstacle cleared. Obstacle two approached.

"What are you thinking? I see that look in your eye." Tuesday was studying my face, tilting her head this way and that, trying to find the right angle that would unlock all my secrets.

If we weren't surrounded by superhuman hearing on every side, I might've told her. I wanted to tell her. Every time she'd looked at Callon today, big, innocent eyes full of trust, I wanted to smack some sense into her. But I couldn't. Three pairs of ears were trained on us, and all of them were ready to report back to Callon.

"Nothing. What are you talking about?" I smiled, relaxing my shoulders, letting my arms hang limp. It was a good thing I lied better than she did.

Even so, she didn't seem convinced as she tried yet another angle.

"Tuesday, I'm good."

Maybe I wasn't that good of a liar, because she was latching on like a grizzly with fresh salmon. I was half expecting her to snarl at me or swat me with a paw.

Koz walked over. "Tuesday, do you need to go to the stream?" He wasn't smiling. He wouldn't be that obvious, but his eyes were mighty gleeful. I'd heard the noises when they'd stolen a few private minutes.

The grizzly suddenly appeared more doe-like. "Sure."

Oh yeah, those two wouldn't be paying attention to anything in about five minutes.

The grizzly made a quick return as Tuesday turned to me one last time. "We'll talk as soon as I get back."

"Sure."

Her and Koz disappeared. I turned to the last two guys, who wouldn't be much of a hurdle at all.

"I'll be right back." I hooked a thumb toward a different patch of trees, knowing they'd assume I needed some privacy.

Hess and Zink didn't glance up, too busy sharpening knives and building a fire. I swung close to Koz's stuff as I walked, plucking up the knife he used to carve up dinner. As soon as I was out of sight, I quickened my steps, knowing the seconds were ticking by.

Callon had said the Magician was probably still tracking us. *That* I believed. The feeling of being watched hadn't left me all day, and I knew the guys well enough that I could tell that they'd been off a bit too. They might be planning on screwing me over, but that didn't mean anyone trusted the Magician. It was a big, murky mess of distrust all around.

I continued to hurry in the direction we'd come from, figuring if they were following us, they would be this way. My legs were already sore from so much use, but I pushed faster. The clock didn't care about muscle aches.

"Harlow?" Not knowing the range of beast ears, even in their human form, I couldn't risk yelling.

A man stepped out of the trees about ten feet away. Three more joined him. None of them were Harlow. These looked more like the men who'd shot at us. Still, if they worked for the Magician, they'd work for my plan.

They didn't approach me, keeping their distance. They probably thought I was bait for a trap. It was smart thinking, because why else would I be here?

"Are you with the Magician?" I asked, needing to get this ball rolling before someone from my group found me.

"Yes," the guy with blazing red hair said, his eyes darting behind me as he tried to figure out what this was about.

These were definitely lower-level men, their clothes not much better than I'd had back at the village. Their hands had the kind of worked-in dirt that wouldn't wash out easy. They'd suit my purpose well enough.

"I'm so happy to have found you." I took a step toward Red. He immediately took a step back. I hadn't been prepared for that. I was going to have to really play this up. "Those horrible people are holding me hostage. They wouldn't let me go!"

I wrapped my arms around myself, trying to look as

meek as possible. They stared at me like I was an eight-foot giant. Weren't balls a prerequisite for being a thug? This was ridiculous. Was I going to have to collapse onto the ground crying?

"Can you please help me?" I tried to pitch my voice as high as it could go.

One of the men, with long, greasy hair, finally took a step forward. He only went as far as Red had. "If we bring her in without Harlow, we'll be the big shots."

"You mean if *I* bring her in. Not we. I'm in charge," Red said. "I don't have to share a fucking thing with you."

Greasy shot a side eye at Red. Red was too busy looking at me, counting up his new favor, to notice.

Red, fearing Greasy might upstage him, stepped forward. "You can come with us. We'll take care of you."

I kept my head down, my arms wrapped around my waist as he approached. He needed to be in range. I couldn't strike until he was close enough. I needed to take him out, a killing shot.

Red's hand came around my shoulder, and I moved my hand to the knife tucked into my waist. Before he could see what I was about, I thrust it at him. It ended up being more of a swipe than a stab.

"What the fuck?" Red screamed, jumping back and putting his hand to where he was bleeding through his shirt, near his stomach.

Dammit. I'd only nicked him. Would that be enough?

"Fucking bitch!" Red continued screaming. "Grab her," he yelled to his three backups.

Greasy was quick to circle me along with his two friends. That was when I knew two of them would die soon. Would one of them die tonight, by my hand? I couldn't tell. Even in the vision, it was hard to make out how they ended up lying on the forest ground, bloody.

I waved the knife, trying to keep them at bay. I needed to take one of them out or it would never be enough. My plan wasn't the strongest to begin with, but if I didn't have a dead body, how was I going to start a war with the Magician and Callon?

One had to die.

They circled around me, and I spun with them. Then the sound of wind chimes tinkled in the air, so soft it was almost like they weren't really there. We all froze. The Magician's men looked at each other while I tried to figure out what the noises were.

"Is that what I think?" Greasy asked Red.

Hand still on his stomach, Red said, "Nah. Can't be. They've been long gone." He was shaking his head, but his eyebrows rose and he was looking all around.

They? Who are they?

The chimes faded as quickly as they'd started. It was as if we'd all taken a time-out that had just ended. I crouched low, wondering who I had the best chance with, when Greasy lunged for me. He took me down easily, knife and all. Pinning both my hands to the ground, he smiled above me as he squeezed hard on my wrist, his stench making me gag.

I didn't let go easy. Once the blade was lost, so were my chances. I had to notch this situation up a thousand degrees for it to work.

All of a sudden, there were screams beside us. Both me and Greasy turned our heads. Before I could figure out what was happening, a flash of silver and black ripped Greasy off me. No one took his place as all eyes went to the beast taking center stage, the one with its jaws on Greasy's neck. The beast gave a violent shake of its head and then dropped a limp Greasy to the ground. Right next to Red's body.

That was it. The other two took off screaming and the beast gave chase.

Well, if this didn't ruin any chance of negotiations, I didn't know what else I could do. I stood there in the clearing, staring at the dead bodies. Something was definitely wrong here. I'd only given Red a scratch, but Callon had killed him. If he'd planned on double-crossing me, that wouldn't have been the move to make.

I sucked a breath in. Well, fuck me. I might've read this one a hair wrong. Maybe, once in a rare moment, trust then verify was in the right order.

There was rustling in the trees, and I gripped the knife I was still holding. Callon padded back into the clearing, fur still glistening, eyes gleaming. He was magnificent. The most beautiful thing I'd ever seen.

His beast walked toward me and then stopped so close that its fur brushed me. Its lips curled back and it growled, its fangs nearly nipping at my neck, as if intentionally trying to cow me.

I wasn't nervous. Maybe that meant I was insane, but I knew this beast. I'd never seen him in this shape, but I *knew* him. He wouldn't hurt me. He'd had too many chances to do it already, and plenty of rage to fuel it.

I met his red eyes without fear but loaded down with remorse.

"I'm sorry." I'd royally screwed up and I knew it.

It was hard to tell what he was thinking, but at least

he stopped growling. Then he was shifting in front of me. He was the man again, completely naked.

I'd seen Baryn naked on more than one occasion. Callon and him didn't even look to be of the same species. Baryn had been all soft roundness, whereas Callon was nothing but sculpted muscles everywhere the eye could see.

I jerked my gaze back to his face before I burned into ashes at being obvious. If he'd noticed my perusal, it didn't seem to matter. All I saw was the intense red of the beast.

"What were you doing?"

I really had no desire to get into the weeds with details. It was bad enough *I* knew my plan. Considering what I now realized, it might be even dumber and more desperate than initially thought.

Meanwhile, Callon was still standing there, very naked, and with heat pouring off him. Or maybe magic? I didn't know which, but it wasn't that warm out, and I was sweating.

"I made a mistake," I blurted out, hoping he'd be gracious and let it go at that. After I blew up his plan, which might've actually existed.

Callon's eyes shifted to my hand with the knife. His hand went over mine, grasping both and then pulling upward.

"Did you think you were going to kill them all?" he asked, trying to narrow down what ludicrous idea I'd had. He stared, trying to read me. "No. This was hasty and stupid, but not that stupid."

He wasn't going to let this go. I was better off getting it out and moving forward than the guessing game. "I was going to kill one."

"Why?"

"Because I thought it would sour the deal and you wouldn't be able to hand me over."

His eyes flashed heat. "I *told* you. I wasn't going to hand you over."

He grabbed the knife from my hand and threw it onto the ground so hard it bounced.

"What else could I do?" I turned and took a step away. I was yanked back by a hand on my arm.

"Believe me when I said I wasn't handing you over? What about that?"

I shoved at his chest. "You made me sit there like a dog on a leash. How the hell could I?"

"I made you put on an act so they'd believe me and I could buy time to save your ass."

Just when I thought I couldn't feel stupider.

I looked down. That wasn't a good idea, so I stared off over his shoulder.

"I'm sorry." This was the most "I'm sorrys" I'd ever said in my life, and I still wasn't sure it was enough. I didn't know what the issue was, but I was either cursing him, screwing him over, or apologizing.

"Why?" he demanded.

I shook my head. I had no answer for him. I didn't know myself.

"It's not like I sit around and think, hmmm, wonder how I can piss off Callon today. It just—*happens*. That's why I need to be alone. I can't be around people." Well, that and I hated most people. Maybe there were a few more I liked than before, but still. And the way I was acting with him proved I needed to be alone.

"You fucked that up pretty well, now, didn't you? You force yourself into my life so that, short of killing you, I can't get away from you, and then tell me how you can't wait to be alone. You're a real blessing there, Teddy." Callon ran both hands through his black hair. "I can't decide whether I want to beat you or protect you."

"That's really not so bad when you think about it. Everyone else just wanted to beat me." I gave a half-hearted laugh, hoping my joke would break the tension.

It didn't. His eyes snapped back to mine, burning hotter than ever. His hands gripped my shoulders, dragging me upward and against his naked form, and his mouth covered mine.

For as much as I'd witnessed sex, it was the first time I'd ever been kissed, or held by a man like this.

Or wanted either of those things.

I didn't move at first. Didn't fight him or make a sound, too stunned and overwhelmed by the feel of him against me. The heat of his body soaked into mine and he felt like he burned at a thousand degrees. He reached up, fisting a hank of my hair and tilting my head to the side.

My spine bowed toward him, like it had when I'd slept beside him, my body seeming to crave the contact. His tongue ran over mine, and I found myself mimicking him.

I'd thought I'd hate this. How many women had I seen silently cry as Baryn or Turrock, sometimes both, took them?

I didn't hate it. Not at all. In fact, I felt like I was being swept away. I wasn't in the woods anymore, only in his arms. And what was that delicious feeling building? No one had ever said anything about that. I pressed my hips against his. His cock was hard and right at the spot I craved friction.

This was what happened to the girls, the ones who followed men around. I'd never understood it until now.

This was something dangerous indeed. This was way worse than a beating because this could take me down. Make me weak when I couldn't afford it.

I stiffened in his hold.

He inched back.

Neither of us seemed to know what had just happened.

He took a step away, his hands leaving me, the cold settling in instantly.

"Go back to the camp."

For once, I didn't argue.

Tuesday was on me the second I walked back.

"Where did you go? Koz went to look for you, but then came right back and said it was fine and you were with Callon."

Koz was by the fire and gave me a halfhearted nod that reeked of someone who'd seen a little more than they should've.

"When did he get back?" I asked Tuesday, already having a solid guess.

"Couple minutes before you." She stepped closer. "You're blushing!"

"Shut up!" I said.

"You're telling me what happened," she said with just as much determination.

"Running down to the stream," I called out. Hess and Zink still didn't look up. They either didn't know something had gone down or they didn't care. Koz nodded, giving us a wave.

I gave Tuesday the general outline but spared her the details of the fight with the Magician's men. She'd probably be as annoyed as Callon had been. Then I was spilling the details about kissing Callon.

When I finally stopped, I thought she was going to climb up on top of her imaginary unicorn and preach to me about how stupid my plan had been.

"Did you like it?" she asked, only caring about the kiss.

I shrugged, searching for words in a panicked brain that was malfunctioning. It really didn't matter if I'd liked it. Getting involved with Callon might be the worst idea possible. I was using him for the year and then moving on.

"Oh, *you* liked it," she said, and then laughed. And continued to laugh.

I shushed her when she got so loud that I was sure the guys could hear. Then I shoved her shoulder to get her attention. "Why is this funny?"

"Just is," she said, winded from all the laughing she'd done.

"There was something else. When I was out there, I thought I heard chiming in the air."

"Your ears were probably ringing from your blood pressure."

"I don't think so. It was chimes."

"Maybe someone hung some in the area. Teddy, we've got bigger problems."

She was right. We really did.

"Come on. Let's get back to camp." I turned and Callon appeared.

We both froze, and I didn't hear a whisper of laughter.

His eyes were narrowed on me. I didn't think he was here to rinse his hands. There was still a haze of red warming the coolness.

"We're breaking camp."

"Now?" Tuesday asked.

I didn't answer for him, but I knew he meant now. I might not have done enough damage to break the truce, but Callon had done plenty. How many bodies had he left bloody in the woods for me this time? How many more were to come?

Callon's eyes never left mine as he answered Tuesday. "Yes."

Tuesday brushed past us as Callon's eyes ran the length of me, red blazing stronger when they landed on my wrists.

I glanced down, seeing the bruises ringing them, and crossed my arms, tucking them in.

His gaze shot back to my face. "Let's go."

I walked forward, eager to break the swell of heat and energy that seemed to still be sizzling between us.

21

"Clarence's isn't too far from here. We'll stay there tonight," Callon said as we set out again after barely a break.

After I'd listened to Callon filling in Zink and Hess, it seemed even more important that we got moving. The truce was over, and no one was sure how many people the Magician had in the area.

"What's Clarence's?" Tuesday asked.

Tuesday's quickness to question was one of the things I loved most about her. I could stroll along as if I hadn't been wondering and still get my questions answered.

"It's a sleep and eat. A lot of traders travel back and forth along this trail," Koz explained.

I hope she asked how far away next. Fatigue had already set in. The tussle with the Magician's men had been short, but it sure had sucked the life out of me.

Tuesday turned to Koz, who was walking next to her. "How far away is it?"

Boom. There it was.

"A few miles." Koz reached and rested a hand on her shoulder.

A few miles? Ugh.

We trudged along. Zink and Hess walked ahead, leading the way with Tuesday and Koz behind them. Then there was me and Callon. We were the only two in single file.

I didn't know what felt heavier, my legs from too much use or my shoulders from the guilt heaped high. I'd trapped him. Then I'd compounded the problem by not trusting him. As to the kiss, I wouldn't even think of that right now. My plate was already full.

It wasn't all my fault. How was I supposed to know he wasn't a liar when everyone else was? When you find a philosophy in life that seems to be working, you can't throw it away because your friend who believes in white knights and happily-ever-after says she's got a good feeling.

Still, there were some rough waters churning between us at the moment, and we had a long way to go. It was not going to be an easy ride.

Especially since I was still holding out. It was time to make a choice. Either come clean or risk burning any chance of a civil relationship with the one person I was stuck with to the ground.

It was also the fair thing to do. First off, he hadn't beaten me. That was pretty big, but I tried not to put too much weight on that since, according to Tuesday, not all men beat women. It was the second thing that had me about to spill my guts. He'd kept me from handing myself over to the Magician, knowing the Magician could kill them all in the end.

Because of that, he deserved the full truth, right? As

best as I had it to give.

I stopped and turned around.

"Can I get a minute alone to talk?" Oh, shit. He better not think I meant about the kiss. We were not talking about that. "It's about the witch and what happened." I spat it out so quickly that my tongue nearly sprained itself.

The rest of the group stalled out.

I was on the verge of repeating the "alone," in case he'd missed that part.

He looked over my head. "We'll catch up."

The group moved away, slowly. I didn't blame them for wanting to hear. This was going to be a doozy.

He walked over and leaned against the nearby tree. Sometimes when I watched the grace of his movements, in even the simplest gestures, it became impossible to believe I hadn't seen the beast in him from the very first second. It was in every line of his body, an agility no normal man had.

"What's going on?" His eyebrows rose.

I glanced around. "Are they far enough?" I pointed to my ears, knowing they could hear everything. Like, *everything*.

"It's clear."

I took a couple of steps around as he leaned, watching me.

"You did me a solid, so I think it's only fair to tell you something." That was a bit of bullshit. I totally owed him. If he asked me to pluck out my eyes and give them to him, I'd have to consider it for a few seconds at least. That was how large my debt was.

"There was something with the witch I didn't mention." I hadn't even told Tuesday this part. It had been too unnerving to discuss, but I had this gnawing ache in my gut that it tied into why the Magician wanted me.

Callon didn't say anything. Just waited. People with that kind of patience always freaked me out. It was unnatural.

"I'm listening," he said, as if he'd sensed I needed something from him.

Shit. Now it was time to tell him, and this was weird shit I was delving into. This was worse than telling him I was Reaper Kissed. Way worse. At least back then, I'd been egged on by the possibility of scaring him, which failed pathetically. This kind of information was, well, really fucking bad, and there wasn't any possible upside.

Just spit it out already. "I think I can transfer life from one person to another."

His brows dropped and he angled his head slightly, as if he, of all people, didn't trust his ears. It took him some more seconds, grueling seconds filled with doubt and dismay for me, before he spoke.

"What are you talking about, exactly? Spell it out for me." The patience dwindled as the ramifications registered.

I was toying with the hem of my shirt before I dropped my hands. I'd forgotten I wasn't a fidgeter for a second. "I can't say for sure. I was only following the witch's instructions, but I held on to two people. The one who was healthy died. The sick one, well, the death vision I'd had sort of vanished, and he was looking a lot better by the time I left.

"I'm pretty sure she had me drain the life out her and pump it into her kid. I think this Magician person must know. Otherwise, why stalk me? Yes, I know that I can tell you when most people are going to die, but is it really that important to go to these lengths?"

He was still relaxed against the tree, but his eyes narrowed as he logged all the new information. He was silent for a good five minutes, not looking at me or saying anything.

I knew he was thinking it over, but he'd been a pretty decisive person in the past. How long did he really need? I couldn't take the calm.

The calmness had to end.

"Well? What do you think? Is this as bad as I think it is?"

He brought a hand up to rub his stubbled jaw. "I'm not sure if it's bad, but there are some problems."

"That's what I was afraid of." I shouldn't have asked. If I'd given him a few more minutes, maybe he would've thought it through some more and decided it wasn't bad.

He looked at me, his head angled. "You do you realize what this means, right?"

"That I could conceivably give someone immortality? Yeah, it occurred to me." I might not fidget, but I could cringe like a motherfucker.

He nodded, finally pushed off the tree, and took a few steps. His shoulders might've been a little tense, but all in all, he'd taken it much better than I had. The day I'd stepped out of that tent, left that woman I'd literally transferred life from, I'd barely been able to walk.

Callon was back to scratching his jaw. "When you did it, did you feel drained? Depleted in any way?"

"No, I don't think so." I'd been shaky afterward, but it had been all nerves.

His jaw shifted and his eyes hardened. "What if you

could do this to an army? Keep fixing them with the lives of their enemy? An army that wouldn't die?"

I'd thought he was talking to himself, but then he turned every ounce of attention on me.

"Do you remember how to do it?"

I shook my head a little too vigorously. "She rattled off all sorts of stuff to repeat. I didn't realize what we were doing until it was done. And it was long, *really* long, and in a language I didn't understand. I'd never be able to do it again." I wasn't going to try, either. This was exactly why I kept secrets. Right here, that look in his eyes. I wasn't going to be a weapon for anyone. He could have my eyes, but not this.

"You can't walk away from something like this." He took a step toward me, the predator sensing his prey was about to take flight.

"Yes, I can." Why had I told him? Why did I think I owed him the truth? I let guilt get to me for a few minutes, and now look at the damage.

"If the Magician knows you can do this, or even suspects, he'll never stop coming for you. You can't tell me this and expect me not to use it. You want to repay your debt? That's the price."

"And if I don't?"

"Teddy, in this world, you either learn to wield the magic you are born with or someone will wield it for you."

He left off the part where he told me I should already know this. I'd been letting someone use my magic for me for eighteen years.

The thing he wasn't understanding was that I wouldn't be trading keepers. He wouldn't be wielding it for me either.

22

Clarence's was larger than the last eat and sleep, but what really got my attention were the smells wafting over from the dining area nearby. My taste buds were screaming in pain, it smelled so good. I stood beside Callon, but the rest of the group gravitated in that direction, Tuesday looking like a bloodhound with her nose raised.

"That'll be three rooms. We have a tub available if the lass wants to use it? Only five coin more," the innkeeper said to Callon. Clarence, I assumed, was pock-faced, with beady eyes that kept darting over to me.

"My *wife* will take the tub." Callon's tone had that extra-deep pitch that always came out when he was irritated.

Wife? My eyes shot to Callon's back, because that was all I saw as he moved in between us. Tuesday might be right. He did tend to block me from people.

He couldn't have said sister, though? It would've had the same effect of getting the beady eyes off me. I wouldn't split hairs, especially not beast ones when his hackles were already up since our last little chat. We'd left things at a stalemate, but I wasn't crazy enough to think that would be the end of it.

Wait, a tub? I poked my head around Callon, willing to deal with beady eyes for the prize I'd heard. "With hot water, too?"

Clarence nodded and then leaned forward. I immediately wished I hadn't asked anything.

He pointed toward me. "You kinda fit the description of that girl people are looking for, except none of the scars."

"What people would that be?" Callon asked, going on a digging expedition.

I would've preferred the subject dropped, but having a little more information on who and how many was worthy.

"Couple guys sent from that bigwig from Newco." Clarence didn't budge his eyes from me as he continued. "They say she's on the run. I'd run too if I were her. The things they want to do to her make a man's balls shrink up into his body. I heard once they get her, they're gonna cut off her legs and then cut out her eyes so she'll never be able to run again."

My skin must've lost all its color, or maybe the horror showed in my face, because Clarence was suddenly raising a finger toward me again.

"You sure you ain't the one they looking for?"

Callon, who'd been fishing for information before, had suddenly heard enough. He pulled me away from Clarence as he stepped forward.

Fisting the front of Clarence's shirt, he dragged him

onto the table in between them. "If you want to keep your tongue, you don't repeat that."

There might've been more, but my legs suddenly remembered how to move. I ran toward the door, waving off Tuesday's concerned look as I did. I only made it as far as the nearby bushes. I dropped to my knees, heaving up all the water I'd guzzled down right before we'd gotten here, and then continued to dry-heave for another minute.

The door opened in the distance and Callon was walking over, slower than his normal pace.

I got back to my feet, wiping an arm across my mouth.

He stopped a few feet away. "Are you—"

"I'm fine," I said, ignoring that I'd run out of the building, my feet not moving fast enough for my liking.

He reached down to his boot and pulled out a knife, then handed it to me, hilt first. "Here. Just in case you decide you need to gut someone."

I took the knife, wrapping my hand around the leather hilt. My own knife. I might not be able to wield it well, but something about having it took the edge off the moment.

"Thanks," I said, trying to figure out where I could put it. Should I tuck it in my pants? My boot? So many options.

"Hey," he said.

I looked up.

He tossed a key at me. "Our room is upstairs, first door on the right. Might be a good idea to stay out of sight. There might be eyes we don't see."

Yeah, that was one thing I'd learned in the village. There were always eyes, and I wasn't worried about a missed dinner when my stomach was heaving like the ocean in a storm.

A noise jolted me awake, before Callon yelled, "Are you decent?"

"I'm not sure about that anymore, but I'm clothed." A couple of girls had rolled the tub away an hour or so ago. I wasn't the type to dawdle getting dressed, just in case.

The words came out and were followed by the realization I was talking to him like I would a friend. When had I started doing that?

Callon walked in, and lay back up into my spot. I'd taken the blanket off the bed and curled up on the window seat. It had a great old oak outside, which would make a wonderful escape route if needed, and a great view of the stars. So many, so very far away. I'd be far away one day too. Maybe not that far, but far enough that when I lay down to sleep, I wasn't searching for a quick exit. I wouldn't be afraid of wrapping myself too tightly in a blanket because I feared it might entangle me if I had to run. One day I would just go to sleep with the only concern being how wonderful my dreams would be.

Callon walked over, handing me a plate. I knew the smell instantly. It was whatever they'd been serving in the dining area.

"I know your stomach is off, but try to eat," he said, already on the other side of the room.

Even if I wanted to argue, I couldn't. My stomach was already telling me to shut the hell up and chew.

I ate as he stripped out of his shirt and laid it over the chair in the corner. He walked over to the bed, grabbed the pillow from it, and tossed it on the floor.

I stopped chewing for a second. "Take the bed. I'm going to stay here."

He didn't say anything for a second and then moved the pillow in front of the door. He looked over at me and, without a hint of mockery, asked, "Is that better?"

"Thanks," I said. I didn't get up right away. I didn't want to look so desperate or obvious as that, even if I was.

He settled onto the floor, crossing his arms behind his head and closing his eyes.

I thought he'd already fallen asleep when he said, "Teddy?"

"Yeah?"

"About what we heard earlier—I promise that won't be your end."

23

We left Clarence's before the sun rose while flurries drifted to the ground. It was clear within minutes that we were going to keep to a more grueling pace. That was when it became obvious they'd gone easy on us until now. But things were different. We didn't have a week. I didn't know how much time we had before the Magician would attack again. How many he would send this time? How many would be one too many and tip the scales?

Callon had said he wouldn't let that be my end. It wasn't a promise he could possibly keep. It was just words. People said all sorts of words that were useless. Maura used to tell me things would work out and be okay. She hadn't meant to lie, but things hadn't worked out. At all.

As if that wasn't enough to preoccupy my brain, Zink kept glancing over at me when he thought I wasn't paying attention. Koz was acting way too happy. Hess kept forming his lips into a whistle that didn't make any noise.

The worst were the looks Tuesday kept giving me. She'd look, scowl, shake her head, but say nothing. It wasn't hard to figure out someone—Koz—had let her in on my freaky magic trick. When she started her fifth repetition of look, scowl, silence, I hijacked her process.

"It wasn't something I wanted to talk about. I needed to get my head around what I'd done, but I was going to tell you."

She held her scowl for another minute before she relaxed. "Okay. It sucked to have to hear it from Koz, but okay."

Tuesday had never been a grudge holder.

"You had a busy morning." My accusing glare shifted to Callon. We'd gotten up at five. When had he found the time to clue his guys in on what had gone down in the witch's tent?

Callon didn't shrink from my stare. "You know I had to tell them."

"So it's really true? You can do that sort of shit?" Hess asked, staring like he'd seen a leopard jump out of a chipmunk suit.

"No. I don't know if I can. It happened and I have no idea how." I hoped this wasn't going to be another *when have you seen your family last* conversation. I didn't want to think about what had happened. I definitely didn't want to discuss what happened, and I wasn't going to try and duplicate what happened, either.

In my peripheral, I could see Zink gearing up with his own questions.

Then Callon stopped suddenly, drawing everyone's attention.

"Smell that?" he asked.

Koz, Hess, and Zink all took a couple more steps in

the direction we were walking before they stopped. A look was passing between the guys.

"Do you smell anything?" I asked Tuesday. I didn't know if my nose was too stuffy or this was a beast thing.

"Nothing," Tuesday said, and then sniffed so hard it was comical.

Koz turned to Callon. "Do we keep going or do we change direction?"

"We keep going. The last one we knew of around here was miles away. If it spread, we should know," Callon said, and started walking again.

"Koz? What are you guys talking about?" Tuesday asked.

Before he answered, a wind kicked up, giving us a partial answer. It was somewhere between the smell of rotten eggs and skunk, with a blend of something equally bad I couldn't quite describe.

"What is that?" I asked.

"A gigantic mess," Koz said. "You'll see for yourself soon enough."

He was right. We'd only been walking about another ten minutes or so when we saw it. There, in the middle of nothing but a light coating of snow, was a sprawling field of mud that looked like it went for miles and miles. Not only was it not frozen, it was bubbling with heat at different spots. It wasn't clear whether it had been a lake once, or it had devoured every tree and life form it had come in contact with.

"What is this?" I asked, for once not waiting for Tuesday.

"We're not sure," Hess said.

"The smell, it's hard to take," Tuesday said, then gagged a few times.

Callon was walking around its perimeter, examining the mud. He and Koz were pointing at the disgusting slop, taking mental notes.

I pulled my shirt up over my nose. Then I dropped it, after it offered no respite.

"I'm glad we're moving on soon," I said, my back to where all the guys now were.

Callon was suddenly beside me, grabbing my arm and pulling me back. "Don't get so close."

The mud was inches from the toes of my shoes. I must've taken a few more steps without realizing it.

Callon was walking back to Koz again, leaving me with Tuesday.

"This is the biggest one yet. They're definitely growing," Callon said to Koz before they were out of earshot.

There were more of these things?

"You know," Tuesday said from beside me, "I figured I'd see some interesting things after I left the village, but, like, cool stuff. This is gross. A bunch of bubbling mud that smells almost as bad as Baryn used to isn't my idea of cool."

She continued talking, and I nodded, but my attention was pulled to a small movement on the ground. Callon had tugged me back a good three feet from the mud. And yet there was a small stream forming in my direction. I watched as it curved around and then flowed uphill as it crept toward me.

"Tuesday, look at that." I pointed toward my feet, where the stream was heading.

She bent forward. "That's strange. It looks like it's heading straight for us. Move away from me and to the side. I'll go this way. Let's see if it follows one of us."

As soon as she said it, I stepped closer, wrapping an arm around hers. "No. Let's move together."

"But that won't tell us anything," she said, yanking away from me. She gave me a shove in the opposite direction and then stepped away.

Please, mud, don't follow me. For once, let me be normal, or as normal as I can be.

The tiny mud stream corrected course and headed right for me. Internally, I was a raging bull. Outwardly, I was as calm as a sunny day. No need to alert the guys. They already looked at me like I was a freak.

I'd divulged too many weird things, in too short of a time. *Too* plus *too* wasn't the same as *two* plus *two*. This addition didn't equal four; it equaled fucked. There didn't need to be any more discussion on what other strange things happened around me.

"Okay, so it's following me. It's probably nothing. The stuff is weird to begin with. I think we step back—"

"Koz! The mud is following Teddy!" she yelled to where Koz was about twenty feet away, trying to get a better view of the perimeters with Callon.

"Why did you do that?" My words shot out in stunned whispers.

Tuesday shrugged, fluffing her already-full hair. "I don't know. It's interesting and he'll want to see it too?"

She was having no problem luring over Koz all on her own. She really had to use my mud allure to get even more attention? If she wasn't my best friend, I might've committed violence upon her.

All four of them swarmed me at once, all watching the mud trying to get to me. Woohoo, look how weird I was now!

Callon took the lead. Of course he would, since he

was the person I'd wanted to hide this from the most. I might be able to convince the others this was nothing, but not eagle eyes. We still hadn't gotten past the whole *you're stuck with me for a year* or the *I can suck lives out of one person and shove them into the other*. I already had the Magician following me. I didn't think mud following too was going to be welcomed.

Callon was standing beside me, staring down.

"Move that way."

"Huh?" I hadn't seen which way he'd pointed as the mud stream burped up a little bubble.

He took my hips and shifted me, instead of repeating himself. He touched me so often these days that I didn't even flinch anymore. I knew it was just to move me here or move me there or move me somewhere else. After all, he had zero patience, so forget having to actually use words to explain what he wanted from me.

"Tuesday, come around and stand here," he said, pointing to a different spot.

She did as he asked, dillydallying her way over. I loved Tuesday to death, but that chick could move slower than a snail crawling through sludge.

He didn't strong-arm her into position, letting her take her sweet old time. Why did he give her more than the nanosecond he'd given me? Wasn't my day bad enough?

She was in her new spot, in between me and the mud stream. The damn thing looked like it was trying to move around her, to get to me.

"Thanks, Tuesday. You can step away from it."

Thanks? Did he really thank her?

He stood, grabbed my wrist, and moved me again as

he positioned himself in between me and the mud. Did he think I was too stupid to take instruction?

"Why do you do that?" I asked, ready to crack like an overcooked egg.

He took one look at me and waved a finger in my direction. "Not now, Teddy."

He turned around, dismissing me as if I would do as he said.

I bit my tongue, acknowledging that he might have a point, even though his delivery sucked. The timing wasn't ideal. I'd hold back my inner tempest until a better time.

I took a few deep breaths, three, two, one. My heart was slowing its tempo from racing to a steady jog.

Callon's hands were on my hips again, moving me. "Dammit, Teddy. Pay attention! That stuff almost touched you again."

Why was he so mad? The mud was following me, not him.

I was officially cracking. "What is your problem?"

His eyes narrowed and all his attention landed on my neck. "There's dirt on your neck."

Huh? He said it like a cardinal sin had been committed. I had some dirt. I'd had a head covered in mud not long ago too.

"So? We've been hiking for miles. It would be more surprising if I didn't have any."

He was moving my hair away from it, staring. "Fuck."

That was all the warning I got before his shoulder hit my hips and he took off at a run. He didn't stop until we were at the nearest normal river.

He dumped me into the waist-high water and then

pushed me down. I pushed myself up with my arms as he planted his hand in the middle of my chest and shoved me down again.

He was finally going to kill me. I'd finally cracked him. I swung at the hand trying to hold me down, scratching at his wrist.

"Teddy, stop. I'm trying to get the mud off your neck."

I froze, my brain readjusting. He wasn't Baryn or Turrock. He wasn't trying to drown me. This wasn't some screwed-up game he was playing to break me.

This was Callon. He was trying to help me. Shivers were still shooting down my spine, but I got a hold of myself enough to stay still and nod. I could see in Callon's face that he'd already noticed too much.

"Hold still." He stared at me, watching to see if I was going to go crazy again.

I nodded, staying still.

He took the sharp edge of a stone he'd picked up and scraped the strange mud off my neck as the water was rushing over it.

He put the stone down and then took some sand and scrubbed the spot for another few minutes. Neither of us said anything about how I'd tried to push him away like he was a murderer.

He finally finished, and I sat up.

"Is it okay?" I asked, shaking now from the cold water.

"I don't know." His head dipped closer, his breath trailing over my skin. Before I knew what he was going to do, his tongue shot out and licked the spot.

"What was that?" I asked, jerking back. "Was that wise?"

He sat back on his haunches. "Whatever that mud is, from what I know, it doesn't seem to affect beasts. And I rubbed your skin raw. My saliva will help it heal. I didn't taste anything off."

He stood, grabbing my hand and yanking me up with him, a little rougher than I was used to.

I didn't need to ask him what his problem was. I'd seen his face after I'd acted like he was going to drown me. I wished I hadn't. Did I say something or pretend?

"It wasn't—"

"I know." He cut me off before I could tell him it was just a reflex.

As soon as we caught up to the guys and Tuesday, Callon grabbed his sack from Koz and dug in it for his pelt.

"Till you dry," he said, tossing it my way. "Let's get going. I want to put as much distance between here as we can before nightfall."

Everyone knew why. If we camped too close to the mud, would we wake up to a river of it right next to me?

I didn't say a word about it, though, and no one else did either.

24

I collapsed next to Tuesday in front of the fire Koz was starting. We were inside the shell of what used to be a stone house that no longer had a roof. There was a stream only a hundred yards away, and I couldn't even make it to my feet again to wash up.

"Is your neck okay?" Tuesday asked, her back propped up against the stone wall.

"I think so." I didn't feel any weirder than I had earlier today, if that counted.

She glanced around. Callon and Koz had both stepped out. Zink and Hess were having their own private conversation across the room.

"Are you two fighting?" she whispered.

"I'm not sure." Callon hadn't said anything to me for the rest of the day, but we'd been moving at a brisk pace. At this point, I had a better idea of the sun's position in the night sky than Callon's feelings for me.

She grabbed Koz's water sack and took a swing before handing it to me. "Well, at least you're okay."

I drank down the last of it, realizing that put me on

the hook to refill it. That meant I had to stand. I didn't know if I could anymore.

"Callon said he couldn't taste it, so I guess so." I flopped my arm down. I'd get up in a couple minutes. I really would.

"You mean smell it?" Hess asked from across the room.

My head snapped up. I hadn't realized they'd been listening. Those beast ears could be awful sneaky.

"No. He licked it. He said something about saliva helping."

Hess and Zink were staring at me, and Koz's head whipped in my direction as he stepped back inside.

Koz stepped closer. "He licked you?"

All eyes were fixed on me. Boom, back to being the center of attention again, and I didn't feel any better about it this time. I shifted in my spot as if I could shake the eyeballs off.

"I know. I was worried about it being dangerous too, but he did it before I could stop him. He said he didn't taste any of it, though."

"His tongue came out of his mouth and then ran up your skin?" Hess asked, like he didn't know what the word "lick" meant.

"Yes, that's the definition, right?"

No one responded, but the undercurrent shooting beneath the three of them was intense enough that even Tuesday, who wasn't the object of their attention, shifted beside me.

"She didn't tell him to do it. He did it on his own," she said, an edge in her tone, warning them.

Koz nodded and gave me a shrug of sorts. Zink and Hess stopped glaring at me and went back to huddling in their corner. There was something wrong here, but damn if I could put my finger on it. If Callon dropped dead, though, it was *not* my fault.

Would he drop dead? He was grumpy, pushy, and bossy, but I didn't want him to die. I was starting to get used to all his irritability.

"Is there something I don't know?" I asked everyone in the room.

"Nope. Not at all," Koz said quickly, before anyone else could think of answering.

Callon walked back in a few minutes later. All the guys were staring in his direction, and Koz seemed to be actively fighting the urge to walk straight over to him.

Koz couldn't keep his feet still for longer than two minutes before he was beside Callon. "Teddy said you licked the spot that had the mud?"

Callon stopped in his tracks and asked, "So?"

I elbowed Tuesday, making sure she was paying attention to this. I needn't have bothered. When she didn't nudge me back, it was because she was too engrossed watching them.

Koz nodded slowly. "So all's normal? Nothing has changed?"

Callon didn't budge. "Yes."

"But what about that thing Bitters said?"

"Bitters is crazy. He was also stoned out of his mind. We're not talking about this again." Callon ended the conversation by walking away from Koz and squatting in front of the fire. He grabbed a stick and poked at it.

"It wasn't a big deal," Hess said, not sounding that sure either but backing up Callon.

It was quite predictable on his part, if someone were

to ask me. Since I wasn't even listening, though, no one would.

Too bad I wasn't a part of the conversation, though, because who was Bitters and what did he have to do with Callon licking mud off my neck? Did Bitters warn them about the weird mud?

"Who's Bitters?" Tuesday nearly barked.

Koz looked in my direction, pausing, before turning to Tuesday. "No one special."

If Koz wasn't going to tell Tuesday, I definitely wasn't getting any answers.

25

I'd gone to sleep that night alone but woke sprawled on top of Callon. How had that happened? I glanced around. I was still in the same spot, so he must've come to me. Apparently that hadn't been enough for my sleeping self. It wasn't happy simply being warm. It had to drape itself over him too.

I slowly detangled, trying to not wake him until my limbs were back in neutral territory. It was quiet, so hopefully the others were still sleeping. The second I cleared the leg I'd draped over his, he sat up.

"You sleep like the dead lately," he said.

I definitely did not. But he *had* rolled right next to me, moved me onto his pelt, and then we'd had a snuggle-fest, all without me waking. Maybe I did?

Callon got up but then knelt next to me. "I want to get going soon."

"What about everyone else?" I asked, looking at the still-slumbering bodies.

"We're going to Hecate's alone, in case we're being watched."

I glanced across the room at Tuesday.

"Don't worry. Koz has her. They'll follow a distance away." Callon stood and held out his hand.

I let him tug me to my feet. Koz could protect her better than I could.

THREE HOURS LATER, WE STOPPED ON THE EDGE OF A field. About three hundred yards away was a huge metal arch. Beyond it, a miniature village. Colorful houses were scattered all about with the greenest grass I'd ever seen. Even from here, the pitched roofs of the houses looked like they'd barely clear my head. Tuesday would've loved this. It was exactly like what we'd both wanted to see when we were sitting back at the village. Maybe we could find our own little place like this?

"What is that?"

"It's an old miniature golf place."

"What's miniature golf?" I asked. Callon spoke like this wasn't something foreign to him. Did they still have this miniature golf where he was from?

He was scanning the trees of the perimeter. "A game they played where they took clubs and hit balls into small holes. Now it's Hecate's home. Come on." He took a few steps away from the direction of the arch.

I didn't move. "I thought we were going in there?"

"We are, but not through the front gate." He turned back around, grabbed my hand, and pulled me after him.

He was doing it again, moving me where he wanted me to go. It wasn't worth fighting about. If this Hecate could undo the death spell, there wouldn't be any reason to mention it. We'd be going our separate ways at that point.

No more tugging me about, or being bossy, or fighting, or waking up next to him.

That was good.

Or better.

It wasn't bad, anyway.

We worked our way around the perimeter of the tiny village until the trees nearly touched the fence that surrounded the place. A portion of the iron gates were rusted and leaning sideways off their posts.

We stepped into the village, which was especially magical up close, even with the chipped and faded paint. The grass was really strange, though, cropped impossibly short and with a crunch.

"Are you sure she's here?" I asked.

He waved me up from where I'd crouched down to feel the funny green stuff. "Yes. We're being watched by her people right now."

We turned another corner and made our way to the largest building. It was modeled to be a small castle, centered in the middle of the tiny village. It came complete with a moat and a drawbridge probably ten feet long. The door to this building was human-sized, as if it had been used for something other than to pop tiny balls into.

Two brawny men exited the building as we approached and stopped outside the door. We walked past them and entered the tiny castle.

The place was nearly windowless except for several colorful windows up high. Candles burned on every surface, and crystals sparkled from the domed ceiling as if they were strange stars hanging low. Pelts lined the floor and tables lined the walls, covered in bottles and heaped high with strange dried plants, a heavy perfume thick in the air.

There, in the center of the room, a young woman lay upon a thick pile of furs. Silk clung to a curvy form, and dark tresses framed an exotic face. I'd never seen someone as striking. She didn't look real.

She unwound her limbs, her leg peeking out from the silk, as if standing itself were a dance of seduction. She glided over, hips swaying and eyes only for Callon.

She laid a finger on his chest and purred. "Where've you been, my pretty?"

My?

He smiled. Until now, I wasn't even sure his facial muscles could pull that off on demand.

"I need your help."

"You know I'm always willing to help out an old friend. What can I do for you?" She ran her palm up to his shoulder and then over the roundness of it, following the dip before his bicep swelled.

Yeah, I bet he couldn't wait to sever the spell and drop me off as quickly as possible. I was surprised I wasn't getting kicked out the door now.

I crossed my arms, watching the two of them.

"Do you know how to transfer life from one person to another?"

My eyes snapped from her fingers back to Callon's face. *What?*

"That's not why we're here." It wasn't what I'd signed up for, and he knew that well. I hadn't agreed to use that magic, so there was no point in getting that spell. I didn't know what he was thinking.

Her hand dropped and the purring was over. "I can't do that spell."

I stepped in front of Callon before he tried to convince her. "That's fine, because we don't really need that. We need you to sever a death spell that joined us together."

Callon picked me up and moved me to the side. There he went again, getting all pushy. He'd have to keep moving me if he thought I was going to stand back and let him hijack this meeting.

I darted around him. His arm shot out, blocking me and then pushing me back.

"Do you know how the transferring could be done, if that type of magic was available?" he asked.

I tried to elbow Callon out of the way, but he was unmovable. All I got for my efforts was another arm in front of me acting as a barricade.

"There's only one reason I can think of that you'd want to know." Her eyes narrowed. She shifted her attention from Callon to focus on me. "You're the one the Magician wants."

Oh, shit. How many people knew about me now? Would she call him? How much did Callon trust this woman? I already didn't trust her as far as she swayed her hips. Maybe less. She really swung those suckers.

Didn't mean I wouldn't try and get what I needed, though.

"Please, can you help us sever this link?" I packed every ounce of pleading I could into the question. I'd thought I was through with begging, but the idea of her giving me up suddenly made it a bit more palatable.

I'd do pretty much anything at this point, because although I feared how I'd fare on my own, I'd made a colossal mistake. When I tied myself to Callon, I'd handed over my fate to someone else. Hopefully, he'd be true to his word and help me get somewhere safe after this, but even if he didn't, I'd still go through with it. Callon asking her how to transfer life proved that I needed to take control of my life, fully. Not in little bits and tastes.

She stepped around Callon, and he didn't try to block her, seeming resigned to losing this battle. He never gave up. Something about that was off, but I'd figure it out later.

As she neared, she took in everything from my head to the soles of my shoes. I saw a depth in her stare that spread goosebumps all over. There was something not right about this one. She might even make me seem normal.

"Don't worry. I've no allegiance to that monster. But even if I did, that wouldn't have worked on me."

She walked back to her pile of furs and reclined.

"I can help you, but I won't separate you." She smirked as if there was some deep amusement there.

I followed her across the room.

"Is it money? He can pay you." I pointed at Callon, knowing he'd pay anything to lose me. Or I'd thought he would. Why wasn't he standing here beside me trying to convince her as well? Why was he across the room as if biding his time until I accepted her answer? That wasn't him. He was as stubborn as I was.

"What's going on here?" This time I was speaking to him. Something about his *accepting* nature was setting my teeth on edge.

"Callon, you should've told her," she said.

He leaned against one of her tables, arms crossed. "Tell her some made-up crap I don't believe? No."

For some reason, Hecate threw back her head laughing. "Always so stubborn," she said once she was done. "Fine, I'll tell her."

"Tell me what?" I asked Hecate, the only person in the room not holding on to every secret like it was their last grain of food.

She reached over to a glass nearby, took a sip, and then swirled the red contents as she spoke. "When the dark trickery rises, the beast must dance among the shadows of death. As the world shudders with wounds unhealed, the reckoning will come at the cost of souls."

I squinted. Callon was shaking his head as if the whole thing was ridiculous. I didn't agree with him regularly, but we were hook, line, and sinker together on this piece of crazy.

"What is that and what does it have to do with me?" I asked.

He shrugged, crossing an ankle as he half sat on the table.

"What does it have to do with you? It *is* you. And now I think we know who the beast is." Hecate sipped from her glass and then laughed again.

I couldn't tell if she'd been tipping that glass too much or if she was insane.

"Do you want me to dance with him? I don't know how to dance, but if that'll get you to help me, fine. I'm all in. I'll do whatever your little poem requires."

"It's not her poem," Callon said.

Hecate licked her lips, becoming almost gleeful. "And not the type of dancing you seem to think. The beast is Callon and you are surrounded by the shadows of death. Dance, well, hopefully you can figure that out on your own, but I'll give you a hint: it doesn't mean waltz."

"You're saying you think if I sleep with Callon, we're going to heal the world?" I pointed behind me. I'd look at him some other time that wasn't right now.

"More like fuck, but yes, that's what I'm saying. It's not only me who believes. Many people believe it. It was foreseen by Bitters, the greatest wizard of our time."

Bitters. I knew that name. I'd heard them talk about him. That was the name they mentioned the other day. They acted like it had nothing to do with me. My cheeks grew warmer, and this time it had nothing to do with embarrassment.

I walked over to Callon and grabbed his arm, pulling him after me. I didn't stop until we were outside. I'd reached my quota of crazy and shady dealings for the day, maybe the week. I walked all the way to the edge of the drawbridge, ignoring Hecate's men.

"What is going on here? Why aren't you trying to get her to break the death spell and why didn't you tell me I'm part of some weird prophecy?"

"It's not worth retelling." He shrugged. "The great Bitters is some stoner wizard that's always going on about something."

I didn't like being part of a made-up prophecy, but I had to agree with him. It was a hard pill to swallow, way too big, with jagged sides. That wasn't the only questionable thing going on here, though. There was a huge, gaping question looming that he still hadn't answered.

"Why aren't you trying to get her to reverse the death spell?"

"It's not the right decision anymore."

"Why? What do you mean? That's why we came. Isn't it? You said—"

He raised a finger and turned his head to the left. His jaw tensed.

I didn't have a chance to ask what was wrong before his hand wrapped around my arm.

"They're coming!" he yelled to Hecate's men as we took off over the drawbridge.

When I tripped, he grabbed me and tossed me over his shoulder without missing a step, and we were zooming back the way we came. He was running much faster carrying me than I could've on my own. The gates of the place flew past us and he kept going.

26

We were deep in the forest again when his pace slowed and suddenly dirt was beneath my feet. They'd barely hit the ground before I flopped down on a mossy bed, breathing deeply, as if I were the one who'd run miles with a hundred-pound weight slung over my shoulder.

"Are we safe?" It was an idiotic question. He would've kept going if we weren't, but part of me, the part that'd been chased since I left the village, had to hear it anyway.

"For a few, but we need to keep moving." He had his ear angled toward the direction we'd come from.

I didn't ask how many he thought might've been chasing. I wasn't ready to ask. Callon had taken on four men by himself without a problem. Knowing the number of men it would take to make him run instead of fight would only lead to panic. Panic wasn't going to help right now. The Magician had gotten close, and that was all I needed to know for the moment.

I pushed up on my arms. "Do you think Hecate got away?"

"I'm sure of it. She'll outlive the Magician, this world, and then whatever comes after." There was a long pause before he added, "But she won't resurface again for a long while."

I got the message. There would be no undoing the spell for the time being. I would've been caught several times already if I hadn't been with him, though. I didn't know what the right thing to do was anymore. Was I better off with or without him? What was complete independence if the Magician swooped right in anyway?

But then again, he hadn't even tried to get our connection severed. Doubt was piling high on whether that was what we'd gone there for.

All those delays, first to get my leg fixed, then to go to a different village. Something was starting to smell wrong. If I hadn't been so intent on worrying about what *I* was hiding, I might've noticed and taken a closer look at what *he'd* been holding back.

He leaned forward, hand outstretched. "Can you walk or do you need me to carry you? We need to get moving."

I took his hand and let him pull me to my feet, but backed up when he would've lifted me.

"I can walk." And I wanted full autonomy of my body until I figured out what he was up to.

Nodding, he took off down the trail, checking that I was staying right behind him several times. He didn't have to worry about that. I was glued to him closer than his shadow. At least for now.

"Why did you say severing our connection wasn't the right decision anymore?"

He turned around, waiting for me to get in front of him. His hand on my back got me moving again, this time in front of him. I hadn't realized I'd stopped.

"Why?" I asked. The silence coming from him was setting my hairs on end. I wanted him to tell me all the horrible things I was thinking were wrong. Tell me that I hadn't confided in him only to get stuck in a prettier cage. That I hadn't finally gotten out of the village to be chattel once again.

"Callon?" I turned and then stopped, not caring if he tried to run me over with his larger size.

"I can't risk the Magician getting his hands on you." There was no give in his eyes, only a determination that sank into me until a shiver ran over my skin.

Had that been the plan all along? All the events came crashing down. While I'd been trying to survive, running around in the dark, he'd been shifting pieces around on the board as new information came to light.

"What business did Koz have at my village? What was he there for?" Tell me it was something stupid, like he wanted to trade for some of Baryn's wine stash. I'd take anything but them coming for me.

"Word was spreading that there was someone in the village with unusual gifts." His jaw was tense.

"You sent Koz there to buy me first? Is that what you're saying?"

"I sent him to check the situation out. I'm not in the habit of buying people." It was the slight shift of his eyes to the right, away from me, that really sealed it. He'd do what he thought he had to, and right or wrong didn't factor in.

Once he decided a course of action, that was what

he was doing, and he wouldn't let a little thing like feelings affect it.

"What happened? Lost interest? Got outbid?"

"He didn't know you were there. Baryn lied to him."

"And if Baryn hadn't?"

"We'll discuss it later. Walk."

I shook my head, not taking a step.

"We don't have time for this. Walk or I'll carry you."

I walked, but only because if he touched me right now, I'd beat him. Or try. We didn't need to discuss it later.

"You lied."

"I told you I wouldn't let him get you, and I won't. You can't play the victim card. I didn't put you here. *You* did." To him, that justified it all.

"But you'll gladly keep me now, huh?" I glanced back at him.

"I do what I have to," he growled, red tinging his eyes.

"When did you know?" I was near shouting at him now.

"I knew something was different from the first night, but I didn't know what. That's not why I agreed to bring you to the first village," he said, his voice raised as well.

I shook my head. I didn't care why. I was too mad to speak. If I spoke, it might unleash the hell I was feeling inside and burn us both to ashes.

I walked, barely paying attention to where we were going. When Callon's hand urged me this way or that, I pulled away from his touch as soon as I felt it.

When he held up a hand to stop, I did so without asking why. I wasn't ready to speak to him. I moved a good ten feet away from him, while he watched. I crossed my arms and shot him a look that said, *I can't be anywhere near you.*

His look called me a hypocrite.

I crossed my arms and ignored the rest of his looks.

Callon made a noise that rumbled through the area and seemed completely out of character for a human. A minute later, a similar growl rumbled back to us from somewhere farther east.

Koz appeared a few seconds later, with Tuesday by his side, Zink and Hess behind them.

It took Koz two seconds to ask, "What happened?"

"The Magician showed. We didn't have time to accomplish anything," Callon said, ignoring me as hard as I was him.

"Fuuuck," Hess said.

Zink ran a hand over his hair, but didn't speak.

Tuesday stepped closer and then paused, trying to figure out where she was supposed to walk and why we were standing so far apart.

"At least you got out okay." With a couple more glances back and forth, she walked over to me.

I nodded, biting down on my tongue.

Koz didn't ask what was wrong with us, but he was staring at where I stood, arms crossed.

Tuesday continued to stare, her eyes intent, and I could see the question about to bubble up.

I wasn't going to say a word. Let Callon explain what the problem was.

Everyone was awkwardly quiet for a few seconds.

"I guess we'll be staying with them for a while?" Tuesday asked.

I wasn't going to say a word. Not now. Not until I got control of myself.

But it was bubbling up and there was no tamping it down. "He didn't even try. It's all a lie. All he wants is to know how to transfer life."

"She said. She. Wouldn't. Do. It." Callon's attention was solely on me.

I swung around. "You didn't even try. You could've made her do it."

"You mean the way you do what I want?" He shook his head.

"You didn't want her to because you want to use me." The accusation tasted bitter on my lips.

Callon turned and addressed the group with fake calm. "Teddy found out that I have a problem with the Magician getting his hands on her to use as a weapon. This seems to be affecting her moral sensibilities."

There were a few "ohs" but I was too busy transferring all my anger to my eyeballs and trying to light Callon on fire.

Tuesday poked my arm. "I don't understand. I thought you pretty much stuck us with them for a year anyway? What's the difference?"

All eyes swung to me, and I could see varying levels of agreement. Koz still looked like he understood, Hess was shrugging, and Zink nodded his agreement with what Tuesday said.

Callon smiled, staring at me. His was a silent *Even your friend sees reason*.

I was about to gag Tuesday but then she said, "But wait, why were you so mad about getting stuck with her?"

I smiled at Callon now. *Yeah, buddy, now what are you going to say?*

Koz leaned down to softly speak to Tuesday. "I think he didn't like being the one stuck."

"Dumping her at our place is a hell of a lot different than getting tied to someone with no say-so," Hess said, laughing as he did.

Koz shook his head at Hess and sliced a hand across his neck, trying to shut up the laughter.

It didn't matter a whit. I was furious anyway. It just kept getting better. It looked like me and Tuesday were the only ones who hadn't been kept in the loop.

"So you all knew?"

Koz shrugged and then looked everywhere but me. Zink nodded and Hess shrugged again.

I swung on Callon and shook my head.

"You did what you had to, and so did I."

"And you gave me hell for it, too." I threw my arms out to the side.

His jaw twitched as he gritted out a reply. "I also saved your ass over and over again, which I continue to do."

I couldn't help a niggle of satisfaction at seeing him start to lose some of his cold detachment.

"So now what?" Koz said, trying to smother the fire building between Callon and I before it burned everyone.

"We get back to home base and we need to get moving. There's a large group on our tail," Callon said in his normal bossy manner.

Hess and Zink started walking.

Callon stared at me, but I didn't budge. He took a step closer.

I took a step closer to him, crossing my arms. "I'm not being used again. Not for anyone or anything."

I gave Callon my back and followed the guys.

Tuesday plowed into me, looped an arm around me, and pulled me forward. "Teddy, this is good news. Now we'll have protection. Why are you so mad?"

"This is not good." Nothing about it was.

"The way I see it, now you're kind of even. You did something morally questionable and now so did he. It all worked out." She smiled as if life was grand.

"Nothing has worked out. It just means we're both assholes. That isn't good." Man, it must be nice wandering around with all those rainbows and unicorns, happily-ever-afters galore, while I was stuck in the mud.

She was still smiling. I glared. After a couple of minutes of watching her scrunch her brow and twist her lips, she gave up and put a hand over her mouth.

I rolled my eyes, avoiding looking at her face again. "I *know* you're still smiling."

"It's not my fault," she said, through cupped fingers. "I'm trying to get rid of it."

"It's a good thing you're loyal."

27

We'd only been walking a couple hours when Callon said, "I've got ten on my side."

"Fifteen or so behind us, maybe more," Zink said.

Ah, shit. We'd just entered a clearing with nowhere to hide.

Tuesday moved so close her shoulder bumped mine. "What's going on?"

"We're being surrounded. I think we're about to be attacked. Don't make a face," I said, as I watched Koz drop back until he was on our right. Hess was slowing down as well, and I was pretty sure trying to casually fall to our left.

I gulped a few times and then glanced over at Tuesday. She had a vacant expression locked down to such an extreme that I wasn't sure if she'd ever be able to smile again.

I bumped her shoulder back, trying to get her attention while knowing every move was under surveillance. Before she set eyes on me, men came rushing out of the forest, so many I couldn't count. There was a war cry and I didn't know if it came from our side or theirs, but it seemed to multiply and grow into an all-consuming roar.

Instinct told me to run. I grabbed Tuesday's hand with my free one and grabbed my knife with the other. I shot forward through a gap in the men in the only direction that looked clear.

I was knocked off my feet before we cleared the fighting. I let Tuesday's hand go before I took her down with me, screaming, "Run," as a body hit me.

It was too late for her. One of our attackers had her by the waist and was lifting her off the ground, her feet kicking the air.

My attacker flipped me over, straddling me. Grabbing my hand with the knife, he pinned it to the ground.

No, no, no! I clawed his face with my free hand while trying to jerk my knee up toward his balls. He pressed further down onto me, trapping my legs between his, as he kept my right hand pinned down as his other hand tried to pry my fingers off the knife. When I didn't let go easily, he pulled back and slammed a fist into my jaw. He was going to have to hit a lot harder than that to make me quit. Compared to Baryn's punches, that had been a love tap.

There was chaos all around and the sounds of fighting as he cursed me, still trying to get my knife. I was sure he had orders to not only keep me alive, but also uninjured, or he would've been striking me again.

With all the screaming and yelling, somehow I still heard Tuesday's voice as she screamed, "Teddy!"

It was a call thick with desperation, and I knew I wasn't only battling for my life. If something happened to her, this was on me. What if the Magician took her instead? What if he tortured her the way he'd planned on torturing me?

Something inside my chest triggered, like a flint sparking onto dry brush. A heat within suddenly burned bright, growing fast. Fingers that had been trying to gouge his eyes felt hot, so hot I thought he was burning them. I didn't know if the heat was from him or me.

He suddenly gasped, releasing my hand. He paused over me, groping his chest.

I lifted my knife in between us as he hovered, shock delaying my action. Before I could plunge it into his chest, his eyes turned empty. Then he fell on top of me, right onto the knife I'd been about to stab him with. His body slumped forward, and I turned my head, trying to avoid his head hitting mine.

Everything froze, even as the battle raged on and I was trapped beneath his weight. Had that really happened?

I thought back to the witch and her spell in the tent, and what felt like years in the past. Had there been heat? Maybe a warmth, but not like this. Maybe my attacker had been sick and died naturally?

In the middle of battle.

Right when Tuesday needed me the most.

Tuesday. The thought of her jerked me back into action. I pushed at the man's body, trying to dislodge at least two hundred pounds. My hands brushed against skin that felt too cool to have only died minutes ago, especially when it had been burning hot only seconds before.

I listened for Tuesday as I shoved, realizing the battle was winding down and I had no idea who the victors were.

My attacker was suddenly jerked off me and Callon stood there, covered in blood. Looking down at myself, I saw I wasn't in much better shape.

He grabbed my hand and pulled me to my feet, the battle putting us in a temporary truce.

I sat up, my eyes racing past him searching for Tuesday. Koz was beside her and she was looking my way. Her sobbing breaths and shaky nods let me know she was okay.

I nodded back, letting her know it was the same with me. Callon knelt near my attacker and pulled my knife from his chest. After wiping it on the dead man's clothes, he held it out to me, hilt first.

I watched, waiting to see if he'd touch the man's flesh. He didn't.

He stood, and I waited. It was a stabbing. That was all. Or a heart attack? That would work too. I certainly wasn't saying anything. Not to him.

He walked toward me, met my eyes with blood still shining in his. He kept staring, and I stood there as if I had nothing to hide.

He didn't know anything. Maybe the guy had just gotten sick. It could've happened. He was running a high fever, and when the fight broke out, his heart couldn't take it anymore. It made perfect sense, right? Except for the burning sensation in me and then him feeling like he'd been on ice for a month. But exposed flesh would get chilly. It could happen.

Then Callon's eyes went to my cheek. And didn't leave it.

It only took a second for me to realize why. I knew swelling when I felt it. Shit. I hoped it wasn't close enough to my eye that it swelled shut. Hard to fight with impeded vision.

Callon knelt down and packed some snow, then slowly brought it to my face and held it there. "Keep it there for a bit."

I moved my hand to the packed chunk he'd made, but only so I could take it off. "I'm fine."

He cupped my hand and moved it back. "Keep it there."

If this would move us past the man I might've killed, I'd hold it there.

Callon turned and walked to where Koz was looking over the bodies, passing Tuesday, who was making her way over to me. She wove in between them, and there were a lot of them.

I knelt, using the snow to scrub myself somewhat clean while taking peeks at Callon. I turned away quickly when his stare landed back on me.

"Did you kill him?" Tuesday asked, her jaw hanging low enough to shovel snow. She couldn't pry her eyes from the dead body not five feet away. "I mean, I knew you had it in you, but I didn't think you could actually pull it off."

"It's not a big deal." I wrapped my arm around hers and began tugging her in the opposite direction. If it wasn't for the super ears around here, I would've spilled all. I certainly didn't need any extra attention in that direction, though.

She moved with me but her body was angled away and her head nearly faced backward. "But wow. How did you do that?"

I looked at the knife I was tucking back into my waist. "I got lucky."

"Are you upset you killed someone?" Tuesday asked, trying to figure out the strange expression on my face.

"No. I had to." What was freaking me out was how I'd done it.

Callon walked toward us, the guys right behind him. They weaved in and out of dead bodies, the blood splattered across the snow like the ugliest painting ever made.

When he stopped a few feet away, I asked, "How long do you think we have before they hit again?"

"They'll have to get more men. These were mercenaries. If they'd come from the Magician, they would've had guns. The next wave will be his own and more." He raised his head to the sky and took a deep breath, looking like a savage king of old. "Storm will be here soon. We need to move."

28

Callon was right. The snow started a couple of hours after we got moving. It came down so hard it was like the Abominable Snowman had a stomach bug and was dumping everything he had on us.

I stumbled and Callon grabbed my arm, keeping me from making the ugliest snow angel in history. I pulled back from him as soon as my feet were solid again, which was harder than you'd think when the snow was up to your knees.

He was trying to be helpful, and I was trying to not tell him to fuck off. It wasn't because I was okay with him. I was just less okay with the Magician getting me and chopping off my limbs for shits and giggles.

I glanced at Tuesday, happy as a clam hitching a ride on Koz's back. She was happy and toasty warm, using Koz as a heater. Why couldn't I be more like her? When she needed help, she took it. How many times had I seen her effortlessly turn to someone and say she needed something? Like it was the easiest thing in the world?

Forget asking—I hated for anyone to know when I was struggling. She wouldn't be fighting with Callon right now, either. She'd be telling him what she needed. What gene did she get that I didn't?

Friend or not, I almost wanted to pull her off his back so she could trudge along beside me. Misery did love company, and I was pretty damn miserable right now.

I wouldn't, of course. Even if she let me, I wasn't evil enough to want to torture her alongside me. I told the little devil on my shoulder to shut up and fuck off. He left, but he'd be back. He *always* came back.

I took a few more steps and crashed. Turned out that numb feet weren't that nimble. I pushed myself up, cold hands getting even colder in the snow.

By the time I was on my feet again, Callon had stopped in front with his back to me. Really? I was struggling enough and now I had to walk around him because he wasn't paying attention? We weren't in a bad enough place? He wanted to antagonize me now as well?

I was going to give the little devil that had already returned free rein and yell at him. I didn't have a chance because he reached around and grabbed my hand, pulling it over his shoulder. I had no choice but to grab on to him with the rest of my limbs or lose an arm. Callon would do it, too—take my arm just to prove a point. He was a bastard like that.

He walked forward, still having an easier time with me on his back than I'd had alone.

Had to admit, this was a hell of a lot better. My pride quickly told me I didn't have to admit shit. Then it took control of my mouth.

"I don't need your help."

"You might not want it, but you definitely need it." He made that scoffing sound he did whenever he wanted me to know how stupid I was.

I hated that sound. It made me want to shove my fist in his mouth.

He grabbed one of my feet and ripped off my shoe.

"What are you doing?" I asked, choking him only a little as I tried to look over his shoulder.

"Keeping you from getting frostbite because you'll let your feet fall off before admitting they're frozen." He tucked my bare foot under his shirt.

I had a hunch that if I did have any feeling in my feet, it would've felt much better.

He did the same to the other, and tucked that under his shirt as well, close to his flesh. He wrapped his hands around them, helping them warm up quicker.

"I could've kept going," my pride told him, refusing to relinquish control of my mouth yet.

My pride had a point. My body would've made it a while longer without his help. He should be thankful that I'd speak to him at all.

"Yes, but it'll be so much easier if you can walk when we get to where we're headed, especially considering I don't have any more witches left for you to kill or run off." His words poked a little hard, but his tone was teasing.

I didn't know why he thought we were on teasing terms. We definitely were not.

"I didn't run that last one off. That wasn't my fault, and you aren't allowed to act like the injured party anymore." Good thing I hadn't thanked him or I'd want to beat him over the head right now.

My arms might have tightened around his neck slightly.

He laughed before he said, "You can't do it."

"You don't know that." I could definitely choke him.

"Yes, I do. I've got a really strong neck. But it is annoying, so if you wouldn't mind? We both know you can't make it the rest of the way without me."

I squeezed tighter.

He ignored me.

We were halfway up the mountain when I saw it. I'd never believed in heaven until I saw the massive building, made out of stone and sitting way up high. There was smoke coming out of the chimneys and the windows glowed in the early twilight. It looked like a painting Baryn had traded for some whiskey once.

"Is that it?" I asked, before I remembered I wasn't going to talk to Callon anymore.

Yes, I was an asshole. I'd done something wrong to him. That didn't mean I had to be nice to another asshole who had his own wrongs to account for. Plus, he'd carried on for days when he'd found out what I'd done. He'd made me feel like the worst person ever. He wasn't walking away from what he did fancy free.

"Yes." His voice was a little raspier than normal.

It took me a second to place the emotion. Then it hit. He was someone who was *happy* to be home. One day, I was going to know that feeling too. What it was like to have a place that meant the world to me that I couldn't wait to get back to. A place all my own.

As we got closer, I saw that there were balconies and lookouts along the building and realized the true beauty of this place. You could see everything coming at you for miles. Something moved, you saw it against the pristine snow. We were staying on a small trail. The rest was pristine. You couldn't take a step that wouldn't be noticed.

He kept walking, and the closer we got, the more I could see the shadowy bodies moving around inside.

"Do a lot of people live here?" Looked like it would hold quite a few. Lots of people meant lots of death. I hated lots of death. It made me awkward and stiff, like the corpses I'd see.

"About thirty between the main house and some cabins scattered about. It used to be a resort before the Bloody Death. Took a while to get it back into shape, but it was built solid, so the bones were all there."

I didn't care about the house anymore. Thirty people, thirty possible deaths to see. *Maybe* thirty. If they were all beasts, there was a chance I wouldn't see anything. What were the odds of that? Probably not good.

Still, it was worth a little more talking to find out. I could go back to ignoring Callon later.

"Are they like you guys? You know, half beast?" Currently, I didn't think he was even half beast. I thought he was a complete animal. But again, answers were nice. I could elaborate on his genetic makeup at a later point.

"About a third."

Twenty humans, then, and twenty possible deaths. Wasn't great, but wasn't quite as bad, especially if they didn't swarm in all at once. But this wasn't like the Gathering. They wouldn't keep their distance. They knew Callon. Probably felt at least somewhat secure he wouldn't eat them. This could get ugly.

He stopped.

The guys immediately turned to look at us, Tuesday barely awake on Koz's back.

Callon nodded at them and said, "Give us a minute."

He waited until they walked inside before he said, "Breathe."

Callon turned his head toward me. "I spent a long time only in beast form. When I first started shifting back, it was a lot. I'd be raw after a few minutes of human company."

I took a deep breath, realizing I'd been holding my breath on and off since I saw the people. I forced the air deep in my lungs, trying to calm myself down and prepare for what was coming.

And then, because my pride still wouldn't shut up, I said, "Don't talk to me like you're my friend. I'm fine." I didn't need help. I could do this. I'd be fine and I'd take care of myself.

"I know. You're always 'fine.'"

He made that *I'm stupid* sound. Then he waited as I dragged in a few more slow breaths.

He took a step forward. "Is there a certain range?"

I let out a long sigh. Was he going to keep talking to me? Of course, I knew why he was asking. If I didn't tell him, I'd be screwing myself.

Damn him. "Depends on the person and the death. Usually, though, I'm safe at about ten feet away."

He nodded before we finished our trek toward the house.

"Being nice doesn't change anything." It was only fair that he realized. Maybe he'd stop talking to me if he did.

We stopped right in front of the two massive wooden doors. Callon turned his head to the side, his voice soft as he asked, "Are you capable of walking if I put you down?"

"Definitely." My feet were still pretty numb, but that didn't mean I couldn't stand on them.

He opened the door.

"Why aren't you putting me down?"

His hand paused on a huge brass handle. "Because I *know* you can't walk."

"Then why'd you ask me?"

"To see if you'd lie about it or if we'd made any progress."

I tightened my arm around his neck, imagining how nice it would be to choke him, just a little. Only until he passed out. I wouldn't actually kill him.

"Still just annoying," he said, laughter in his voice.

I didn't say anything else.

Then I couldn't as I took the place in. It was a haven of warmth and wood. We walked into a room that only had a staircase and no furniture. This part alone was the size of Baryn's shack, and it was only for the stairs?

He made a right and came to a room that had stuff, and not only wood but furniture covered in fabric and a huge table. A fireplace, so large I could've lain down in it, took up a huge chunk of the wall. Curled metal grates stood in front of a roaring fire. That was the best thing. It was warm.

A short, stocky blond guy walked into the room. "Callon!"

"Hey, Shifty," Callon said, stepping back when Shifty stepped forward.

Shifty lost a little of his smile.

"I'll explain later. Where's Issy?" Callon asked, his shoulders tensing underneath my arms.

"Issy is fine," came a weak female voice. Shuffling steps preceded a woman walking into the room. If I'd been standing, I would've stepped back to stay out of range, although no one would need my vision to see this death coming. The grey of her skin and the dark smudges under her eyes told you everything you needed to know.

I couldn't put an age to her, because the sickness had stolen so many years already. I couldn't tell if she was thirty or forty, but I had a feeling it was the former, since her hair didn't look to have a strand of grey in the chocolate brown.

Callon didn't budge as she got in range, and I didn't blame him. I was probably the last thing on his mind right now.

She stepped over to a chair and put a hand on it as she dragged a breath in. It whistled as she forced it back out, each rise of her chest seeming to steal a little of the life she had left.

I braced myself for her death. And braced. And waited.

Finally, when nothing hit me, I began to relax. She might look like death, but the reaper wasn't on her doorstep. It didn't add up, though. She even smelled of death, her skin pulled too tight over her bones. Her hands shook and her head looked too big for her body.

"Are you—"

"I'm fine." She waved a dismissive hand, tired of a question she was probably getting constantly, from the looks of her.

She smiled at Callon, finally getting her breath back from the short walk. "Zink and Hess are in the kitchen getting food. Koz is getting his girl settled." Issy looked at me. "Who's this?"

If she'd ever been involved with Callon, she didn't have a jealous bone in her body. Although, as her attention shifted to me, I tried to untangle my legs, realizing how idiotic I must look clinging to his back.

Callon's hands kept my legs wrapped around him, thwarting my attempt to stand on my own and regain some dignity.

"This is Teddy. She's going to be staying with us for a bit."

"You all right?" Issy asked me. She had kind eyes that reminded me of Maura.

Issy's eyes went to where Callon's hands were holding my feet captive under his shirt.

"A little frostbite but nothing too bad," Callon explained, answering for me.

"There's water on in your room. I told some of the boys to bring it up when they saw you making your way up the mountain." Her voice held a whisper of worry.

"Thanks."

Huh, guess Callon did know that word.

Her eyes shot back to where Callon was grasping my feet. "Do you want me to help?"

The woman could barely walk. He'd have to carry us both.

"She won't let you. I don't know if she'll let me,

except I'm going to make her," Callon said, watching Issy as she nodded, sitting in the chair she'd been holding on to.

The sound of voices getting closer had me trying to untangle my legs again.

"I'm going to go get her settled and I'll be back down," Callon said.

"Come by my room instead. Feeling a little tired."

His entire back stiffened. "Sure."

Without saying anything else, he carried me up the huge flight of stairs and then down a long hallway.

"Is she your…" Sister, friend? I didn't get the sense it was romantic.

"She's family." The words were clipped.

I bit my lower lip. I shouldn't have asked. I, of all people, knew when you should keep quiet. I didn't even know why I'd talked to him. I was still mad.

He walked to the last room on the right and pushed the door open with his hip. A huge bed took up the center of the room that had massive windows arching high. A wood-burning stove stood in the corner, with several buckets of water on it. The smell told me this was Callon's room, and the view told me why. There wasn't a threat you couldn't see coming from those huge windows.

He set me on the edge of the bed and then turned around.

"I don't need your help. You can go."

He watched me for a few seconds, and I kept my eyes toward the wall, not returning the look. He walked to the door and then paused, and then walked back to me.

This time I knew I wasn't going to be able to get rid of him easily.

"I wasn't going to buy you. I had to find out what was going on. There was too much talk."

I didn't acknowledge he was speaking.

"Would I have kept you here to stop the Magician from building an immortal army and killing everyone he came across? Yes. You'd do the same, whether you admit it or not. If I walk, you don't have a shot in hell. You know that or you wouldn't have gone along with Hera in the first place."

I wasn't ready for this conversation. Not yet. The knowledge of how I'd been duped was still too fresh and strong. I knew what he was saying, but I couldn't accept it yet.

He squatted in front of me, forearms resting on his thighs, and eyes on my feet.

"Can you feel them?" he asked, looking at the skin that had turned white.

I knew what this really was. An olive branch.

I was angry, but the steam had been let off enough that I wasn't ready to snap the branch. Everything he said was true. I wasn't ready to admit to that yet, but I'd take the branch until I decided the next course of action. Maybe I'd take it and then beat him with it later.

"Yes." Feeling had been coming and going in the forms of pins and needles a little while after he'd shoved my feet up against his skin.

His head stayed downward but his eyes shot to my face.

I shrugged. "More than I did."

He got up and walked over to one of the buckets, testing its temperature before bringing it to me.

"It might sting a bit, but it's not that hot," he said as he put it down in front of me.

The warning didn't prepare me. I sucked in some air between my teeth as my feet hit the warmth. My ankles thought the water was lukewarm, but my feet thought it was boiling.

"How bad?"

I tried to unclench my teeth. "Not horrible."

Those steel eyes called me a liar in a thousand different ways, all without saying a word.

"Stay there for a while. It'll subside."

I nodded. I couldn't walk, so I wasn't sure where he thought I was going.

He turned to leave. As much as I wanted to punish him for everything I'd discovered, I couldn't. As he kept pointing out, I wasn't completely innocent in this situation. My gut kept agreeing with him.

But there was one thing I needed to know before I said anything else about the other thing nagging me.

"Callon, did you want me here so I could to steal a life to save Issy?" I asked, stopping him before he got to the door.

He turned around and slowly shook his head. "No. Even if I wanted you to, she wouldn't."

I bit my lip. I didn't like the idea of giving anyone false hope. That had never been an issue before. People didn't usually come to me when they were looking for hope. They came looking for death. But no matter what secrets he'd kept, I owed him this if I could give it to him.

He was waiting. "Was there something else?"

"I've been wrong in the past." I gripped the blanket underneath my hands, wondering if this was a mistake but knowing it was too late not to say it. "I didn't see her death."

He angled his head toward me, eyes narrowing as if his super ears hadn't heard me right. The shape Issy was in, I wouldn't have believed it either. It didn't make a whole lot of sense. Last time I'd seen someone that looked as sick as her had been Maura, and she'd died in a matter of days.

He took a step back toward me. "Are you sure?"

Living as I had, I knew what was running through his mind. If I didn't know Callon so well by now, it might've sounded like he didn't want to believe me, but I knew that wasn't it. He was afraid to. Hope could be a mighty scary thing. I'd been there and done that for the first eighteen years of my life.

I'd never told Tuesday this, but the first time I'd run hadn't been my first opportunity. I'd had another a few months earlier and choked. The possibility of getting out and then not making it, as had happened the next time, had been as horrible as I'd feared.

But maybe it had all happened like that for a reason. Maybe I'd been meant to wait for Koz and then Callon? If I let my thoughts run away with me, I might start believing Bitters' crazy prophecy that the witch had repeated. Maybe I was losing my shit and going to start searching for unicorns in the forest too.

"When someone is very close to death, I pick up on it easier and from further away. If I was going to sense it, I would've as soon as she walked in the room."

He looked as confused as I was. How she was going to live didn't make a lot of sense, but my cursed gift didn't come with a medical diagnosis.

He nodded. He didn't believe it, even though I knew he'd wanted to.

Well, that solved one problem. I hadn't given him *that* much hope.

29

I fell out of the closet as someone ran into the room. After I'd soaked my feet back to life, one excruciating inch after another, all I'd wanted was sleep. I hadn't cared about food or people or whose room I was in. I'd crawled into the bed and passed out.

I'd woken a short time later, imagining that someone was staring in at me through those big windows. Since it was still dark, I hadn't gotten nearly as much sleep as I wanted. That was when I'd decided to relocate.

Callon stood at the door, looking about the room, trying to find the problem. "Are you all right?" He leaned forward, looking right at the open doors of the closet and the pillow on its floor.

"Were you—"

More feet sounded in the hall. Callon backed out of the room, the door still in his grip. "She's fine. She tripped."

I couldn't see who was there, but the loud grumbling and general moans sounded like Zink and Hess.

The footsteps retreated. Callon shut the door and made his way to where I was getting up from the floor.

"What happened?"

"Nothing. A dream, is all." Shaking hands gripped the blanket as I pulled it tighter around me.

Nothing had been the beating Baryn gave me at twelve. I hadn't dreamt of that moment in a long time. If I had, I didn't remember it. Or maybe I hadn't wanted to. That was when he'd crippled me the first time.

I also couldn't forget what he'd said. *You won't use your wiles on another person. You ask for help again, and it'll be both legs.*

Callon walked farther into the room, jerking me back to the present.

"Were you sleeping in the closet?"

I pulled the blanket tighter around me. "There's a lot of windows in this place and not a lot of trees for a quick escape. It was a rational decision."

He stared at the closet, not responding. His brows dropped lower over his eyes.

Maybe for him it seemed weird, but it was a big, comfy closet by anyone's standards. Maybe he needed to get out a little and see how the rest of the world lived before judging.

He was scowling by the time he stopped staring. It was probably only a few seconds, but it was long enough to get awkward.

He stood there, hands on his hips, as if he were coming to terms with something.

"I was coming in here to crash. We're short on rooms and the bed's big enough that we won't even know we're sharing."

His hair was mussed like he'd already been sleeping. I didn't ask him about it. I just said, "Okay."

Why did I have to say that so quickly? Now he was going to think I wanted to be in bed with him, which I didn't. I didn't even want to talk to him. It was simply easier to sleep when I knew there were beast ears listening for threats.

I climbed back on the bed and watched to see what he'd do. If he left, I was going back in the closet.

He walked over to the side of the bed and sat there for a few seconds. Was he going to lie down?

"Aren't you taking you shirt off?" He always took his shirt off when he slept inside. Was he trying to fake me out?

He didn't say anything, but he pulled the shirt off, threw it to a nearby chair, and stretched out.

I settled deeper into the mattress. Sleep was calling back to me, and I knew I was going to be out for the count soon.

I curled onto my side, feeling sleepier by the second. "Just so you know, we're still fighting."

"*We* aren't fighting. *You're* fighting." His voice softened as he added, "It's all right, though. I get it."

Was he admitting he was wrong? Sounded like an admission of guilt. It didn't fix anything, but it soothed the wound a bit. Although when I'd apologized, several times, I'd been very clear. None of this wishy-washy business. His apology was falling short of the mark, but I was too comfortable to fight right now.

He sounded as relaxed as I did. Why was it so comfortable to sleep near him? Had to be that he could kill people with a snap of his jaws. That was awfully convenient in times like these.

I turned onto my back, facing the ceiling. As mad as I'd been, there was one thing that tempered the anger, besides the fact that my hands weren't exactly clean in all this. He really wasn't going to hand me over. I believed it now, beyond a doubt. Otherwise he would've tried to get Hecate to get rid of the spell. He hadn't even asked for it.

There was one thing that puzzled me, though. "Why wouldn't you have tried to strike a deal with the Magician that would keep you and your people safe?"

There were a lot of people here. I'd screwed him over to save the soul of just one person.

He groaned, slightly exaggerated if you were to ask me, before he asked, "This again?"

"Yes. You never answered." I turned to look at him. I'd stare him into a confession if need be.

He was lying on his back, his eyes drifting shut as his head rested on his arms. "Issy has this necklace she wears that dates back to the Glory Years. Can't even imagine what it went through before she found it, and she's been wearing it for a decade at least.

"The gem has notches and chips on every side, and a crack that runs almost completely through it, except for this one spot that somehow holds it all together. The thing refuses to break, and for all its flaws, when the sun hits it, it's the most vibrant thing you'll ever see."

He paused, his eyes staying closed. It was really nice that Issy had some jewelry but what did that have to do with me?

"You remind me of her necklace," he finally said. "Maybe I don't want to be the one who strikes the final blow that breaks you. Maybe I'm afraid of what I'll become if I do, because we're both hanging on to humanity by our fingertips."

I watched him, his eyes closed, and I finally got it. *Really* got it this time.

We were more alike than I'd realized, both of us afraid of what we might become in this crazy world in an effort to survive.

"Go to sleep, Teddy."

The door creaked. I squinted one eye open and watched Issy walk in the room. She put a pile of clothes down, rested a hand on the dresser, and bent over slightly, pausing to breathe.

"You didn't have to do that. I would've come down," I said, sitting up in the large bed, the late morning light streaming in.

"I wanted to check on you." Issy turned, smiling.

I must've slept fifteen hours. All I'd wanted to do last night was lay my head down and never get up again. All the days of traveling, of pushing unused muscles beyond their limitations, had built up until they demanded payment.

Issy took a step toward me before she bent over, a coughing spasm stealing her words. She braced her hand on the bed.

Forget me. She needed someone to check on her.

"Are you all right?" I reached out, unsure how to help her, even as I worried direct contact might bring on a vision that would make a liar out of me.

She waved off my hand and straightened, albeit with

a struggle. I sagged back on to the bed and let out a breath, glad I wouldn't have to find out.

The wheezing noise abated after a few minutes, and her chest stopped heaving. The pendant Callon had talked about last night hung around her neck.

"I'm fine," she said as soon as she got her wind back a few minutes later.

Her "I'm fine" felt a little familiar. No wonder no one ever believed me. I hoped I pulled it off a little better than she did. I had a bad feeling about that, though.

"Callon said you're going to be around for a while?" she asked, punctuating the question with a smile, in contrast to the eyes that were still watering.

He'd definitely told her a lot more than that. The fact that she was still being pleasant said he must've softened it a bit.

Did she know that the Magician was on our tail? Might be following us here right now? Because I couldn't imagine how anyone would be welcoming to someone with that kind of baggage tugging along behind them.

"Not sure how long, exactly." The witch said around a year, but the date hadn't been etched in stone.

Issy waved her hand and then took a seat on the bed beside me. "I see your face and know what you're worried about. That's not your fault. That was going to happen. It's in the prophecy."

I smiled. She had to be talking about Bitters' prophecy. If there were any more weird wizards floating around talking about me, I didn't want to hear it. Were Callon and I the only ones who didn't believe in prophecies?

It was a bit convenient at the moment. Could I let fate take the fall for all this? It wasn't really my place to tell her what to believe in.

I was still debating when another series of coughs had her bending over. As soon as they paused, she got up, grabbing on to the dresser as she made her way out of the room.

"I'll be letting you have your privacy now," she said in between her lungs rebelling. She waved her hand toward me, her eyes tearing as she left.

I wanted to help her, but I knew she'd only tell me she was "fine" again. I hadn't realized that could be a bit irritating.

I gave her a few minutes' lead, for her pride's sake, before I stuck my head out the door to make sure she hadn't collapsed. It was empty. Looked like Issy had made it downstairs.

The hum of voices reached the hallway, along with the smell of food. My stomach wanted to charge forward. My gut wanted to go back to the pile of clothes she'd brought, throw on the heaviest thing I could get my hands on, and run out into the raging snow until there wasn't another soul around. I knew what was coming for me, and the idea of standing still seemed foreign.

I sat down on the top of the stairs. Elbows on my knees, I planted my face in my palms. Hera's words drifted back to me again, as they did so often now. Callon could protect me. He was my only shot. I couldn't run without him now anyway.

He wasn't running anymore. He'd found his spot to take a stand, and I was pretty sure it was fight time.

Callon had been right, too. I either wielded my

magic or someone wielded it for me. I didn't want to embrace what I was, but my gut was taunting me and calling me stupid if I didn't try.

My gut was also telling me what our best shot was. I hadn't dreamt of Baryn's breaking my leg when I was twelve for nothing.

I stood and then trudged along as if I were going to my last meal, telling myself that this wasn't the end of the world. I'd learn to wield my magic and I'd be in control of it, right? I'd lay out parameters, lines I wouldn't cross. I'd make it work because it had to.

Why was I so averse to it, anyway? Was it really so bad to save good people using the lives of the evil? My morals weren't as pristine as the snow around this place. They'd been dinged up and dirtied before, and even more so recently.

I continued to follow the sound of voices, one in particular, which were conveniently in the same direction as the smells. My stomach was growling almost as loud as Callon's beast did.

Callon was at the head of the table, boots kicked up on a chair. Zink was sitting next to him. Hess and Koz were standing a few feet away, plates in hand.

A few other people, including Shifty, were also there, as well as two tall, dark-haired men who looked like brothers. I was pretty sure Shifty was human, but I pegged the brothers as beasts. I was getting better at spotting them.

Callon had been watching the door as I entered, as if he'd known I was approaching. Everyone's talking faded as I walked in.

Keeping my shoulders square, I made my way over to Callon. His eyes shifted to my feet. I figured he was looking for blisters. He was right, of course. I had them, but nothing I couldn't tolerate.

I pulled out the heavy chair next to him. "We should probably talk."

He nodded.

The room cleared.

He sat there, eyes looking smug. I couldn't say why they looked smug, but somehow they did. Smugness was oozing across the table, nearly smacking me in the face.

He really didn't make anything easy and then he acted as if I were difficult. Still, there was a massive problem lurking on the horizon, so I would be the bigger person here.

"Before recently, I didn't know who the Magician was. I won't pretend to understand the threat heading toward us as well as you do. But what I do understand is we're in this together at the moment. I wronged you. As I've recently discovered, you've wronged me as well. Is that a fair statement?"

He crossed his arm in front of his chest but relaxed his shoulders. "I guess I could agree with that."

I sat a little taller. Not bad so far.

"For the time being, I'd like to make a truce, at least until we deal with the Magician. We'll leave our bad history alone and call it *sort* of even."

Both eyebrows rose. "Sort of even?"

"Your wrongdoings might be slightly worse than mine"—I threw my hands up—"but okay, we can call it even if that's important to you."

He tilted his chin down but let that go.

I continued. "For the time being, I won't poke at you and you'll refrain from giving me a long list of all my faults."

I already knew the list by heart, and it was a mile long. He lifted his hand, scratching the shadow along his square jaw, then sucked air in between his teeth as if that last request was going to hurt.

Seriously? This was going to be the stumbling block for him?

He pointed toward me. "I think we should leave that part alone."

That did leave me open to continue to poke at him. I could live with it. "Okay. Agreed."

"Then agreed."

"You might be right about some other stuff. I need to get a handle on my magic. If we can figure out how to practice without having to kill someone, I'm game."

"And we both know you might not need that much practice."

He definitely suspected I'd killed that guy with magic when we'd been attacked. He could keep on suspecting. I wasn't quite ready to lay every card on the table yet.

Callon's face didn't move a fraction of a millimeter, and yet I knew he wanted to smile. That made me want to scream for some reason. As expected, both of us did neither.

"Even if we can figure out how I did it, no one dies to save someone else unless they're going to die anyway. That's a hard line, and I won't cross or it breaks the truce. I'm in control of my magic. No one else."

"That sounds pretty reasonable. Any other hard lines?"

"Yes, but I haven't thought of them yet. If I find something appalling, I reserve the right to raise issues at a later time."

"Sure." It was an offhand comment, as if he'd

already thought this all through, as if he'd known what I was going to do before I came down and told him.

I sat back, giving him narrowed eyes. "And don't expect me to trust you right away, either. That's going to take a while."

He leaned forward and touched my face, his thumb brushing my lower lip. I didn't know what he was going to do, but he stopped short of kissing me.

With a light in his eyes and a straight face, he asked, "How'd you sleep last night?"

Bastard. A good night's sleep had nothing to do with trusting him.

"So so." My voice didn't lack for bite, but it wasn't only because he thought he was smart.

Some part of me, not a part I was on board with, but couldn't quite disown, had thought he was going to kiss me. That same part might've hoped he would. But no part of me was admitting I trusted him even a little bit when he was going to act like this over desperately needed sleep.

He leaned back, but that spark was still in his eyes as he looked at me. The one that had made me think he would kiss me.

For whatever reason, he seemed to be in a good mood. If I was going tell him, this was the moment.

"I think I have an idea what to do with the Magician."

"Which is?"

"You remember Hecate said 'it won't work on me'?"

"Of course." He uncrossed his arms. "Continue."

He was taking this a lot more seriously than I thought he would. I'd imagined battling it out with him to make him listen. I wasn't sure if this made me feel better or worse.

"I thought she meant asking her for help wouldn't work, but I think it went deeper than that. I remembered something the other night, but I'm not sure if I made it up or it's true. I need a test subject. I think it might work better if I show you. If I can, that is." It might be easier, too. I wasn't sure if I could quantify what it was I thought I could do. I certainly didn't know how to explain it that well.

"Can you get Zink back in here?" He hated me. He'd definitely be the best option to test this out on.

Callon's eyes narrowed but he nodded. He walked into the hall and said, "Zink, you got a minute?" He walked back into the room. "He's coming."

I hadn't heard Zink respond, but I believed Callon. I made my way over to the couch on the other side of the room while I waited, knowing it would be a better test situation. Plus, if I humiliated myself, the light here was dimmer and I could blame the sweating on being too close to the fire. It was perfect.

A second later, Zink walked into the room. "What's going on? You call?"

The whole thing felt ridiculous, but I had to try. I looked up, focusing all my energy on him. "Zink, we need a little help figuring something out. Can you please help me?"

He walked across the room and sat down on the couch beside me. And not at the other end, but in the center, right next to me. "What do you need?"

It was, hands down, the nicest he'd ever spoken to me, and we'd been stuck traveling together for more days than I could count.

"You already helped. Thanks."

I hadn't imagined it. I'd stopped asking for help when I was at the village and people stopped looking at me, but maybe it hadn't been as clear-cut as I'd realized. When I asked, the people who'd tried to help had sometimes paid with their lives.

"What did I do?" Zink asked, looking confused.

I glanced at Callon, who was standing across the room. "I—"

"You lured him in."

He understood exactly what had gone down. I couldn't tell what he thought about it, though.

"She *lured* me? What?" Zink's head was swiveling back and forth, in jeopardy of unhinging from his body. "What are you talking about? I walked in the room and sat down. Nobody did anything."

Callon walked closer, leaning on the mantel. "Look where you're sitting."

Zink looked down and realized he was mere inches from me, when he normally kept at least six feet in between us. *And* he grabbed my hand.

"What the fuck?" He jumped up and took a bunch of steps away, restoring our normal buffer.

"She's a lure of some sort," Callon said calmly. "It makes sense. If you can pull life from someone, why wouldn't you be able to draw that same life close to you?"

When he put it like that, it did make sense. It also made me want to vomit. I was a perfect killing machine. Or I could be if I knew what I was doing.

Zink pointed at me. "She's starting to scare me. I might have claws, but her beast is way scarier."

There was always a silver lining somewhere.

"I think we call the Magician here. I can lure him over and you can kill him."

I'd try first, but they didn't need to know that part of the plan quite yet. Baby steps.

"No one knows for sure what he is. He was human once, but that doesn't mean he is now. It might not be that easy to kill him."

"Is that how she got Koz to break her out?" Zink asked, rubbing his hands through his hair, still hung up on what had happened to him.

Callon shook his head. "No. She might've had a pull on him, but he had to go back of his own accord. She would've lost the pull as soon as he was away from her."

"How do we know for sure?" Zink asked, staring at me.

"Because that's how that kind of magic works," Callon said, sounding as impatient with Zink as I was. We had bigger issues, and he was afraid he'd gotten cooties. "It might not work on the Magician. He's strong. He'll most likely sense it before you draw him out. Even Hecate said it wouldn't work on her."

I stood and walked toward Callon, and Zink stepped back. "It's worth a try. We have nothing else."

"If you can pull it off." Callon looked toward Zink. "Give us a minute."

"Not a problem." He left in record time.

Callon followed him, shut the doors to the room, and then immediately turned his intensity back on me. "How did you not know you were a lure? I can understand the other, but this would've shown."

I crossed my arms. "I just didn't."

"Truce, remember? It's only a question."

Callon continued to stare at me, trying to unlock all my secrets. I backed away.

He took a step forward. "How bad was it before you shut down?"

It had taken a while. There had been a time I'd been open to all. Way back when, until it had been chipped away at.

Whispers of a memories trickled into my mind, but I stomped them back down. Some memories weren't worth the room they took up. All they did was bring on the hurt and make it sting again. I'd had enough of the stings.

He tilted his head, as if he were delving into my soul.

"Callon, I thought we called a truce?" I asked, throwing the T-word right back at him.

"I didn't know that included bullshitting each other."

"Is it possible for you to let anything go?" I brushed past him, heading toward the doors.

"I can. Doubt you'll be able to."

30

I went to bed alone and woke up alone. But I hadn't slept alone. Callon had been in the bedroom. I could smell his scent and see the dent left in the pillow next to me. The biggest reason I knew, though, was because I'd slept through the night.

A slip of paper sat on the table beside me, and I picked it up.

Meeting in the great room after breakfast.

I flipped it with my fingers, letting it sail back to the surface of the table. Tuesday would need to know. I got up and dressed, then made my way to Koz's room. Tuesday was walking out his door before I got there.

She stopped dead center in the hallway. "You know about the meeting?"

"Yep. Was coming to tell you. We better eat up. Who knows what's coming next."

"Oh yeah," she said, then turned toward the direction of the smells.

"I've got some stuff to catch you up on," I said, following her.

"After breakfast. I'm too hungry right now," she said, not even slowing down now that food was close.

We hit the stairs and I slowed to a stop a few steps down, hearing all the people below.

She looked toward the sounds and then back to me. "Is it too much? You want me to grab something for you and we can eat upstairs?" she asked, hand on the rail, waiting for me.

People were walking in and out of the great room, glancing up at us.

It was going to happen eventually. I wasn't going to be able to avoid everyone unless I sat in Callon's room all day and night, so the question was: slow and steady or all at once? Was it that big of a difference?

"No. I'm coming." I walked down the rest of the stairs, catching up to her.

We made our way into the great room. Bowls of food and a stack of plates were set up on the massive table.

So many people were here, except for Issy, and that sat like a stone in my gut. I kept telling myself I hadn't seen her die, but she was the sickest-looking healthy person I'd ever seen.

I didn't have much time to think of her lack of death vision, as we moved into the room and none of the diners kept their distance. As we weaved our way through the crowd of curious eyes, I knew exactly which ones were shifters. I didn't pick up anything from them. Wished I could've said the same for the rest.

In rapid order, five separate deaths hit me until I wanted to fall on my knees, sweat on my brow.

Guts pouring out of bodies.

Skulls caved in.

Pools of blood.

All of it happening on this mountain.

Tuesday took one look at me and went into cover-up mode. She pointed out two empty seats, and we walked toward them. A minute later, she shoved a plate of food in front of me, trying to make me blend.

I took the fork she'd stuck by my hand and toyed with the food, pretending more than eating. People waved and said hello, and I did my best to fake it, even with the ones who I knew wouldn't be here much longer.

By the time Callon walked in, most of the people had left and the guys had filed in. I was still sitting in front of a full plate of food but with no appetite left.

Zink and Hess were on the other side of the table from me. Koz slid into a chair beside Tuesday while Callon pulled two doors shut.

He turned, instantly getting everyone's attention.

The first words out of Callon's mouth were: "Does everyone here know what Teddy did to Zink last night?"

It was the last thing I'd expected, and I was less ready for the consensus of nods. Even Tuesday was nodding.

My face scrunched up as I watched her.

"Zink told Koz and then Koz told me." She shrugged.

Callon walked to the head of the table but didn't sit. "Everyone in this room knows what's heading our way. The only idea on the table is using Teddy as a lure to entice the Magician into a spot we might be able to take him out. Either I'll kill him or we get him close enough to take a shot at him. I'm not sold we'll be able to get him close enough for either. Any thoughts?"

"I don't think we should stay here," I blurted out before anyone else had a chance to speak. We needed to lure the Magician away from this place before every death I'd just seen happened, and maybe more. I couldn't see the beasts. How many of them would die?

Callon crossed his arms. "No. This place is our best defensive position. Leaving isn't an option."

Okay. He had a point there, but I still had a major problem. "Then we should send everyone else away."

"We need as many people who can fight as possible. Any other ideas?" he asked, looking at everyone but me.

My hands were fisted underneath the table but I didn't go crazy. He didn't know the full outcome. I'd get him alone. I didn't want to blast out a list of names that one of the guys might go and repeat. Hearing you were going to die through the grapevine could make a person real sour. I had some experience with these things.

"What about the people who can't fight?" Tuesday asked.

"They're better off riding it out here. The basement is fortified," Callon said. "There's a tunnel that leads to the other side of the mountain, and we rigged the entrance on this side to implode if needed."

Koz moved his arm to the back of Tuesday's chair. He leaned in and whispered something to her. Tuesday seemed to relax into her chair, putting her palm on his leg.

"Do we have any other options?" Hess asked.

"We hit him head on as soon as he shows up," Callon said.

Hess rolled his eyes, and the other guys looked down. Clearly, no one thought that would work.

"I didn't get out of the village to end up caged somewhere else. I want him dead, and I'll figure out how to do it myself if I have to. I'll use whatever I have on him." I scanned the room, stalling when I hit Callon's gaze.

There were a handful of people I didn't mind killing if the opportunity arose. The Magician was one of them. Callon wanted me to wield my magic? Get me near the man who'd bought me, had been stalking me, and I was going to give it my best shot.

Callon walked over and leaned his hands on the table. "What if that doesn't work?"

"I thought the witch couldn't help? You don't have the death spell. How could you *possibly* make it work?" Koz asked, Zink and Hess all ears.

Tuesday shook her head and covered her eyes with her hand. She'd already figured it out, and it was groan-worthy. "Oh no. This was the talk, wasn't it?" she asked softly.

"Because it might," Callon answered for me, the two of us staring at only each other.

He'd known. My gut had told me he did, and I'd told my gut to shut up. Never tell your gut to shut up. It's clued in to a lot of shit you can't even imagine.

"Huh?" Koz looked at me.

All eyes were on me, except for Tuesday, who was now reclining, staring at the ceiling and mumbling something about how I made it so hard sometimes.

I turned to Koz, because sometimes he was the

easiest person in the room to deal with. "You know the guy I stabbed in the fight right before we got here? I might've sucked the life out of him somehow before I technically killed him with my knife."

"Oh, is that all?" Hess asked, eyebrow up.

"You knew?" Zink asked Callon.

"Suspected. I know blood, and there wasn't enough. Blood spurts from live bodies." Callon looked back at me, straightening but no less daunting in his expression. "You didn't necessarily kill him. He might've had a bad heart or a weak blood vessel in his brain."

All things I'd considered myself and found highly unlikely, and I was sure he did as well.

I stood, my chair scraping. "That went at just the moment he grabbed me? Look, I don't want this to be true, but let's accept it and use whatever we have."

He tipped his dark head toward me. "It was a high-stress moment. That's when a bad heart would go."

"You don't think it was me?" Bull. I knew he did. No one else had a plan, but he wanted to shoot mine down and go with nothing? What was his problem?

"I didn't say that. I'm not sure." He turned and walked away from me. "Which was why I don't think it's a valid reason to have you go and try and use it on the Magician, someone who might know it's coming and plan accordingly. Not to mention, you have no control over it." His voice rose and grew sharper with each word.

"That's all fine and dandy, but there's no other plan," I yelled.

"Sending out Reaper Jr. over here might be our best bet," Hess said, shrugging.

The room was silent.

Zink leaned back and kicked his feet up on the table. "Anyone else notice she's getting scarier every day?"

No one spoke. Tuesday shrugged. I took that as a yes.

"Maybe a little," Koz said, confirming my impression a few seconds later.

Tuesday smacked him in the arm for me.

"Thank you," I said.

"Of course," she replied. "It's one thing to think it, but it wasn't nice to say."

Callon let out an annoyed sigh. "We need something else."

Except there wasn't anything else, and I wasn't the only one who thought so. No one said anything as he looked around the room.

He shook his head, looking disgusted by everyone, and walked from the room.

I was the only one who got up and followed him. "Callon, you need to send some people away. I saw some things this morning—"

"I'm not a babysitter," he snapped, turning.

It was the man talking. I wished the beast could speak. I was starting to think I got along with it better.

"What is your problem?" This wasn't about my list. He hated my plan but had nothing better, and all he wanted to do was shoot down my ideas.

Callon seemed to realize it himself. He took a deep breath before he said, "Give me a list of names. I won't force them, but I'll tell them what you said."

31

The table in the large room was nearly empty as Tuesday and I sat and ate dinner. Only Shifty was sitting with us, at the other end, and that was close enough.

"Are you and…" I didn't want to say, *Are you and Koz a real thing?* with the company.

"Uh huh." She took another bite.

"Is it…?" It was the most awkward conversation we'd ever had, but our audience was hanging on to every word.

"Oh yeah." She took a look around the enormous room that might've been able to fit everyone from our village at one time. "Where is everyone?"

I chewed as I thought it over. I'd left Callon after the meeting and slept another few hours. I wasn't sure if it was exhaustion or depression. By the time I woke up, the place had gone quiet. "Maybe we missed the normal dinner?"

I glanced down to Shifty. He was eating.

He looked right at me with a smile. I smiled briefly

and hoped it wasn't too late to seem engrossed in my food.

"You that girl Bitters talked about?" he asked.

That prophecy was turning out to be a plague on my life.

"Not sure." I shouldn't have smiled. Nothing good came from pretending to be social. What were the odds he'd shut up now? Probably low.

He leaned forward. "Everyone says so."

"Couldn't say for sure." Why did people always have to talk so much? Constantly filling the air with stupid chitchat. Silence was a beautiful thing, if people only gave it a chance.

Shifty opened his mouth, gearing up for his next question, when Tuesday beat him to it. "What about me? Does this Bitters guy say anything about another girl?"

"Nah. Just her." Shifty leaned back.

Tuesday scooted her chair closer. "Are you sure? Do you have his stuff written down somewhere? What else is said? You can't know for sure that there isn't another girl and maybe another guy."

Shifty shoved some food in his mouth while shaking his head. I knew the food tactic well.

"Hey, why do they call you Shifty?" Tuesday asked, and now I knew for sure she was screwing with him.

"Because he has unethical card-playing habits," Callon said from the door. He walked in and stopped beside me. "You almost done? It's time to work."

Callon stared at me, eyes cool, without a hint of fire, but intent nonetheless. If I said no, was he going to stand there until I was done? There was a full bowl of whatever this meat and gravy was sitting in front of me, screaming for someone to take a second helping.

I finished chewing my last bite, feeling like everyone in the room was listening to me swallow. Another glance at the bowl, then him. How was a person supposed to eat under these conditions?

"What work?" My chair scraped the floor as I stood. I didn't have a job here. Or I hadn't. Maybe he'd decided our truce was the shortest lived ever and he was going to send me to scrub toilets because my plan had pissed him off?

"Come with me." He walked out of the room.

I gave Tuesday a shrug before I followed him.

The place was a maze of hallways, and I wondered how big it actually was. We took a couple lefts and then a right before he opened a door to a small room with a desk, a few chairs, and a couch. A bookcase lined a wall, filled with actual books.

I didn't have a chance to look at them before he was pointing at a chair. "Sit."

"You know, I really dislike it when you do that."

He walked toward a second door in the room and stopped. "Dislike what?"

I was still standing, and he didn't even know what he'd done. He had no clue how bossy he was. Was it worth debating when I wanted to sit anyway?

"Nothing." I sat in the chair he'd pointed to.

The corner of Callon's mouth ticked up along with a half laugh.

I gasped. "That wasn't nice."

"If you wanted to sit, then why would me telling you stop you? Doesn't that seem a bit absurd?"

"No." I stood and switched to the couch. He hadn't told me to sit here.

From the raised eyebrow, my action was taken for exactly what it was.

"What are we doing, anyway?" I asked, spreading my legs out on the couch. Now I wasn't even sitting anymore. I was almost lying down.

"That thing you did with Zink, if you want to use it on the Magician, I need to see how consistent you are—and how strong."

"We're going to use my plan?"

"Only if you don't suck."

That sentence made the vein in his neck pop out.

He opened the door and Koz was standing there, shoulder slumped on the side and a line of people behind him down the hall. Callon didn't only want me to do it again, he wanted me to do it again and again and again.

"Get in," Callon said to Koz.

Koz walked in the room, and Callon shut the door on the line of people all trying to peek in.

Nope. Not Koz. I couldn't do it with Koz. What if somehow or another Callon was wrong about it going away easily and what I did got *stuck* in the "on" position. What if Koz ended up following me around, trying to help me constantly?

Tuesday would be crushed. Not that I thought what I was doing made people romantically inclined, but Tuesday wasn't going to want to see him, of all people, following me around.

Zink had been different. Zink was too much of an asshole for him to be giving for long, magic or not. Even if it did last a little while, I wouldn't feel so bad tormenting him.

Koz stood there, looking at Callon and then me. "What's going on? Why are we all lined up?"

I turned to Callon. "He doesn't even know we're practicing?" I definitely was not doing this to Koz.

"No, he doesn't. They might suspect something, but I'm trying to get an unbiased pool."

I shook my head. "We have to go to the next unbiased person."

"Why?" The tone Callon used already told me the answer wouldn't matter. He was going to insist I try on Koz.

I was going to insist I didn't.

"Do what with me?" Koz asked.

"Because I *can't*," I said, getting to my feet.

Callon took a step toward me. "Of course you can."

"No. I. *Can't.*"

"What the hell is going on?" Koz asked, looking back and forth.

Callon didn't budge, and Koz was waiting for an answer. I walked to the door that didn't have the line of people waiting.

"Where are you going?" Callon asked, as if shocked I'd walk out of a room on him.

"With *you*, to talk." I opened the door and waited for him to follow me.

He did. He probably only did so because he was going to explain how wrong I was.

I held up a finger to Koz and then shut the door.

"What's the issue?" Callon asked.

"He's Tuesday's guy." I crossed my arms.

"No. Koz is *my* guy and *I* need him." He crossed his arms.

"If this goes wrong and Koz is following me around, are you going to tell Tuesday why?" He wanted to play it all loose and crazy, let him fix it if it blew up.

"It's not going to go wrong. If there's a lag of some sort, she'll understand."

"Oh, yeah, I'm sure it'll go over well when I tell her he's lying in my bed because of a lag." I might've actually huffed and looked up at the ceiling. My knee decided it needed to get into the act as well and bend with some attitude.

By the time I looked back at Callon, he had a stubborn tilt to his head and his jugular was bulging. "How would he end up in your bed?"

"See?" I waved my finger at him. "That's *exactly* what Tuesday will ask."

"You didn't say *how*. Are you attracted to him?"

That was an interesting question. I'd never even thought of him in that way. Koz was cute, but he wasn't really my type—if I had a type. "He's a good-looking guy, but—"

Callon opened the door before I finished. "Koz, we don't need you."

"Need me for what?" He was scratching his head with both hands. "I'm so damn confused."

"I'll fill you in later." Callon pointed at the door we'd just used. "Get out. We've got work to do."

Koz walked out of the room shaking his head and muttering something about waiting in line for some secret and then he didn't even get to find out what it was.

I sat in the chair, waiting for Callon to open the

other door again. It was a young man I'd glimpsed passing in the hallway, who looked like he'd barely hit manhood.

"Teddy, this is Mark."

That was all Callon said before he turned to me expectantly. Okay, the show was on.

I cleared my mind of everything except imaging some great need. It wasn't hard at the moment, since my life was balancing on top of a pin. "Mark, could you help me with something?"

Mark's eyes shifted from curious to pliant in an instant. "Of course. What can I do?"

Mark rushed to my side but was stopped short.

"Far enough," Callon said, holding out a hand in front of him.

I looked at where I was sitting and tried to figure out the distance. I'd say it was just about ten feet. Callon remembered me telling him I could see death when people got closer than ten feet. I shut down the warm and fuzzies that thought brought on. He was probably afraid my list would get longer, that was all.

"She doesn't need you anymore. You can go," Callon said, then motioned to the door.

Mark looked over his shoulder, and I nodded, encouraging him to exit. He smiled and left the room like he was fighting his way out of quicksand.

"We good?" I asked, as Callon shut the door on Mark.

"Not even close. I've got them lined up according to how difficult I think they'll be. Get comfortable." He walked back to the door and let in the next person.

There were women and men, human and beast.

Each time, it had the same effect. They came in confused and then didn't want to leave me.

I was yawning by the time the twentieth person walked out.

The door clicked shut. "Well? Now are we done?"

Callon walked over and sat on the edge of the desk. "You're consistent, but I'm not sure if it's strong enough with someone with a lot of magic. It didn't work on Hecate. Odds are, it won't work on the Magician."

I heard the words, knew the logic was sound, but the desperation inside me didn't want to hear any of it. This had to work.

"Maybe Hecate was an anomaly? You said yourself she'd survive anything. Why don't I try it with you? You have magic and you're strong."

"No. It won't be the same."

"Why? I think that might be a good idea to try."

"Teddy, I said no."

He still thought I couldn't do it. I was too weak or something. Worthless. That was what Baryn had called me over and over again. Pathetic and worthless as I sat there cowering.

"I can do it," I said, standing.

"I'm sure you can, but don't." He was staring at me, a warning there.

He didn't believe me. He thought I was dead weight that he had to carry. A lifetime of horrible words churned around in my mind, gathering steam. The urge to prove Callon wrong won over logic. I wasn't going to be controlled anymore, told what to do. I'd spent years like that. *Do this. You can't do that. You're stupid and dumb, worthless.*

I was strong, and fuck him for thinking otherwise.

"Callon, I need you." I laid it on thick, every desire I had lacing my words. The years spent in abject misery layered my voice, the lilt of my tone. Every beating, the hours of loneliness, everything I had piled up in the dark crevices of my mind filtered through me, aimed at him.

His eyes flamed red. He walked toward me, nothing like the others had. When they'd come, it had almost been like children to a loved caregiver, submissive. This was more like an animal stalking me.

Startled, I tripped around the chair, feeling for the wall behind me as he closed in. His palms landed against the wall beside me, caging me. His head dipped low, his chest rising and falling, and I could hear a rattling in his chest from strain. Heat was exploding off him. Power and magic so thick it licked at my skin and teased my senses.

"I told you not to do that." His voice was low, guttural. His right palm fisted and the cords in his neck popped. "You need to go."

I didn't move. I wasn't sure if it was my fight-or-flight making a bad call and telling me to hang close or something else, something dark inside myself. His beast was right there, trying to break the surface. His darkness was about to come into the light as red swirled in his eyes.

I didn't know what it would do and I didn't know if I cared. The monster inside me wanted it to come out and play. It was lonely, so tired of being alone.

I arched forward, my hips brushing his.

His whole body tensed. "You don't know what you're asking for."

I wasn't so sure of that.

He leaned forward, pressing his entire length against

mine until I was pressed back against the wall. It felt good. Better than good.

It felt like the darkness in me had found a home.

The feeling was so startling that it sucked everything good into a vacuum of fear.

"Go." He grated out the word, and I knew it was my last chance.

I slid down the wall, under his arm, and fled the room.

32

It was late, and the place was quiet except for the occasional creak from one of the people on watch. From what I'd heard, they always had someone on post. Now they had twice as many because sooner or later, probably sooner, the Magician would show.

Callon hadn't been seen for hours. At first I'd been trying to avoid him, until I realized I didn't have to. He'd left right after I had.

So I'd tried to sleep but tossed and turned instead, blaming my wakefulness on the recent binge of shut-eye.

Another hour came and went before I found myself knocking on Koz's door.

Koz answered, leaning against the frame, slightly breathless and with nothing but a blanket wrapped around his waist.

"Have you seen Callon?"

"He went to run a perimeter check." He kept looking over his shoulder back in the room. "He'll be back in a few hours, I'm sure."

"Teddy, do you need me?" Tuesday shouted from deeper in the room, sounding as winded as he was.

"No, I'm fine." I gave him as good of a smile as I could.

He took it as if I meant it, and the door swung shut.

Knowing sleep was useless, I wandered the house until I stumbled upon a lookout balcony. Zink was leaned over the railing, but it was large enough to ignore him. Plus, he didn't speak to me anyway.

I opened the door and curled up on a cushioned bench, glad I'd brought the blanket from the bed.

Zink gave me a glance and then went back to watching the horizon.

"You do some *weird* shit," he said.

I glanced at the door, expecting to see someone else had joined us. They hadn't. "Are you talking to me?"

"Obviously. Who else does weird shit like you?"

"Why?" I blurted. This was Zink, after all. He'd called me a dog.

"I don't know. I must be really fucking bored."

I could understand that. Watching the horizon for enemies wasn't the most riveting thing ever, especially if you didn't see any.

"Talking about weird shit, did your beast want to come out when I did that thing to lure you over?"

He looked over his shoulder with his eyes narrowed, as if he was trying to figure out why I'd ask that. "Why would it?"

"I don't know. Just figured maybe it would want to."

"My beast knows better than to do that." He tipped his head back, letting out a belly laugh I didn't think existed within Zink.

"What's so funny?"

"I'd tell you, but I doubt you'd find it as humorous." The dickhead laughed a little more.

I'd definitely picked the wrong place to straighten out my head. I liked Zink better when he was grouchy, mean, and silent.

Luckily, Zink didn't say anything else, having used up his ten civil words for the day.

After another few minutes of silence, I curled on my side, watching the moon rise over the mountains.

Even in the chilling night air, bundled up in my blanket, it was calming. The Magician would be coming, but this was a gift of peace, maybe the most peace and sanctuary I'd ever had.

The door opened and footsteps sounded on the wood behind me a little time later.

I knew it was him without turning around. The smell of the trees and pine air preceded him, along with some indefinable energy that could only be described as the magic of his beast.

I wondered if he'd go back inside. If he'd stumbled upon me by accident. Then I reminded myself of who this was.

Zink reverted to his silent ways and left his post. He evacuated the balcony as if he knew Callon was there to talk to me.

Callon walked toward the railing, admiring the same view of the moon rising, glittering on the snow.

He turned, resting his hips on the railing. His eyes had that slight otherworldly glow they got when the beast was still lingering.

"Were you looking for me?" he asked.

I didn't bother denying it, and I wasn't surprised he knew. Koz had probably run him down the second he came in, even if he had been mid-thrust. I pulled the blanket over my shoulders as I sat up.

"I didn't mean to…"

I wasn't even sure *what* I'd done, but I'd meant to do it. It had been intense, almost as if I'd summoned the beast within him.

I'd liked it, too. The beast fit. It wouldn't fear what I was, or the darkness I had inside me. It wouldn't calculate like the man did and tally up lives, decide who should go where like everyone was a chess piece.

When the beast had found me surrounded by the Magician's men, it hadn't decided what was the smart move. It had simply killed.

I'd *wanted* to see if the beast would come to me.

"Don't do that again," he said, as if he were reading the thoughts as I worked through them.

"Why?"

"I don't know if I'll be able to pull back the next time."

I opened my mouth, about to ask him what he'd pull back from, but not because I didn't suspect. I wanted to hear it. I wanted him to tell me that he couldn't always control everything.

The man could be cool to me. He functioned on logic and what needed to be done. The beast was raw emotion. The beast understood me, maybe even wanted me.

I didn't have the nerve to come out and ask him, afraid I was wrong, so I hit it from the side.

"Why didn't Zink react like that? Or any of the other shifters that came in?"

"Their beasts won't touch you."

"Why not?"

Red swirled intensely in his eyes as he gripped the rail behind him. "I think you already know."

There it was. And there was the problem, too. The man was trying to overrule the beast. I guessed we'd find out who was stronger.

I needed to decide who I was rooting for.

33

Hess was sitting next to Zink in the great room the next morning, talking quieter than I'd thought them capable. Hess was speaking but Zink's mouth was turned down, and not in his usual angry way. I knew sadness when I saw it.

I marched right over to them. "What happened?"

Hess looked up and shook his head. "It's Issy."

Ah, shit. When I hadn't seen her at breakfast, my gut said it wasn't good. But she wasn't supposed to die. I hadn't *seen* her die. How was this possible? I'd never been this off before, except for the furred ones. Was I going haywire?

"Where's her room? I want to see if she needs anything." I needed to see if she was really dying.

Hess rattled off a few turns, and I took off at a fast walk.

A young man called Tommy, one of the many that I thought would die, was leaving her room as I got there.

"You can go in if you want to pay your respects, but she's sleeping," he said in hushed tone.

"Thanks."

Callon was already in her room, standing along the far wall and watching her sleep.

I might not have seen her dying in my visions, but looking at her now, she *looked* like she was already dead.

I took a step and then paused. I didn't know if I should go to her, as I'd planned, and see if something triggered a vision, or go to him and apologize. I never should've said a word. He'd wanted to believe me. I'd seen it in his eyes, his mouth, his fucking soul.

That was what you got for trying to give someone hope. From here on out, I'd stick to my comfort zone and only dole out death and despair. Hope was too dangerous. Hope could hurt worse than a thousand expected disappointments.

I forced another step, going toward him, trying to not hear the agonizing breathing coming from Issy, each one making me a liar.

I stopped beside him. He glanced at me but then looked back to her. When he'd looked at me, his wall was up. I didn't take it to heart. That was how he was holding it together, and I would've done the same. *Had* done the same. Was still doing it.

"I'm sorry. I never would've said that if I'd known. I screwed up."

He shook his head. "You have nothing to apologize for."

I leaned on the wall beside him, not sure what to do to help.

"I've known her since she was a little kid," he said. "Took her in when she was only six or seven."

I'd thought Callon was maybe thirty, tops? How the hell did that math work when Issy looked older than him? I couldn't ask. Even I knew the timing wasn't right to quiz him.

He pushed off the wall, pent-up energy spilling off him. "Can you stay with her for a few?"

"Yeah, sure." He had to go for a run. That I knew it was a little disturbing.

He moved toward the door.

I went to Issy's bedside, watching her breathing pause and then start up again, as if she was at the end of her fight. How had I not seen this? Could still not see it? With Callon and his men, it was one thing. They were barely human. But her?

She struggled with a breath, her eyes fluttering open with the effort.

Did I scream for help? Call Callon back? Was this the last moment?

Her eyes opened and focused on me. She lifted her hand, and I took it.

"I'm here with you," I said, going on instinct and what I would've done for Maura.

"Take care of him."

Take care of him? Me? I was a mess. I couldn't take care of *myself*. The only person I'd tried to take care of was Tuesday, and I'd been dragging her through a swamp of shit. No one was safe around me. I was on the verge of getting Callon's men killed, and maybe him.

"Promise." She squeezed my hand, her grip weak and her fingers bony.

What if she really was dying? Then this would be a *deathbed* promise. I didn't like breaking normal promises. What the fuck would I do then?

I laid my other hand on top of hers, sandwiching her frail one between mine. Meeting her gaze straight on, I went with the only thing I could think of. Stall a promise I was doomed to fail at.

"You aren't going to die. Do you hear me? You. Are. Not. Going. To. Die."

"Teddy, it's my time. I'm okay with that." Her smile was feeble at best and a bit mocking.

I got it. She was barely able to take a breath and I was insisting she'd carry on. I would've looked at me the same way. But I was desperate and not giving up easily. There would be no deathbed vows.

I moved even closer, my hip grazing hers as I held on.

"You will not die on him, so rest and get better."

Her hand, so cold in mine, grew clammy.

Her lids fluttered again. "Promise me you'll watch out for him?"

"No. You aren't dying. I told you that." Holy shit, was I a horrible person? I was breaking out into a sweat, all so that I didn't have to taint my already dingy soul a little darker. What was worse? A broken promise or refusing to let her die in peace? My moral compass was so broken that I couldn't tell which way pointed to hell anymore.

Her eyes closed again. Crisis averted—for a couple of minutes, anyway.

Damn, it was getting hot in here.

The door creaked open and Carla walked in. "I saw Callon leave. Thought maybe Issy would need someone."

It was clear Carla wanted to be there, definitely more than me. I stood, willingly giving up my spot.

"Teddy." Callon was standing by the bed.

I sat up, stretching. I'd been hiding in this room all afternoon, not wanting to stumble across any more deaths by accident. Tuesday had been hiding out with me until she switched rooms to hide out with Koz instead.

"How's Issy?" I asked. It was better than coming out and asking if she was dead yet. Was that why he was here? To tell me she was?

He stared down at me with a guarded expression I couldn't pin down. His eyes were narrowed but he wasn't mad.

"She's sleeping."

I shoved some hair out of my face. I remembered watching Maura at the end. The longer she'd slept, the more I'd waited and hoped. Every day she hung on, I'd thought maybe she'd pull out of it. It was almost harder.

"Was there something else?"

"The Magician's men have been spotted. Zink went to send word that we want to strike a deal and hand you over."

I sat up fully. And so it began.

He let out a long sigh and dragged a hand through his hair. "I can't think of a better option."

"How long do we have?"

"Him and his group aren't far now. Probably until morning."

By tomorrow, my world might be completely changed. I'd be free—or the alternative that would be worse than anything I'd experienced yet. I'd been through some serious crap, but it could always get worse.

"Callon, if things go bad, I need you to do whatever it takes to—"

"I'm not killing you."

I thought back to what I'd heard at the eat and sleep. It had become a thorn in my memory, always jabbing unexpectedly. "I don't want to live like that. If he gets me, promise—"

"I. Won't. Let. Him."

"You promised me you wouldn't let me end up like that."

"I won't." He stared at me as if he'd do whatever he had to. But what if that wasn't enough?

I reached over to where I'd made a list of the people who were most in danger of dying and handed it to him.

He opened it and looked down. He took a lot longer looking over that list than it should've taken to read. The overwhelming death toll that might be coming was getting to him.

I shoved my hands in my pockets. "I couldn't remember the one guy's name, so I described him."

He nodded. "I know who it is. I'll let them know before tomorrow." He tucked the list away. "Time to get ready."

34

Everyone was preparing, whether it was boarding up windows or moving supplies to the basement. Every person who wasn't able to fight would go there as soon as the Magician approached the final stretch. The entrance was rigged with explosives so they could close it off if things went bad and then make their way to the other side of the mountain.

I was carrying a box of supplies down when Zink walked into the main hall, his jaw set, shoulders tense. Everyone that had been coming and going froze. Then more people filtered into the hall, as if sensing the impending doom.

Zink was usually a steady eight on the "geared up and ready to fight" scale. Only recently had I seen him dip down to a six. Right now, he was at a full ten. His hands were fisted and he could've been gripping my stomach for how I felt.

My plan was set in motion and about to play out. It was strange to have been fighting for this, all the while never really wanting it to come to pass. If I dug deep, which I didn't really like to do, I knew this was our best shot.

Callon stepped forward. "Well?"

Zink unlocked his jaw. "He'll be here within the hour."

Zink didn't have to say he preferred to have attacked already. The blood in his eyes made it obvious he would've rather ripped the Magician's people apart than speaking to them, trying to lure them closer.

I understood. If I was a beast, I might want to attack like that too. Difference was I knew what defeat was like, the shitty taste it left, and I'd do whatever I needed to stack the odds on our side.

I turned, feeling more urgent now than ever to get things ready.

"Get everyone in position. Anyone not fighting needs to go to the basement now," Callon said.

I watched as people headed toward the basement, and I didn't see the people from my list heading that way.

Tuesday rushed me from the side, wrapping her arms around my neck. "Don't do anything crazy."

"I'll try not to. That's the best I can offer." Tuesday would be heading below, and I was grateful. I wanted at least one of us to be able to hang on to a rainbow or two.

"Can you still see my death?" she asked, looking for reassurance that we'd both make it out of this.

I nodded, afraid to tell her my theory was probably wrong after my big screw-up with Issy.

Koz stepped forward, took Tuesday's hand, and walked her the rest of the way. I left them, going to the window that had a partial view in between the boards.

All the way in the distance, I could see the Magician's group working their way up. There were at least a hundred of them. They might've agreed to a trade, but they were ready for a fight, and they didn't look like they were planning on losing.

Callon stood behind me and took in the same view. "You don't have to go out there."

If only.

"Yes, I do. It's the best shot of getting him close enough."

Callon might not realize the threat he looked like, but I did. The Magician wasn't going to willingly get anywhere near him.

"If I give you the signal, you run for the house."

I wrapped my arms around myself. "How many men can the average beast take on?"

He stepped close enough that I could feel his heat. "It depends on the man and the beast. If we can kill the Magician, a lot of them will scatter."

The Magician's men climbed the mountain, getting closer and closer, rifles slung over their shoulders and pistols at their hips. "What about the guns?"

"We've got gunmen in place. We're ready."

I didn't think it was possible to be ready for this.

We watched in silence as they continued toward the house. Then they stopped, too far away for the gunmen to get them, at least with the guns we had. We needed to get the Magician a lot closer, but he probably knew that.

"It's time," Callon said.

WE STEPPED OUTSIDE ALONE. EVERY OTHER ABLE body had circled into the woods or were in position around the outside of the house, ready to flank the magician's group. The others were positioned in the house with whatever guns we had. All guns were aimed for the Magician but with orders to not take a shot unless they were completely sure they could take him out. If they missed, they'd bring on the wrath of the horde that still had a head directing them.

Callon stood beside me, gripping my bicep, giving the Magician the impression that I wasn't a willing participant.

We walked about thirty feet outside the house and stopped. The Magician stood another two hundred yards or so away. He had people flanking him on either side, holding metal umbrellas to shade him. They were offering protection from bullets more than the sun.

I hadn't known what the Magician would look like, but it wasn't the man standing there. He looked—unassuming? Not overly tall or broad. His hair was a salt-and-pepper mixture with a part to the side. *Plain* was the only word I could think of.

"Send her forward," the Magician said.

This was it. Do or die. I felt Callon's thumb graze me, trying to offer the only support he could.

"Can you help me?" I asked, laying the lure on as thick as I could. Everything I had, I piled into those words, hoping it would be enough.

It wasn't. He didn't budge. But he did smile.

It wasn't going to work. I wasn't going to be able to get the Magician in range, not for the unreliable guns we had, or for Callon to take him out.

Callon moved his hand off me when I'd expected him to pull me back. I was waiting for the signal, but it didn't come.

I turned to look at him, knowing something was off. He was staring at me but his face was frozen, his lips parted, as if he'd stalled out right before he had a chance to tell me to run. Red was burning so bright in his eyes that I couldn't believe he hadn't changed into the beast.

"Teddy, I do wish you'd pay attention to me," the Magician called from across the field.

I whipped around to face him.

I stepped closer to the Magician, my legs moving without my say-so.

I'd thought I would be stronger. I'd lure him to me. I'd be in control.

I was a child at this. I had the magic, I knew it in my gut, but I'd been playing checkers against his chess, and now I was his puppet.

I heard chaos erupt around me as I was being marched forward. Our people charged out of the surrounding woods, some in beast form. Guns firing, bullets flying past me from both directions. Screams exploded, blood sprayed, and I couldn't do a thing about it.

Step after step, my legs moved without my permission. I couldn't even turn around to see if Callon had freed himself.

The Magician never stopped smiling as he watched me walk toward him. He'd kill everyone to get me, and then he'd be immortal. He'd never die. He'd carry me around like a lump of flesh and I'd live day after day, remembering what happened here, unable to end my own life to stop the misery.

I was halfway to him. If he could control me this

much without touching me, what would happen once he did?

The only other times I'd been able to pull life out of someone else had been when they were willing to offer it and the witch had been directing it, or when I'd been desperate.

This definitely fell into the desperate category, but the Magician was much stronger than me. He'd known what was coming. I had a pretty good idea of how this was going to go down if something didn't happen soon, and I didn't need a drunk wizard to tell me. The only way I, and those around me, might have a chance was if I changed up the plan, and soon.

I blinded myself to the chaos all around and struggled, fighting the pull forward as much as I could. I'd have one shot of taking him out. I had to do this. I'd done it before. It was in me somewhere.

And then it hit. If I stopped fighting, for just a second, I might have enough strength and freedom to do something he wasn't expecting.

I couldn't leave this to chance. My need had to be so great that it could war with the pull of the Magician. If it didn't work, I had to make sure he couldn't use me.

It was a risk, but the only chance left. I stopped fighting his pull and stepped forward of my own volition. Relinquishing that fight freed up enough movement that I was able to grab the knife tucked under my shirt.

His smile dropped as if he were confused. Then he rushed me, but it was too late. I'd shoved the knife upward into my chest.

I might've been killing myself for nothing. No, even then it wouldn't be for nothing. It would save me from a fate I'd never be able to escape, and I'd be saving the world from contributing to this man's domination.

He grabbed for the knife, yanking it out of my chest at the same time I latched on to him.

"Die," I said, hoping my words would lend my magic power.

We fell to the ground together, him landing on top of me as I held on to his wrists, then his neck. We struggled, and I went for any exposed flesh I could find and keep a grip on.

"Did you really think you could match me? That you could steal my life? Mine?"

He smiled and then his face shifted, the skin darkening until it was black. His eyes no longer had any whites. He was a hairless creature without a hint of the human I'd seen.

I felt warmth building in my hands. I could feel the heat of his life draining into me, and then pulling back out. My blood pooled, and I realized this might not have worked.

His eyes flared. I kept my grip on him, in spite of the flash of burning and then freezing cold. Magic was ping-ponging between us as if it were a tug of war. I felt a surge of it pull back toward me and I latched on with all I had left. I thought of everyone here, all the lives that would end if he won, Tuesday, Koz—Callon. I even thought of Zink.

My hands grew warmer still, and his lip curled back as he growled with teeth of ebony. He pulled off me, and then he was speeding off so quickly he appeared to be a wisp of smoke disappearing into the trees.

I lay there on the field, my clothes soaked with blood, feeling like my life was pouring out of me.

"Teddy?" Callon's hands were on me, running over my torso.

Air surged into my lungs and life pulsated in my heart, pushing into my limbs.

Callon knelt beside me, covered in blood and guts, looking like a true barbarian. "What the fuck was that stunt?"

"I had to get creative." I put a hand to my chest, feeling the blood that soaked my shirt. I reached underneath it, but there was no hole.

Had I died? I thought I had. I'd gripped the Magician, and crazy magic like I'd never felt had poured out.

"So you thought stabbing yourself in the heart was the thing to do?"

All around us, there were bodies and blood-red snow. It was becoming a familiar scene.

"Did you see him take off?" I asked, looking toward the trees.

"Zink went after him, but I don't think he'll catch him. He was moving too fast."

"What about his people?"

"Half of them took off."

I looked around. I knew what happened to the other half. Callon and his people. I searched the ground, spotting at least one of ours that I'd known was going to die.

Koz and Hess, along with the other survivors, were going through the bodies.

"I can't see them. Not yet." I tried to get to my feet and wobbled.

Callon's arm went around my waist and I leaned into him.

We were walking around the bodies, on our way to the house, when Issy walked out the front door.

Her eyes were bright and her skin was rosy.

She looked all around. "What the hell happened while I was sleeping?"

I WATCHED FROM THE WINDOW IN THE GREAT ROOM AS Callon and Hess worked alongside other surviving warriors, digging the graves for the fallen. The sun setting behind them cast long shadows over the growing number of mounds of dirt. Bodies, wrapped in white, lay beside each of the holes that marked their final resting place. The corpse of our enemies had been dragged farther away and buried in a mass grave.

Zink made his way toward them, Koz beside him. They'd both tried to pick up the Magician's trail but had come back empty-handed after nearly eight hours of tracking.

Issy fluttered into the room, as if not only did she feel better, she'd gotten a hit of crack when she woke up. Her resurrection from the almost dead had caused quite a stir. No one openly spoke of how suspicious her miraculous recovery was, but I was receiving more side-eyed glances and hushed conversations than ever. I had an idea of what happened, as I was sure a few others did. The life I'd taken had gone to good use, it seemed, tucked away until needed.

"They're ready," she said, before moving on to tell the rest of the house.

We walked out of the house, walking past spots of

red snow that were already getting a new dusting of white as flakes drifted down.

We gathered around the many graves as the bodies were lowered in. My brain was too stunned to hear what was being said by friends and family. No one talked for long, though, as sorrow and exhaustion met in some unbearable place.

Then they were drifting off again, back to the warmth of the building.

I remained, along with Callon and the guys, and Tuesday by my side. It was different for us. We all knew this wasn't the end. There would be more battles, and more deaths to come. I might've wounded the Magician, but I hadn't killed him.

"Every one of them, huh?" Tuesday asked as she stopped beside me.

"My list and then some." All the people on my list were gone, plus another shifter I hadn't seen coming.

I looked over to Callon, wondering how he was doing and knowing I shouldn't care as much as I did.

He lifted his eyes to me, and we stood there for a few seconds staring at each other as if we were the only ones there.

Then Zink walked over, drawing Callon's attention away.

"What's going on with you two?" Tuesday asked.

"I'm not sure," I said, but it was a lie. It was something terrifying and invigorating, something that made me want to run to him and from him at the same time. It was something that might break me or make me whole, and I didn't know which.

Look for the continuation of Teddy's story, in early 2019.

Sign up here to be notified of new releases by Donna.

Donnaaugustine.com
   https://www.facebook.com/Donnaaugustinebooks/
   https://twitter.com/DonnAugustine

ACKNOWLEDGMENTS

You might write a book alone but you never get to the finish line that way. I've Camilla J., Lori H., Christine J., Donna Z. and Lisa A., I'd be a mess without all of you pitching in. Soobee D., you are the best cheerleader ever.

ALSO BY DONNA AUGUSTINE

Ollie wit

A Step into the Dark

Walking in the Dark

Kissed by the Dark

The Keepers

The Keepers

Keepers and Killers

Shattered

Redemption

Karma

Karma

Jinxed

Fated

Dead Ink

The Wilds

The Wilds

The Hunt
The Dead
The Magic

Wyrd Blood

CPSIA information can be obtained
at www.ICGtesting.com
Printed in the USA
LVHW081303231118
598054LV00017B/352/P